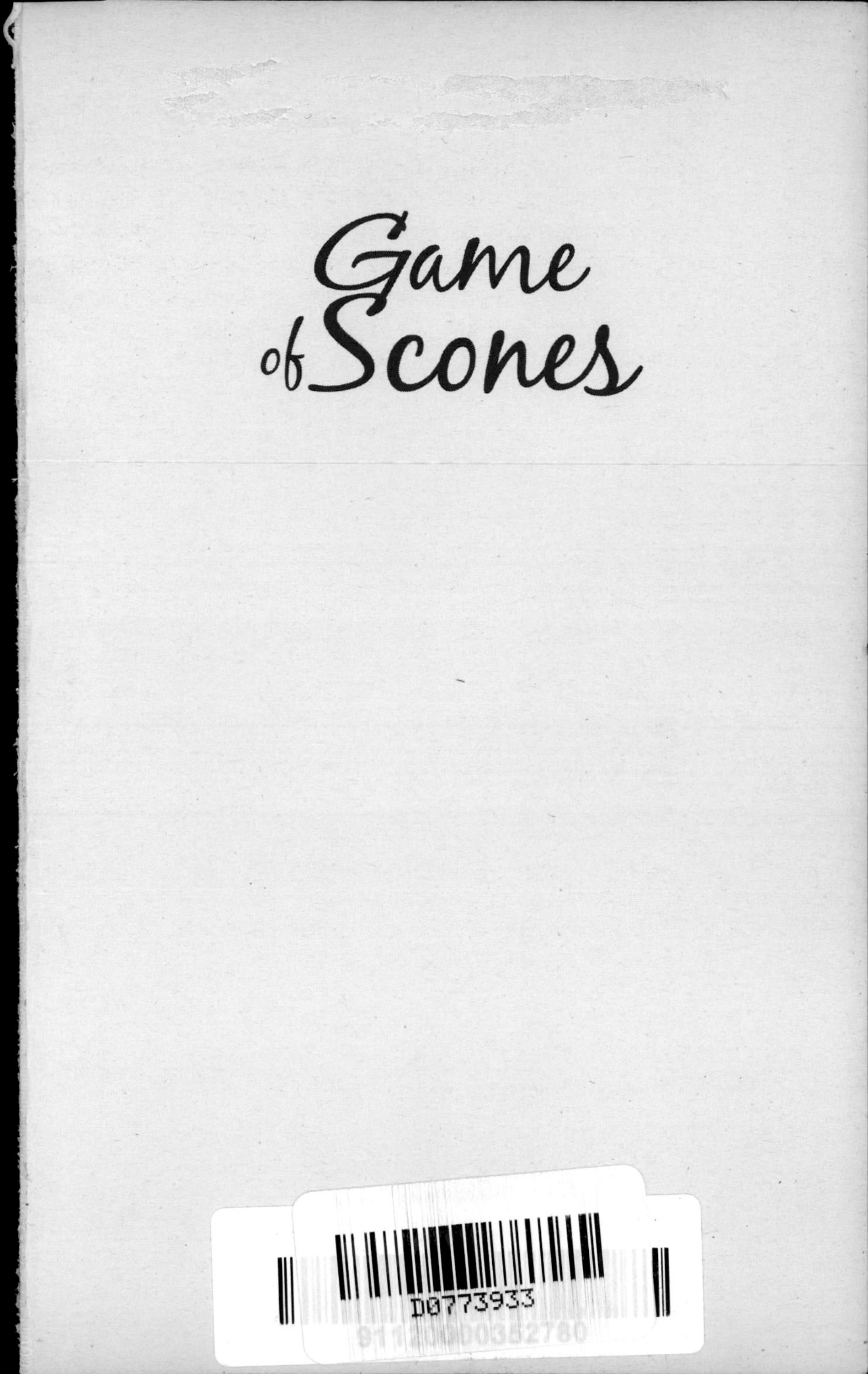

Game of Scones

Available from
Samantha Tonge

DOUBTING ABBEY
FROM PARIS WITH LOVE
MISTLETOE MANSION
GAME OF SCONES
MY BIG FAT CHRISTMAS WEDDING

Game of Scones

SAMANTHA TONGE

CARINA™

This edition is published by arrangement with Harlequin Books S.A. CARINA is a trademark of Harlequin Enterprises Limited, used under licence.

First Published in Great Britain 2016
by Carina, an imprint of HarperCollins*Publishers*
1 London Bridge Street, London, SE1 9GF

ISBN 978-0-263-92245-5

58-0416

Our policy is to use papers that are natural, renewable and recyclable products and made from wood grown in sustainable forests.
The logging and manufacturing processes conform to the legal environmental regulations of the country of origin.

Printed and bound by
CPI Group (UK) Ltd, Croydon, CR0 4YY

Samantha Tonge lives in Cheshire with her lovely family and a cat who thinks it's a dog. Along with writing, her days are spent cycling, willing cakes to rise and avoiding housework. A love of fiction developed as a child, when she was known for reading Enid Blyton books in the bath. A desire to write bubbled away in the background whilst she pursued other careers, including a fun stint working at Disneyland Paris. Formally trained as a linguist, Samantha now likes nothing more than holing herself up in the spare room, in front of the keyboard. Writing romantic comedy novels is her passion.

samanthatonge.co.uk
twitter.com/SamTongeWriter
facebook.com/SamanthaTongeAuthor

My darling Immy, this one's for you!

CHAPTER ONE

Word to the wise: never Google "Dutch" and "Sex" in the same sentence. Mmm, tempted you, haven't I? A graphic image hovered in my mind after I closed the page on my browser. *Really?* How was that even possible? With a brief smile, I put my phone on the coffee table and snuggled back into the black leather sofa. On my lap lay a pen and sheet of paper. For important decisions, I had to map out my thoughts the old-fashioned way. On one side I'd scrawled a list titled HEAD: *reasons for staying together.* On the other, HEART: *reasons for breaking up.*

Breaking up, that was, from my six-foot-four boyfriend, Henrik from Holland. Okay, so he was only half-Dutch, thanks to his mum Greta, a divorced liberalist, who strutted around her house half-naked. However, he showed several of the stereotypical characteristics of a Dutchman that I'd just discovered on the internet, in a bid to come to a decision about our future. Despite Henrik's ever-increasing earnings as a real estate developer, he counted every single penny. Plus he could be direct to the point of sounding rude – although I just called that honesty.

On the plus side… what can I say, his lack of inhibition in the bedroom had rubbed off onto missionary-position me. Talk about fifty shades of yay! In fact, on hearing that Christian Grey's safe word was "red", for a joke we'd set ours as "pneumonoultramicroscopicsilicovolcanoconiosis", the longest word in the English language. Just as well our love life, whilst adventurous, didn't really include risky whips, clamps or cable ties.

A picture of Henrik came into my mind, with his slicked-back oat-coloured hair, Atlas shoulders and Titan height. This guy had the swoon-factor in excess – or at least that's how I used to feel, until recent months. The first time our eyes had locked, his crinkled in a way that made me feel like a teenager crushing on a boyband. What's more he was ambitious – for both of us – could wire a plug, kept fit and cooked a mean bowl of pasta…

Gushing now, wasn't I, as the list under HEAD (to stay with him) grew longer? It sounds shallow, but hands up, I've been constantly bowled over by his Hollywood looks – until lately when, for some reason, his super suave appearance has grated. I know. Ridiculous. Talk about picky. Yet, thanks to my maths degree, I am analytical to the extreme, which means weighing up *all* the evidence – including my gut feelings. So I'd almost come to a decision – that just this once, I should listen to my heart and tell myself I'm actually *not* being silly. Despite Henrik's considerable physical assets and appealing personality traits, my head needed to listen to my heart shouting that our relationship no longer felt right.

With a sigh, I stood up, went into the bedroom and slipped out of my trouser suit. I yawned. Would my body ever get used to the six a.m. starts, one-hour commute to work and busy days in my power suit? Without concealer, dark rings circled my eyes and at night my brain found it hard to switch off. Henrik was the same, both of us often working in bed on our laptops. But that was good, right? Showed we were motivated and getting the most out of life?

Carefully I hung up my suit, pulled on cut-off jeans and a T-shirt, and headed into the open-plan kitchen. I tied a cake-themed apron around my waist. After one last look at my list, I tucked it into the front pocket. Now, flour, butter, milk, sugar… what flavour of scone would I bake today? Late afternoon sunbeams warmed my face and I gazed out of the window, onto the small regimental garden. Such a bright summer's day called for sun cream-smelling desiccated coconut with a zing of fresh lemon juice…

I sieved the flour and rubbed in the butter, enjoying the sticky sensation. Scones were brilliant – like a blank canvas, you could colour with either a savoury or sweet theme. What's more, gently kneading the dough, after adding the milk and sugar, never failed to lessen worries… It was the one time of day I took an hour out and emptied my mind of sums and equations. Stressed or happy, nothing beat creating something scrumptious out of such basic ingredients. However, you had to be careful not to pummel the mixture too much. Ideally, before you cut out shapes, the dough should still feel crumbly. Over the years I'd picked up the tips for perfect scones – keep the butter cold to improve the rise, too much milk would make the dough tough, and scones do best on a hot oven's top shelf.

I jumped as the front door to our swanky ground-floor Notting Hill flat opened and slammed shut.

'Had a good day?' I said and turned around to face Henrik. He leant down to brush my lips with his. At five foot ten, my inner cavewoman had always loved the rare experience of a man towering over me. I used to think he'd make a heartbreaker of a uniformed hero, like a scrubbed-up surgeon or cabin crew member.

'The best, thanks – but nothing compared to this evening when I'll reveal a surprise.'

He put his shiny briefcase on the laminate floor. Not for the first time, I appreciated how well an expensive suit showed off his athletic outline. Henrik removed his jacket, slipped off his tie and undid the top two shirt buttons. This revealed a patch of tanned chest that I'd have once found tantalising, in the extreme. Henrik led me to the sofa. My stomach had lurched when he mentioned a surprise, thanks to a recent night out with Greta, who'd texted, asking to meet.

'My boy is about to propose to you,' she'd said after too many gins. 'Marriage can get messy – make sure you carefully consider your reply.'

Despite feeling annoyed on his behalf at her indiscretion, I secretly appreciated the heads-up – but hence the pressure on me to make up my mind about her son. I'd rather break up with him before any proposal, to avoid bruising his pride even more – to not witness the hurt on his face if I refused to accept a ring. My mind swirled for a moment. But what else could this surprise be? His eyes shone and his smile exuded warmth, so it was unlikely to be something he'd dislike announcing such as... a promotion abroad or *him* wanting to break up with *me*.

'Tell me about your day first, Pippa Pattinson,' said Henrik. 'How is the new team that you're overseeing?' We sat down, hips and legs touching. The list in my front pocket rustled and with a grin he plucked the sheet of paper out of my apron. 'I can't believe you still have to consult recipes, after all the baking practice you've had. What's on the menu today?' He waved the list in the air, before turning away to unfold it.

With a squeal I draped my arms around his taut waist, jostling for the paper. My heart thumped. What if he read it? Did I really want to split up? Would he be upset or agree with me that things between us had changed? Either way, I wasn't yet ready for a confrontation.

My knotted stomach unfurled as he chuckled and gave it back.

'It's, um, also a surprise,' I said, cheeks burning as I stuffed the list back into my apron pocket and folded my arms.

His lips twitched into a smile. 'Bet it won't be as big as mine.'

Henrik had the knack for surprising people, as his mum found out last month. He arranged an amazing fiftieth birthday spa morning for Greta and her best friends, followed by afternoon tea at The Ritz. My arms loosened and out of habit, our fingers intertwined. In truth, his caring nature had been the biggest turn-on of all, although just occasionally I wished conscientious Henrik could be a little less perfect and forget someone's birthday. Again, urgh! Talk about ungrateful. The prospect of a proposal from such an impeccable lover should make me super-happy.

'Today was okay, thanks. Although the customer service supervisor is twice my age and probably considers me too young to be training for management.' I shrugged. 'But that's not new territory for me. She seems hardworking…' Plus had the cutest photo of a cat on her desk – must ask her about that.

'And the vending machine?' he asked, with a serious expression.

I smiled and gave the thumbs up, my heartbeat having returned to its normal pace. It was our little joke – whatever office we worked in or visited, we rated it by the supply of drinks. A rich mochaccino or creamy latte never failed to perk up a gruelling day.

Henrik tucked a loose strand of hair behind my ear. 'I'm so proud of you, Pips, you're zooming through the bank's trainee manager internship. It seems like only yesterday you graduated from university.'

My eyes tingled. More supportive than an underwired bra, how could faultless Henrik not be the ideal man?

Yet over the last few months, a slight sense of unease had crept over me, because of phone calls he'd leave the room to deal with… Then there were really late nights at the office and unexpected trips that totted up more air miles than ever… But then why would he bother cheating? He could just end the relationship. When I'd asked, Henrik said, in an excited voice, that the company was developing fast and it meant more man hours if he was going to get a promotion.

I sighed. Okay. Really my suspicions were unfounded – Henrik hid nothing in life, including his One Direction CD and tub of anti-ageing cream. So onto the main reason that I'd recently felt he and I fitted together no better than a phone with the wrong charger… If you'd only ever had one proper relationship to talk of (um, life's been busy,) how do you know if you're really head-over-heels? Movies rave about love at first sight… Sex scenes on telly show couples tearing each other's clothes off. Occasionally I still felt leg-trembly over my boyfriend's movie star looks, but physical attraction aside, what remained? *Was Henrik my soulmate out of bed, or even in it?*

Lordy, now I sounded like Carrie Bradshaw typing questions into her computer in Sex and the City… But tons of thoughts had swirled in my head these last few weeks, without getting answers. Perhaps I'd overdosed on romantic novels, which talked of fairy tale meant-to-be's. Plus, I should be grateful for our fancy executive lifestyle, despite dreaming as a youngster I would one day own an old-fashioned afternoon teashop.

I know – mad idea, wasn't it? My lips tugged upwards. High-flying Mum and Dad were having none of it. They'd pushed me to do my maths degree, little knowing I attended baking classes on the quiet. Just as a hobby, of course, not that Henrik understood why I'd waste my mathematical brain on creating something that fed your body and not your mind.

My chest glowed as I thought back to many summers spent in Taxos, a little fishing village on the northern coast of the Greek island, Kos. Having been sent to boarding school from the age of seven, it was the only time I saw my jet-setting parents consecutively, for every day of a whole month. 'What are you thinking about? asked Henrik, as I felt a dreamy look come over my face.

'Taxos. Georgios and Sophia.' Mum and Dad's good friends who used to be like a second set of parents to me.

'Ah, yes. Pleasant people.'

'You got on well with them in January, didn't you?'

Henrik shrugged. 'I guess. Not that I could spent much time at their taverna. Jeez, dead as the tourist market in the Ukraine, that restaurant was,' he said. 'If the people of Taxos have poor summer takings, it must be a real struggle to make ends meet during the low season.'

Urgh, that was a harsh comparison, but remember what I said about the Dutch speaking their mind? A trait that could be highly uncomfortable or rather refreshing... In fact, it was one thing I'd always found attractive about him – his total transparency.

'Although Georgios did take me to the wetlands, to watch wading flamingos... Never far from his binoculars, is he?'

I grinned. 'Sounds like some things haven't changed. Dad used to tease him about looking for dollybirds.' I don't think we ever did explain that joke.

'You might get a shock when you see Taxos again.' Henrik shook his head. 'The recession has taken its toll.'

That's what worried me. I bit my lip. Six months ago he'd gone over as a favour to Mum and Dad when they received word that their villa had flooded. Henrik had a business meeting on the Greek mainland anyway, and said his employer – ThinkBig Development – could pay for the detour. He was always flying off to meet foreign builders or architects, since ThinkBig had branched out into Europe.

'I never asked – did you at least try Georgios' homemade retsina?' I gave a grin.

'Yep – didn't think you'd want the details as I was as ill as a dog the next day.' He pulled a face. 'Have you ever stuck your head down a Greek toilet? I can confirm that the flushing system copes with vomit as poorly as it does loo paper.'

I giggled. Yet I'd always envied everything about my Kos friends' simple lives; rearing their own meat, growing vegetables and fermenting their own wine.

'How long is it exactly since you've been there?' asked Henrik and stretched back against the sofa, hands behind his head.

I thought for a moment. 'Wow. Nine years – the last time I was fourteen and had just chosen my GCSE options. Then life got busy with exams, sixth form, university, getting a new job, renting this gorgeous flat with you…' My chest tightened as I recalled comments Henrik had made about empty Taxos properties and rundown businesses… Of Georgios and Sophia's home needing a good lick of paint… Although I cheered up as an image of their cheeky son Nikolaos – Niko – popped into my mind.

'It'll be a change for you, to be on a beach during your days off, instead of on the piste, during one of our usual ski breaks.'

I nodded. Even our holidays were busy these days, navigating snowy slopes or trekking up challenging mountains. Relaxing images floated into my mind of the many summers Niko and I had spent together, climbing olive trees, chasing goats or diving for pretty shells. The clear waters and marine life inspired a love of tropical fish, and ever since my thirteenth birthday I'd owned the biggest heated tank I could afford. My current one was home to three angelfish, two mini shark fish and some colourful snails. I sighed, almost smelling the briny air of Taxos beach.

'On my last visit, Niko would have been fourteen like me and was sponge-diving and fishing with his Uncle Christos and helping out in the taverna... What's he doing now?'

Henrik shrugged. 'Much the same, from what I could tell.'

No surprise there. Niko never had aspirations to leave home and travel the world. Even as a young boy, he'd say "Like fertile soil, Taxos will provide everything I need for a lifetime of happiness".

I kind of admired the confidence he had in his little hometown. And despite me studying and ultimately heading for university, we'd still had lots in common, that last summer – a love of nature and food plus the ability to tease each other mercilessly. Niko would call pink-hating teenage me Tomboy and being the tallest, I named him Shorty. We used to spend hours watching turtles and both joined the World Wildlife Fund.

'It was good of Mum and Dad to invite me on their annual visit this August,' I said and loosened my ponytail. And for three consecutive weeks! I'd never left my desk for that long, but since my chat with Greta, since my feelings for Henrik had shifted, I needed a good amount of time away from the daily grind, to think about our relationship. Fortunately, work had insisted it wasn't a problem, even though I'd just moved departments, due to all the unpaid overtime I'd happily put in over the last two years. 'I've always loved Taxos for being so untouched by the glitzy eighteen-to-thirty crowd. You experience a real slice of authentic Greek life.'

Henrik's jaw tightened and he fiddled with his designer watch. 'I'd say it was short-sighted of any Greek village to hark back to the old days, in these economically-challenged times. Taxos didn't look to me as if it was doing well on feelings of nostalgia and the earnings from selling fish and olives.'

My head told me he was right, but the just the thought of puking, drunken tourists invading that community made *me* feel like throwing up. I shook myself. 'Anyway, it's a shame you've got that big contract to work on and can't go.' I cleared my throat. Truth was, I felt as relieved as an ice cream finding shade that I only had seven days to go until I left. With that marriage proposal on the horizon, I needed to come to a decision about him, without the distraction of his seductive slate eyes. They only reminded me of how I'd felt about him when we'd first started dating.

My own eyes misted up as I thought of struggling Taxos with its turquoise waters and shortbread sand – of my imaginary teashop where I'd do the school run, dance in the dark and wake with the birds. Oh, the hours Niko and I had spent thinking up ridiculous names for it: Scones Sweet Scones; Teacakes Ahoy; She Shells Cake; Shiver me Sandwiches. In the end, I'd plumped for Pippa's Pantry. BORING, Niko had declared – cue a generous handful of hot sand down his back.

I leant up against Henrik, wondering if I would miss him whilst out in Greece. He wanted kids, but not until our thirties and, like my parents, thought boarding school fitted the executive life best. A bustling family home like Georgios and Sophia's wouldn't suit him one jot.

'Funny you should talk of Taxos, you see my surprise...' Henrik sat upright and turned to face me.

Eek! Greta's words rung in my ears. Was her son about to propose and take me to Greece on honeymoon? Because his surprise certainly wouldn't be chocolates or extravagant bouquets. Henrik wasn't the chivalrous, romantic type, and would consider such gifts a waste of money. Which was good, right? I was a successful, independent woman, not a Disney princess – although if I was, it would have to be Snow White, with her love of birds and forest life. Not that I've, um, thought that through at all *clears throat*. Knights – or princes – in shining armour, I knew, belonged in fiction books, and Henrik always respected my modern outlook. He rarely gave out flowery compliments either – said I was far too intelligent to be patronised by such "tosh". Neither of us could understand why I loved reading anything with a romantic theme.

'Oh, goodness, is that the time…' I rambled, desperate for a speedy exit. I moved forwards, to the edge of the sofa. 'Sorry, I've got to go out right now, forgot I have Zumba and–'

'Whoa! Slow down, Pippa! Surely an exercise class can wait two minutes?'

Aarggh! There was no way out of this. As if already feeling apprehensive about an engagement ring, my left hand curled into a fist.

'Guess what? Thanks to your parents and my boss, you're in for a great holiday abroad.'

Like the detergent-blue Greek tide coming in, a growing sense of uneasiness washed over me.

'As a thank you for me heading over to sort out the flooding mess, your mum and dad insist we have the villa to ourselves this summer. They will visit your aunt in Canada instead. My boss said he can just about afford to let me go for three weeks as long as…' Henrik fiddled with his watch again, '…I find a few days to head off to Kos Town to tie up some business at our new offices there.'

'Since when did ThinkBig have offices on Kos island?' I said, for a minute forgetting my total relief at him not having proposed.

'Ignore all that for a minute – didn't you hear? I'm coming with you, Pips! It'll be just us, cocktails and waves… And who knows what could happen.'

Voice husky now, Henrik took my hand and – uh oh – ran his thumb over my ring finger.

CHAPTER TWO

'Us split up? Why?' said Henrik, and his well-defined jaw dropped. He put down our cases in the lounge of our villa and straightened up. His head almost touched the ceiling built by much shorter Greeks. To avoid an answer, I gazed around. Nothing much had changed since my last visit. The wooden coffee table in the middle of the floor, on top of a mosaic rug… the cream sofa and armchairs… the paintings of fishing boats on the whitewashed walls… the vases of dried flowers… I glanced over at the kitchen with its gleaming white units, deep cornflower blue cupboard doors and spotless silver appliances. Plus the sturdy, rectangular breakfast bar in the middle, surrounded by high stools. The eating area had hardly been used seeing as Mum and Dad preferred to dine out. On the rear side were French patio doors, revealing the Aegean Sea in the distance, beyond a small dusty patio edged with trees and shrubs.

'Um… I need to stretch my legs and could pick up some essentials like bread and milk. You've worked so hard this last week, Henrik, why don't you unpack and take a dip in the pool?' I gave a bright smile, knowing this would appeal to his practical side. 'We've got the next two weeks in each other's company. A couple of hours apart won't kill us.'

What? Did you really think I'd break up with him minutes after arriving in Greece? Where would be the sense in that, and talk about cruel? Plus…*sigh*… thanks to my head and heart tug-of-war, I still hadn't quite come to a decision.

'Okey doke.' He shrugged. 'Whatever suits. I know you get twitchy if we stay anywhere that doesn't stock flour, milk, butter and eggs.'

Which was true – the scone-maker in me was never far away.

Henrik jerked his head back towards the corridor, leading from the front door. 'Which room is ours, that big one on the right – your mum and dad's?'

'No way! That would be *wrong*.'

Henrik grinned. 'The English are so uptight about things like that. So what if your parents have shagged in that bed?'

My shudder only fuelled his laugh.

'We're in the spare room, on the left, which has a lovely big bed.' I led the way in, walked past the huge mosquito net, which draped down from the ceiling, and headed for the round window. Like a small child trying to spot Santa's sleigh, I peered out. Henrik came up behind me and, as he let out a whistle, his breath brushed my skin.

'I'd forgotten this view of the sea. Talk about peacock blue.' Gently he ran a hand up and down my bare left arm. 'Sure I can't tempt you to stay a bit longer? I've been dying to get you out of those shorts ever since we got off the plane. Why don't I turn down the bedcovers?'

He kissed my neck, pulled away and within seconds uttered an expletive. I turned to see him fighting the mosquito net. Eventually he burst out laughing.

'Jeez! This stuff makes the best form of contraception! Just look at my cool moves.' He karate-chopped his long arms and became even more tangled.

I couldn't help giggling. Suddenly his phone belted out the Dutch national anthem – a nod to his roots, him being a mad fan of that country's football team. Then, as had become his way of late, he mouthed "sorry" and after a moment's more struggle, left the room to answer. Hooray! This gave me the perfect opportunity to head off into Taxos.

What with my doubts, I'd found it nigh on impossible recently to… well, ahem, just "go through the motions" in bed, so it really was just as well we hadn't signed any kind of Christian Grey contract. Call me old school, but I truly believed sex went hand-in-hand with love – unless there had been partaking of Prosecco. Fizzy alcohol had a lot to answer for in my life, including a Brazilian wax, one tiny tattoo (don't ask where) and a snog with a university professor.

My chest squeezed. Henrik being Henrik, he never complained. He'd simply ask, in his straightforward way, if it was that time of the month or bought Paracetamol when I'd pleaded stress headaches. On a relaxing holiday, sweetened by sun and cocktails, it might prove harder to avoid his flirtatious touch. Tip-toeing, I picked up my floppy hat and big bug-eye sunglasses from the lounge. Henrik didn't look up as he sat next to a large folder, having brought work papers with him – or at least I'd assumed that's what it contained. He'd kept the folder well sealed, muttering something about confidential documents.

Suited me. I'd come away for a break from that office stuff and left my mobile phone on the kitchen worktop, before heading out of the front door. I admired terracotta pots bursting with bubblegum-pink flowers, and strolled past our gleaming white car – ThinkBig had left it at the airport for us, having apparently signed a good deal with Range Rover for their company's transport. I made my way down the dusty road to my left, having glanced at the fire station opposite. A skinny tabby cat scooted past. It would be fifteen minutes' walk before the village appeared. I suppressed a yawn. Although I'd slept on the four-hour flight, it had been a ridiculously early start. It was only just half past twelve now – and the hottest time of the day. Yet after all these years, curiosity reenergised me. Would Taxos live up to my memories?

Mum and Dad's villa had been built on the outskirts, for privacy, as part of a cluster of four. Over the years, the others had always been full during the summer but now I noticed that two looked quite derelict, with worn "for sale" signs out the front. Smiling at an old woman wearing a black dress and headscarf, I took in the wooded pine forests either side. As perspiration glistened on my skin, I inhaled. Mmm. What a fabulous combination of cedarwood and salt.

Some things hadn't changed one iota – like the gentle island breeze and chirp of cicadas. Memories once again came back: Niko pointing out a glimmering shoal of sardines as we sneakily snorkelled, instead of helping out of with the melon harvest; the two of us munching on honey pastries in his parents' taverna, sipping crafty sips of the grown-ups' ouzo, whilst guests circle-danced. A grin spread over my face, as I realised just how much I was looking forward to seeing my former partner in crime.

'Pippa!' called a voice from the distance.

Uh oh, Henrik must have expected me to stay longer. Despite the early afternoon heat, I sped up, wishing I'd worn sun cream as well as my shades and hat. Eventually the wooded area thinned, and the dusty road forked into three smaller, paved-over pedestrianised avenues, which I knew all led to the small port and postcard-perfect sea. Behind me a bus pulled up, at the last stop. No vehicles ran up and down the streets of Taxos. The only transport from hereon was bicycles and donkeys. The latter's dung gave the village a distinct odour when the weather became really scorching.

I gazed down the left fork, trying to remember the exact layout of the village. Let's see… Down there would be the supermarket, post office and school, with great views of mountains in the distance, towards the south of the island. Then I turned my head to the right and far away spotted the blue dome of the church. That road led to a pottery workshop and gift store, run by Demetrios who now, ooh, had to be in his late thirties. He'd given up a bank job in the city to follow his artistic dreams, and with his last generous bonus had bought the premises and the equipment he needed. He'd let me and Niko make small pots and paint them. I narrowed my eyes at a maze of further avenues, lined with small whitewashed houses with blue painted doors and window shutters.

Even more quickly now, I made my way down the central walkway ahead, past houses and a cake shop run by Pandora – a friendly, fashionable woman. It still had the gilt painted window sills, and colourful potted plants outside, plus the sign swinging in the breeze, bearing a delicious looking drawing of chocolate cake. Then I passed the Fish House and Olive Tree restaurants... Moving on, I glanced into the cycle shop owned by middle-aged Cosmo, whose back faced me. I remembered his skinny build and penchant for his mouth harmonica. I could just see him, through the dusty window and frames of bicycles leant up outside. The walls of his shop looked grubby and chipped.

Right at the end, nearest to the boats and the water's edge, stood Taxos Taverna, belonging to Niko's family. My heart lurched at the cracked windowsills and door frame and decidedly weatherbeaten blue and white paintwork. The place looked empty inside, despite it being lunch time – in fact, the far half of it, the other side of its kitchens, looked completely closed down. I swallowed. The Olive Tree and Fish House had been the same – not buzzing with catchy Greek string music, nor pre-dinner smells of garlic and oregano. How tranquil it was for a Saturday.

Just before reaching its front door, I stopped and stood in the shade of a nearby palm tree, a must thanks to my pale skin, smattering of freckles and red-tinted hair. I picked up one of the large, fallen leaves and fanned my face. It had been so long since I'd enjoyed a foreign summer break, I'd forgotten how sensitive I was to the Mediterranean rays. Niko used to tease me for living in a cap and long-sleeved blouse. Our complexions couldn't have been more different, with his caramel skin and curly black hair.

Feeling slightly queasy, despite my hat, I decided to visit Georgios and Sophia when I felt on better form. So I headed straight to the port and, as soon as I could, left the concrete path and jumped down onto the beach. I approached the breaking waves, stepping across spiky sand lilies. Impatiently, I slipped off my ridiculously impractical high heels. Phew. I felt so much better once I'd sat down and cool water lapped over my toes. Fishing boats bobbed gently nearby, now all tied up due to the heat sending everyone indoors. The local fisherman always used to head out first thing. The beach was empty, as was Caretta Cove, an inward curve of sand down to the left, named after the endangered species of turtle that used to nest there – the loggerhead turtle, to you and me.

Taxos residents knew better than to sit out at midday. As the breezed lifted my fringe, a tightness inside me loosened up. It was good to be away from the stresses and strains of London life: my computer; the musty train journey to work; the artificial lighting in my office block. When was the last time I'd kicked back and relaxed without a phone or pen in my hand? I lay down, pulled my sunhat over my face and closed my eyes, revelling in the sound of lapping waves.

'Oi!' shouted an irritated voice from behind, '*Me sinhorite*!' which I vaguely remembered meant "excuse me". Really? The beach was deserted. Why would anyone need me to move? I kept my eyes firmly closed and pretended to sleep.

'Woman! Move yourself, please. Now…' said a man's voice, in what could only be called Greeklish, pronouncing the consonants very strongly, with a slight roll on the Rs.

Opening my eyes to roll *them*, I sat up and turned around. From behind my big glasses, I spied four men, heaving a small boat. Oops. I now realised I'd been lying directly on a path leading from a boatshed to the nearby ramshackle jetty. I jumped up and grabbed my shoes as they puffed past and was just about to say sorry when a young man at the back muttered "*vlakas*".

My cheeks felt hot and I folded my arms. Idiot? Me? How dare... Ooh, now my head started to throb and my mouth felt as if last night I'd drunk a litre of ouzo. I caught his eye as he stood knee-deep in water, the bottom half of his face hidden by a small mast. Feeling a bit weird, and not at all like myself, I held up my palm, fingers spread out (a milder equivalent of giving someone the finger in England).

Without waiting to see his reaction, I spun around, just a bit too fast. The beach swayed, as if I really had drunk a bottle of that aniseed liquor. Bile shot up my throat. This has happened to me once before when I'd actually been sick and spent a day in bed with the headache from hell.

'Oi! Not so polite, huh? But *you*, woman, were in the way.' A man loomed into view. My vision was kind of blurred but, phooey, even I could see he was one hot stud! Perhaps he was a mirage. Just a bit taller than me, he stood, mocha eyes fiery, yet a hint of a smile on his lips. Plus a tight vest top that showed… well… You could tell he did physical work for a living. He was earthy, kind of ruffled – the opposite to well-groomed Henrik. I had a sudden urge to squeeze his neatly formed biceps, but instead pulled down my sunhat, worried my tongue might be hanging out like a puppy dog's.

'I'm not usually so rude, but you called me an idiot!' I muttered.

'Sorry, but I was struggling with half a ton of wood. Of all places to sunbathe, why you choose the runway between the–'

'I didn't realise…' I said. 'It was an easy mistake. And I wasn't sunbathing.'

'You no looked as if you were about to budge.'

'Budge? Good word,' I muttered.

He chuckled. 'Okay, all is forgiven.'

'*You* forgive *me*?' I shook my head, feeling too icky to remonstrate further, plus, oh God, any minute, this sun was once again going to make me throw up. If he didn't get out the way, revenge for his *vlakas* comment really might be sweet – or rather sickly, and all down his shirt.

The stranger stared at me and then, with a surprised tone, muttered something in Greek. With one swift movement, he leant forward to remove my glasses and hat.

'It is you!' He gasped. 'I recognise that feisty tone anywhere – yet you have no idea who I am.'

But I was hardly listening and in reply promptly vomited over his leather sandals, before everything went black.

CHAPTER THREE

If this was heaven, then sorry Mum, Dad and Henrik, but I'm reluctant to come back to earth. Eyes still closed, I breathed in the comforting aroma of tomato and beef. Foreign voices muttered in the background. Cold air fanned across my face. Someone held my hand so gently, as if I were as valuable as a Fabergé egg.

Eventually I opened my eyes to wooden beams above my head and ochre walls all around. Guitars, pots and plates filled slightly wonky shelves. A ceiling fan spun above. Squinting, I averted my eyes to focus on the person who sat by me, their fingers curled around mine, a leather bracelet around their wrist.

Mmm. Caramel skin... a man with curly dark hair and mocha eyes full of concern… slanted lips... would they taste of olives or baklava?

I shook myself. Honestly, I was practically engaged! The sun must have warped all sense of reason. Clearing my throat, I focussed again. Ah yes, the tight vest top… those frayed jeans… This was the guy who'd called me idiot; the guy whose shoes must be covered in sick. My stomach twisted slightly. Something was bugging me. The thick eyelashes… the way his head cocked slightly to the left… A voice in my head whispered that I'd seen him before today.

'What happened?' I mumbled.

My vision sharpened and behind him stood two short middle-aged figures. The woman patted my shoulder before passing me a glass of water. I sat up and took a large sip, then set the drink on a scratched mahogany table. I looked up to say thank you and gasped.

'Sophia?' I gazed at the man next to her. 'Georgios?' Of course, I was in Taxos Taverna! I'd been lying on a sun lounger they must have brought in from outside. The wonky shelves… the familiar ochre walls… It all made sense now. So this man holding my hand had to be…

'Niko?'

'*Ya sou*, Pippa,' he said, eyes dancing, probably because of my dropped jaw. I scanned him from head to toe. Of course. How hadn't I recognised him earlier? Despite the fuller build and inches he'd grown, there was no mistaking the slightly bent nose and mole just above his left eyebrow. Laughter lit up his eyes. I grinned back, leant forward and gave him a big hug. Eek! How embarrassing, that just for one minute earlier – well, a second… no, a nanosecond, really – I'd considered him hot stuff.

'It's great seeing you all again,' I stuttered, hoping my breath didn't smell of sick. 'My parents send their love.'

'They shall visit us this evening, no?' said Georgios. 'We are so happy to see you. Tonight we celebrate.'

I loved the sound of the locals speaking English. Thanks to tourism, most people in Kos knew a smattering of my language – and many, like this dear family, much more than just a few essential phrases.

'Afraid not. They are visiting my aunt in Canada. It's just me here, with my… boyfriend, Henrik.'

Niko's body stiffened, like a dog that had suddenly got a whiff of a cat.

'Ah yes. We met him last winter.' Georgios' smile widened. 'I introduced him to retsina. He was a little ill afterwards.'

'Talking of which, sorry about your sandals, Niko,' I said.

Georgios' deep laugh bellowed out. Sophia punched her husband's arm.

'My little meatball, it is not funny. Poor *Pippitsa* has not been well.' She came forward and kissed me on the forehead.

Sophia hadn't changed, apart from being just a little fuller around the waist. My chest glowed at the familiarity of her floral skirt, long hair scraped into a bun and friendly heart-shaped face.

Playfully Niko shook a finger. 'What a welcome you gave me, Pippa, although… sorry for calling you *vlakas*.'

My cheeks burned. 'Sorry I palmed you – must have been due to sunstroke.'

'Enough of the apologies,' said Georgios and ran a hand over his round, hairless head before stepping forward to give me a hug. He'd been bald as long as I'd known him, and still tried to make up for that with a big, black moustache. 'Pippa, to see you back in Taxos after so many years, warms my heart. But before we exchange news, you eat, no? Let me fetch moussaka, or a fresh feta salad, with toasted pitta bread, like you always preferred.' He raised his bushy eyebrows which were grey and didn't match his moustache.

'Both dishes sound lovely – although that moussaka smells divine. *Efharisto*.' Some words, like "thank you", had stuck in my mind.

Sophia insisted on helping me to one of the tables, then took the sun lounger outside as a couple of blonde tourists trickled in – a rare sight, I suspected, in Taxos nowadays. On her return we chatted about my job and parents. Niko headed over to the diners, two young women.

'*Ya sas*, ladeez,' he said and soon they were laughing with him. Neither could take their eyes off my Greek childhood friend. No idea why. The fact that I couldn't either meant, um, nothing at all.

'Apollo?' I said to a black cat that strolled over and meowed. I picked him up and tickled his chin, before running my hand over the soft fur. Niko eventually came back, carrying two plates of moussaka – not without winking at the tourists, as he passed them. Sophia left us alone at the table to catch up. Carefully, I put the purring cat down.

'I can't believe Apollo is still around.'

Niko forked up the juicy layers of meat and vegetables as if he'd not eaten for a week. Henrik would not have approved – back home, he never ate without a full set of cutlery and napkin.

Several mouthfuls later, Niko paused for breath. A chuckle escaped his lips. 'Sorry, hunger wins over manners when I've been out fishing all morning... Yes, Apollo does well – he is eighteen this year and still catching mice. And I can't believe you've come back, Tomboy…' His eyes shone. 'Although I cannot call you that any more.' He put down his fork and reached for my hand. 'Those manicured nails – so mature and sophisticated, no? And your neatly tied-back hair… Where are those cute spots on your cheeks?'

'You mean freckles? I've discovered foundation – and hairbrushes. So, guilty as charged – I've grown up.'

Like two teenagers, we giggled.

'That I see,' he said, and for some reason the way he stared made my palms feel hot. 'You happy, no, with your fancy bank job and living with Henrik, in London? In January he told us all about it.'

Gosh, I'd forgotten how intense his gaze was. I'd also forgotten Henrik until just now. But that was normal, right? I'd just blacked out. Ignoring the guilty twinge in my chest, I decided he was no doubt tucked up in the mosquito net, sleeping off several hard months of work and today's early start.

'Hmm my colleagues… London… Me and Henrik, it is… very nice.'

Niko burst out laughing. 'Remember all those summers you taught me English? Rule one was NEVER use the word "nice". You said it meant nothing at all.'

I bit my lip. 'Well, my English teacher drilled that into me. He was my idol. I was a bit of a language geek back then.'

'But still…' Niko picked up his fork again and toyed with a slice of melt-in-the-mouth aubergine, ignoring the cat's hopeful stare. 'You and Henrik… All you can say is it's *nice*?'

'Yes – unlike you,' I replied, in the frostiest voice I could muster.

Sophia glanced over as once more we laughed. She looked from Niko, to me, then back at him and her mouth downturned for a moment. She exchanged a glance with her husband. Sophia's whole demeanour couldn't hide a sense of… not exactly disapproval but something negative. Niko seemed to sense it too and jerked his head towards my empty plate.

'You and me – let's get some fresh air,' he said. 'We take two orange granitas down to the beach. Siesta is almost over, it will be cooler and I know a shady spot.'

'Under the fig tree, by the disused boatshed, just before Caretta Cove – is it still the same?'

Niko's face lit up. 'You remember?'

I went to the bathroom to freshen up and when I returned Niko had prepared the slushy ice drinks. We went outside and I stared at the drinks in sealed paper cups, with straws.

He shrugged. 'We do takeaway drinks and food now. Times have been hard.'

‘The other half of the taverna is closed down...’

‘Yes. On a good day, we are lucky to fill just the half that is now open.’

I slipped my arm through his, enjoying the breeze which blew stronger. It was as if the last nine years apart hadn’t happened. In fact, I almost expected him to drop a beetle or handful of damp seaweed down my back. I sucked up the refreshing granita as we strolled down the left side of the beach and eventually came to a sprawling fig tree by a dilapidated building. In the distance stood the ash and green southern mountains, all hazy at the top. We sat on the sand underneath the tree. I removed my floppy hat and sunglasses and swatted away a wasp.

‘That was weird,’ I said.

Niko raised an eyebrow.

‘Walking together, with you now taller than me. I couldn’t give you a piggy-back any more.’

‘And look at you, in those fashionable heels.’ He gazed at my feet.

‘I forgot to change into my sandals,’ I said and kicked them off.

Niko took my drink and put the two cups down by his side.

‘I no criticise, Pippa. You are a beautiful woman – more striking than the orange blush of a sunset. But then I always thought you were out of the ordinary. I…’ He shrugged. ‘I never thought I’d see you again.’

For a moment I lost myself in his mocha eyes and swallowed hard. Henrik would never say something like that. I shook myself. And quite right too. It was okay in books, but what modern woman needed to actually hear romantic mush? Yet my heart raced like it never used to years ago, in my Greek friend’s company. What was going on? Clearly the strong Aegean sun had a lot to answer for.

I cleared my throat. ‘So, um, come on then – what’s the punchline?’ I leant back on my elbows.

‘Huh?’

‘The joke… after that compliment.’

Niko’s eyes lost their intensity for a second and he grinned. ‘We used to laugh a lot, no? Okay… Would you feel happier if I said you look very *nice* instead?’

‘Don’t you dare!’ I laughed and turned onto my front. ‘Does Cosmo still play his harmonica?

Niko smiled. ‘All the time.’

‘How about Demetrios? Remember the awful, wonky pots we made – is he married yet?’

‘No. But he adopted four stray cats. How they are spoilt – he made each a food bowl with their name.’

‘And is his shop still the only building in the village that isn’t painted white and blue?’

Niko nodded. ‘Yes, it is still the colour of aubergine, with ivy growing across the roof. Before the recession hit, Demetrios laid fancy tiles on the floor and bought a new kiln... So inside it has changed, but from the outside it still looks about one hundred years old, with the unlevel foundations that make it sink to the right.’

I grinned. ‘It’s good to be back.’

‘How long for?’

‘Three whole weeks.’

‘Ah, yes is good. We can get to know each other again. I have missed you these last summers, Pippa.’

My stomach fluttered. I realised I’d missed him too.

‘You and Henrik…’ He bit his lip. ‘It is true love… forever, no?’

‘Niko!’ I grinned. ‘We haven’t seen each other for so many years and within minutes you cut straight to the chase!’

'Huh... chase?' His gaze bore straight through me. 'We haven't seen each other for nine years, Pippa. Time isn't to waste. You are sure he's good enough?'

I raised one eyebrow. 'Why would you ask that?'

Niko glanced away. 'It's just... Ay, ignore me, Pippa. You are an intelligent woman who wouldn't waste time on the wrong man.' He stared at the sand. 'No one could believe his size, when he visited in January. The village's children called him Gigantes, after our country's mythical giant tribe.' A muscle in his cheek flinched. 'And the women couldn't do enough for your Dutch goliath. Young Alysia from next door managed to build up a secret album of photos of Henrik, taken on her mobile phone.'

I gazed sideways at him. 'So, if we're being so forthright, what about you? Has Nikolaos Sotiropoulos found the woman of his dreams?'

His cheeks flushed. 'For a long time I've doubted I ever would, but life is full of surprises. Perhaps now...' He squeezed my hand. 'Fate has been kind to me.'

My stomach flipped. Surely not...? Could he mean *me*? No. This was Shorty, just a family friend, who used to scare me with grass snakes – at his peril, I might add, as I knew spiders gave him the shakes.

I breathed in and out. Clearly the sun was messing with my brain.

'So... Taxos... How are you all managing, with the recession?' I mumbled, not quite sure what to say next.

'Huh? Oh...' Niko's brow wrinkled and he drew circles in the sand with his finger.

'Not good. I help Papa and Mama where I can, as a chef and waiter. Plus my cousin Stefan and I take out my uncle's boat every morning to fish – after siesta we sponge-dive. But the locals watch every euro and there are only so many sponges you can sell to the neighbouring villages.' He too lay on his front, so close it reminded me of when we'd hide, stretched out under tarpaulin, in the bottom of his uncle's boat, to avoid our parents calling us in for bed.

Niko nodded across the sand. 'See Mrs Dellis, over there?'

The old lady was easy to pick out as the beach was still empty. Dressed in black, from her scarf to her shoes, she sat in a deckchair, under a large parasol. Two young children built sandcastles at her feet. By the side of them lay two red lilos.

'I'm surprised to see them out in this midday heat,' I said.

He shrugged. 'Two young boys must be hard for her to keep entertained. Their family is typical of many – her son-in-law lost his job as a website designer in Kos town. He's gone back to farming the little land they have, with his wife, who makes cheese. They trade with farmers in neighbouring villages, try to sell jam and pickles as well, but is hard, especially in winter. More than ever grandparents look after children, whilst both parents work all hours.'

'How do your uncle and cousin manage – just by fishing?'

'My cousin and I have more physical strength now, so we've taken over. Uncle Christos gets shift-work cleaning, or as security at the airport, when he can.'

My eyes ran over Niko's solid body. Despite being short as a child, he'd always been strong.

A relaxed silence fell between us as I glanced at houses lining the beach, each blue and white, like the sand, like the sky; each with a boatshed that could have done with a lick of paint. Henrik had been right – the village did look run down. Henrik. With a sigh I realised it was time to return to the villa. I hadn't even bought any milk or bread.

I glanced up at the tree branches overhanging us. Their big leaves shimmied in the wind. Plump, green figs drooped down, as shapely as any Kardashian bottom, a clear sign they were ripe. Niko followed my gaze, stood up and easily plucked one off.

He lay down next to me again, caught my eye and I nodded. Just like in the old days, he rubbed it against his vest top before taking the first bite. Juice trickled out of the corner of his mouth as he passed me the other half. The cinnamon flesh glistened. I pushed it between my lips. Slowly I chewed, savouring its sweet lushness.

'I'm glad you haven't become too posh to eat the skin,' said Niko and his mouth slanted into a smile.

'I haven't changed that much,' I mumbled, as with his thumb, he gently wiped away juice from my chin. His hand lingered. Our eyes locked. The strangest sensation ran up and down my spine. As his pupils dilated, I wondered if mine were doing the same.

'You still have those thick eyelashes,' I murmured.

'Remember you'd beg me to give you butterfly kisses,' he said, eyes teasing. 'You'd say "Niko, lean forward close and bat your eyelashes against mine". The tickling sensation made your laugh sound like a braying donkey.'

I chuckled.

'Go on – let's do it, for… what do you say? For old clock's sake.'

'Old *time*'s sake…'

His grin widened. 'Unless… perhaps Pippa Pattinson is boring in her old age?'

I snorted. 'Fine. Go ahead.' Our faces neared by a centimetre. Then another. Despite the shade, my body felt as if I were lying on volcanic rock. He pressed right up close, his breath blowing against mine. Our eyelashes touched.

What would happen if my mouth tilted just a few millimetres forwards? It was as if every cell in my body was magnetised to his. Oh God, all I could think of, right at this moment, was him. The memories, history between us, the laughter, silly arguments, the small scar above his lip…

I shut my eyes, to be met with a kaleidoscope of colours, as if magical fairy dust swirled in my head. Wow. What was that? Unable to stop myself, eyes open now, I leant further forward, calling on all my willpower not to press my lips against his – although if I didn't soon, my insides would surely explode... By now we held each other's hands. Gently our noses met. It was as if time had stood still to shout "all those moments from your childhood were leading to this". Was I still out cold from sunstroke? Was this all a dream?

'Pippa! I thought you were shopping,' hollered a familiar male voice, from behind. 'What on earth are you doing?'

No, I was wide awake and with a jolt pulled away.

CHAPTER FOUR

I swung around and got to my feet. Henrik approached, the wind almost blowing off his cap. He removed it himself to reveal Top Gun sunglasses. Behind him smiled a young Greek woman with a purple flower in her hair.

'Sorry, Henrik,' I stuttered, as he reached the fig tree. I brushed sand off my shorts. 'Georgios and Sophia looked after me, you see, I fainted, then–'

'I know,' he said. 'They assumed you two had gone shopping for the food we need.' He held out a hand to Niko. 'Good to see you again, mate. Thanks for looking after Pippa.'

After a momentary pause, Niko held out his hand. I got the feeling Henrik's "mate" was the last thing he wanted to be.

'Niko's granitas are hard to resist,' said the woman as she eyed the empty cups. '*Ya sou* Pippa. I am Leila, pleasure to meet you – I guessed you two had come here to cool off.'

Oh the irony – during those butterfly kisses, I'd never felt so hot.

Deep lines appeared in Henrik's forehead, as he scanned my face. 'I should have reminded you to put on sun cream. Why don't you head back to the villa? I'll get the groceries in.'

But I couldn't stop staring at petite Leila. Not remembering her from my childhood, I studied the gathered skirt and blouse, the shiny raven hair draped down one shoulder and the small gold hoop earrings. She had a flavour of the exotic about her and what friendly eyes… Leila came forwards and with a shy expression hugged me tight.

'Often Georgios, Sophia and Niko have talked about the Pattinson family, since I moved here with my parents six years ago – and Niko's grandmother, Iris, tells tales of the tasty scones you baked her.'

'How is Grandma?' My chest glowed at the thought of Georgios' mum. I couldn't wait to see her again. Nine years without her fiery words – but caring heart – had been too long.

By now Niko had sat up, fig juice still at the corner of his mouth, vest top ruffled… His shoulders sagged. 'Not the best, what with her being ill, the last year.'

Ill? My mouth went dry.

'Whilst successful...' his voice wavered, '...the treatment has been harsh. We see very small signs of improvement, of her blossoming back into the old Grandma – it is a gradual process, like the growth of oregano, a most slow-developing plant.' He exchanged a look with Leila. She walked over as he stood up and squeezed his arm.

'But a visit from you would cheer her up, Pippa,' said Leila.

I returned her nod, barely able to breathe for a moment. Grandma was strong. It couldn't be that bad, otherwise the Sotiropoulos family would have surely contacted us back in England.

'She talks of you often,' said Niko. 'I remember how you used to tell her everything.'

'Yes. Grandma was a great confidante.' I gave a small smile. Which was true – Mum did her best but her mind often seemed elsewhere (the office, probably), whereas Grandma, who never stopped cooking or cleaning, still had the knack of knowing when to call me in for a fresh pastry and ask what was wrong. Like the summer after I'd fallen out with my best friend, or the year of my OCD phase. Gently she'd asked why I kept disappearing to the bathroom to wash. No one else had noticed. Grandma worked out I was fretting about the approaching autumn school term. I was due a new form tutor with a fearsome reputation. Grandma gave me her own Greek stress beads – but just talking about my worries had helped. And as usual she'd been right – rumours always tainted the truth and the new teacher turned out to be all right.

'She'll be okay, I'm sure,' said Leila, in a voice as gentle as rustling olive tree leaves.

Yes. She was right. No doubt when I visited, Grandma would still be baking and ordering everyone about – and asking me to sing (or at least whistle) her favourite Greek song about a sleeping cuckoo... I nodded at Leila, now unable to take my eyes off the way she easily held onto Niko.

Henrik held out his hand. 'Come on, Pips. Let's head to the supermarket. I'm sure Niko and his fiancée would like some time alone, before the sponge-diving boats go out.' He grinned at Niko. 'Leila filled me in on your daily routine. It's clearly not for the faint-hearted.'

My throat constricted and the oddest expression crossed Niko's face.

Fiancée? Engaged to be married? For some reason, an unpleasant sensation pierced my chest. Wow, what a flirt he'd become, for someone on the verge of exchanging marital vows. Pursing my lips, I stood transfixed to Leila's right hand and a diamond, obvious now, twinkling in the sunlight. That explained why Sophia had looked uncomfortable, in the taverna, at my easy closeness with her son. My eyes scanned her face, those elegant arms, the tiny waist... What was not to like? No wonder my childhood friend had fallen for her charms. Plus she was softly spoken and had the prettiest smile... I swallowed hard and for the first time in a while, momentarily wished my frame was more petite.

Niko spoke rapidly in Greek to this fiancée for a moment and then cleared his throat.

'Look, Henrik, I don't think Pippa's up to shopping just yet – Leila will take you to the supermarket, yes? We'll meet you back at my parents' taverna.'

'It's true,' said Leila, 'you look a little off-colour, Pippa. It makes me happy to help Henrik. I promised to look after my small cousins today, but not for another hour.'

'I'm absolutely fine,' I replied in a bright voice. So, she was kind-hearted as well.

But the happy Greek couple (who me, sarcastic?) were having none of it. Plus Henrik took little persuasion when Leila hinted Georgios might shout him a free beer. Within minutes the two of them were gone. I picked up my hat and sunglasses and turned to go. However, Niko grabbed my hand.

'Pippa. Look, don't go, I should have…'

Gently, I pulled away my fingers. 'Whatever… Your personal life – it's… it's nothing to do with me.' I coughed. 'Congratulations. She seems lovely. Your parents must be thrilled.'

'Yes, but… look… before… about the butterfly kisses…'

I forced a laugh. 'Look at us, trying to relive old times. What are we like? I'm… I'm glad you've found someone, like I've found Henrik.'

'About Leila… I was going to tell you, but–'

Urgh, give it up Niko, otherwise… too late. Prepare for an Epic Fail when it came to pretend civility.

'But what? I saw the way you flirted with those guests back at the taverna. "Ladeez"? I mean, *really*? Then with me on the sand… all those mushy compliments… you never *used* to talk like that.' I shook my head. 'You were the last person I expected to turn into one of those bull-shitting Greek waiters determined to charm their way into customers' good books and wallets.' Damn my voice for wobbling, but what was he playing at?

He stepped forward, eyes dull. 'You really think that of me, Pippa?

I bit my lip.

'The things I said about you… every single one I meant.'

Yeah right – as beautiful as the blush of a sunset? Did I *really* fall for that rubbish? Henrik may not be the most romantic man in the world, but at least he was dead-straight. And for that quality alone, he was worth hanging onto.

'Oh come on, admit it,' I said, voice calmer now. 'You've not given me one thought over these years. And I... I'd practically forgotten that annoying boy who used to pinch my sweets and ping the straps of my bikini top. It's okay. Life moves on.'

'You're even more attractive when angry,' he said and smiled.

I shook my head. 'You could learn a lot from watching a famous film my mum loves, called Shirley Valentine… You might pick up some tips on how to get into foreign women's knickers more quickly.'

Cheeks flushed scarlet, he scowled and promptly lifted off his vest top. He threw it on the ground.

'Oh God, what now… Am I supposed to be impressed?' I muttered. 'Honestly, you're unbelievable.' Although… wow. Look at those pecs, clearly visible, as he'd not become nearly as hairy as his dad. Niko's eyes sparked and he pointed to a line of small scars down the right side of his abdomen, an imperfection which contrasted Henrik's smooth, unmarked chest. Annoyingly I longed to run my fingers – or my tongue (eek, did I really just think that?) across his deliciously firm, caramel skin.

'You remember, no?' he demanded.

I stared for a moment, praying for some cold shower to hover over my head, like the snowman's personal cloud in Frozen. Then it clicked. The jellyfish attack. It had happened during that last summer, when we'd both just turned fourteen. One stung me and I panicked. Swiftly Niko had swum over, through a cluster of them and dragged me out of the water. In the process he got trapped by tentacles and injured ten times worse than I was.

'I would do it again in a heartbeat. And I'm grateful… This scar is a constant reminder of happy times – of our friendship. And–'

'Here we go, bullshit again. That's like the Greek waiter in that film saying he loves Shirley Valentine's stretch marks.'

'Stretch marks?' He shrugged. 'I don't understand the words but get your tone – after all those summers together, now you dove-hole me as some shallow playboy?'

'It's *pigeon*-hole,' I muttered. My stomach twisted. 'Yes, well, I wouldn't worry. Clearly Leila thinks you're fabulous.'

'*She* is the fabulous one,' he snapped.

My throat ached as I thought back to her exotic appearance. What did Leila do for a living? Probably something super sexy, such as painting portraits or dancing.

'Unlike Henrik,' he continued. 'You should know that last time he was here–'

A bloodcurdling scream pierced the air and, dropping my glasses and hat, I span around. Old Mrs Dellis paced up and down, howling and pointing at the waves. The beach was still empty so I followed her finger and gasped.

Mrs Dellis' two small grandsons balanced precariously on red lilos, far out at sea, wailing almost as loudly as her. Niko ran towards the old woman. I followed his cue. Within a minute we were by her side. He spoke rapidly in Greek and in between more howls she responded.

'*Na para I eychi*!' muttered Niko ("damn" to you and me) and in a flash slipped out of his sandals and jeans.

'Exhausted Mrs Dellis fell asleep,' he barked. 'Those kids snuck off with their inflatables, even though they are not allowed in the water on their own. This wind must have blown them out towards a current. Neither is good swimmer. If one of them falls off…'

We exchanged a brief look before Niko charged into the waves.

Two hysterical kids and one adult? Nope, that wasn't going to work. So thanks to the mathematician in me – and to the amazement of a few elderly locals who must have heard the commotion and come down to the beach – I pulled off my blouse and stepped quickly out of my shorts. Thank God I was wearing matching underwear and had recently waxed. Blocking out thoughts of jellyfish, I ran across the sand, to make up the numbers, flinching as one foot landed on something sharp before I hit the warm waves.

Trouble was, that wind seemed twice as strong in the water, which increased the height of the waves – for every half-metre forward, I had to navigate a half-metre into the air.

Bobbing up and down, I got flashes of the children's faces scrunched up, lilos colliding. As saltwater filled my mouth, I suffered a coughing fit and Niko turned around.

'Pippa? You crazee woman! Go back!' he hollered.

'Not likely. You'll need help,' I shouted. A scream cut through the air from the beach. I stared at the lilos. One of the children had fallen off – the eldest, by the looks of it.

'Theo!' shouted Niko, before disappearing from view himself. I also dived under the water. Just a few more metres and I'd be at the inflatables. Hundreds of white bubbles blocked my vision, but eventually I could just make out Niko's muscular legs and the black curly head of a child. He dragged the boy up to the surface and we all came up for air.

Spluttering, I glanced again at the lilos, whilst Niko tried to calm down Theo. Nausea backed up my throat. Both were empty, now. The youngest must have fallen in too. Oh *skata* (rude word, you can guess which one).

I took a deep breath and dived again, leaving Niko to deal with Theo, who kept gagging and flapping his hands. Frantically I paddled my legs, arms tearing through the relentless current. Within seconds I was under the red plastic rectangles, exhausted, despite having only progressed a couple of metres. A clump of seaweed floated past and my eyes stung as I forced them to focus towards the inky black depths. With brilliant timing I recalled the film Jaws. Were great white sharks common in the Aegean?

With all my might I pushed myself further downwards. Now all I could think about what how much I needed oxygen. Luxurious, fragrant Greek cedar air, wafting into my lungs… My chest burnt as something grabbed my leg. I pirouetted around, throat aching as I ran out of breath. Little fingers reached up. In one swift movement I ducked and put my hands beneath the boy's armpits. Legs kicking wildly, I propelled us to the surface.

'Pippa…' Niko's voice broke as my head shot above the water's surface. Theo was back on one of the lilos.

'Help!' I yelled, my open mouth taking in more briny liquid. Somehow we dragged Theo's brother onto the other lilo and turned him onto his side. The little boy suffered a violent coughing fit. Water and saliva spewed out of his mouth. He gagged several times and burst into tears. The knots in my stomach unfurled as crying probably meant he was all right.

Niko ordered the children to lie on their fronts, on the lilos, and hold tight.

By this time a group of fishermen had sailed out, towards us. Thank God. My whole body felt as heavy as the anchor I spotted on the boat's side. After what seemed like five hours, not five minutes, they arrived, first hauling the boys to safety. Niko insisted I went next. He followed, panting for breath, and the four of us crouched on the wooden seats, me in between the two boys.

A young fisherman, in a checked shirt, altered the angle of the sail, whilst his grey-bearded companion wrapped the boys in towels and passed me a spare one. He avoided my eye. Ah yes. Of course. Just remembered my outfit consisted of one lacy bra and high-leg knickers. I wrapped the towel around my body, sarong-style, and wiped my mouth. Urgh. I hated that salty taste, and was that a slimy lace of seaweed down my back? My hair hung in rats' tails, the tight bobble lost, as I slipped my arms around the children and cuddled them tight. My cheeks pricked and tingled like only fair skin does under the sun. Niko spoke to the crew, a couple of whom had clapped him on the shoulder.

Whilst the boat swayed from side to side, I spotted two adults with Mrs Dellis, on the beach. All three waved madly. As we neared I could see their tear-stained faces. The young couple must have been the boys' parents. A bigger crowd had assembled near the old jetty. As the boat hit the sand, the boys' mum and dad rushed forward, wading into the water. Old Mrs Dellis was still wailing and wringing her bony hands.

'*Efharisto, efharisto,*' the boys' family kept saying to me and Niko. In turn, we thanked the fishermen.

A while later, Niko gave me a wry smile. 'So here we are again,' he muttered.

Having escaped the congratulations of the crowd and beady eye of the local doctor, we stood under the fig tree, me back in my shorts and blouse. I picked up my hat and glasses. He leant forward and ran a thumb over my cheeks.

'They'll be painful later. Grandma swears that yogurt helps sunburn.'

I shrugged and turned to go, like I had a couple of hours before.

'Pippa… No leave it like this…' He held out a hand. 'How you see me… it is not true. I'm no playboy. It's just… I'm so pleased to see you again. Stay a while. Tell me about your life. Let's catch up on the time we've been apart.'

I fought the urge to slip my hand into his.

'Look, it's great to see you too,' I said, now over the shock of the change in him. Almost losing those boys gave a bit of perspective. 'But I'm a Londoner now – part of the rat-race. An office worker. A suit wearer. Whereas you…' I gazed around at the island… the lapping waves… the squawking seagulls… 'We couldn't be more different. And I'm here to spend time with Henrik. I mean, you are happy with Leila, right? Committed to spending the rest of your days with her?'

'Of course,' said Niko quickly and for some reason averted his eyes.

'Just like I am committed to honest, caring Henrik,' I continued, shifting uncomfortably. Well, I hadn't made my mind up yet.

'Henrik? Honest? Pah, I can keep quiet no longer.' He sneered. 'This Dutch giant is up to something. Back in

January he kept meeting Stavros Lakis, our local mayor. He is a sly figure, well-known for zooming around in his new white Range Rover, smoking fancy cigars and tricking people out of money. Wake up, Pippa, your tall, handsome boyfriend whose charm is legendary, is in fact a scoundrel, making some deal with the most corrupt man on the whole of Kos island...'

CHAPTER FIVE

I wrapped my arms around Niko's neck. My fingers played with his curls. The teasing mouth quirked into a smile and like a mirror reflection, I'm guessing my lips quirked back. I couldn't be more grateful to him, for pointing out the dark ways of clearly unwholesome Henrik. I mean, fancy him speaking to the dodgy town mayor. Without hesitation, I stripped off and lay down on a carpet of fallen fig leaves. Holding my hand up, I muttered 'Ravish me, my little sea urchin… let your feelers do their work…'

Hmm. As if that was going to happen – me play right into that gigolo's hands? Yes, "gigolo" – all civility had left me the moment he insulted my boyfriend. I'd snorted in Niko's face and flounced off, dignity lacking due to my high heels wobbling in the sand. It was laughable. Henrik talking to an underhand mayor meant nothing, because as everyone else on this planet knew, corruption throughout the Greek establishment was rife. In fact it would be more suspicious if Henrik had talked to an official whose reputation was still intact.

I glanced sideways, across the shell-white pillows. Slowly Henrik's chest rose and dipped. Yesterday we'd spent just a quiet Sunday together, by the pool, managing with basic food provisions and… okay, if you must know, we finally made love again and it was... nice.

Aarggh, and now I'd used a word that reminded me of Niko. But me realising what a jerk Niko had grown into forced me to abandon my doubts and realise Henrik really was a catch. My head told me to grow up – that like oysters, not all men had something priceless inside. My man had lots of good qualities, like his honesty, and that should be enough.

I jumped as someone knocked at the villa's front door. Henrik yawned and went to sit up. I shushed him, slipped through a gap in the mosquito net and headed towards our little blue-painted front door, which I unlocked and pulled open.

'*Ya sou*, Theo!' I squinted in the sunlight and bent down to ruffle the black hair. The little boy stood next to his dad.

'Miss Pattinson…' Mr Dellis bowed his head.

'Please, call me Pippa.' I smiled and smoothed down my nightdress. Eek, by the position of the sun, it must have already been late morning. I yawned again. 'Excuse me – we got woken up by the fire station last night.'

'Ah yes... There was a fire in a nightclub, further north – our crew went to help out. My brother is one of the team. Fortunately no one was hurt.' Mr Dellis cleared his throat. 'Pippa… again… Saturday – *efharisto*. It was dangerous. Like firemen, you risked your life – for my boy.'

'*Efharisto*,' mumbled Theo, in a shy voice, from under the green sunhat he'd just put back on.

'No problem,' I said, chest glowing.

'But as a thank you, we put on a little meal tonight and have booked Taxos Taverna for eight o'clock. Please say you and your boyfriend will be there. My family and I will treat you and Niko like the greatest of gods.'

My stomach twisted. Niko? Could I really face seeing him again, without my temper urging me to shower him with retsina and…. Oh no. Did I really just imagine what it would be like to lick it off?

My ears burned. 'There is no need, honestly–'

'That is exactly what Niko said.' Mr Dellis took my hand. 'My wife and I, my mother… so grateful. Please. Let us honour you in this small way. We have arranged for Georgios and Sophia to put on a modest buffet.'

Bags bulged under his eyes and his nails had split, no doubt from working the land. 'Okay. Um… lovely, thank you. But please let me bring something… for dessert.' I didn't want to hurt his pride by saying don't spend money you can't afford.

His face lit up. 'We look forward to it. Eight o'clock. Until later!'

I closed the door. How great to see Theo looking so well, although I doubted he'd go back on a lilo any time soon.

As I walked through the hallway, gentle snoring wafted out from the spare room. Both Henrik and I had slept like exhausted Olympic torchbearers since arriving in Greece – no doubt the months of a hectic London life catching up with us. Humming, I headed into the kitchen and filled the coffee maker. Mmm, those ground beans smelt good. Soon it was percolating and energised by just the aroma of caffeine, I opened one of the cornflower-blue cupboards and took out the flour, butter and sugar that Henrik and Leila had bought on Saturday afternoon. We were almost out of milk, but I wouldn't need much for even a large batch of scones.

Leila. How long had she been going out with Niko? Did they laugh together like I used to with him? Who'd made the first move? Did she, too, like wildlife?

My heart pumped as I recalled Niko's face, up against mine… Could I avoid him forever? No. For a start, food was running low which meant a trip into Taxos. Talking of which, how on earth would I flavour the scones? Not that much beat a plain, well-risen one with melting butter on top, but I had a bit of a reputation to uphold with the Sotiropoulos family, particularly Grandma.

My gaze fell upon a large bar of chocolate on the low wooden table, in the middle of the lounge. Henrik had bought it at the airport. He liked it dark. Surely he wouldn't mind me using a little if I replaced it at the local supermarket? I gazed out of the patio windows and for the first time really studied the plants, especially a wide, roundish tree with emerald leaves and what looked like orangey-red peaches… Of course – apricots! The last fruits of the season hung in August and we used to gorge on them for breakfast when I was a child. Chocolate chip and apricot scones would be a perfect combination of bitter and sweet flavours. I slipped into my flip-flops and drew back the patio doors.

As I walked onto the paving stones, the tolerable morning sun kissed my cheeks. I still winced as Saturday's sunburn had not quite turned brown. Cicadas chirped and I inhaled salty sea air. Bliss – a heavenly change from the stuffy smell of the London underground.

I tucked strands of unbrushed hair behind my ears, only for the breeze to release them once more. On reaching the apricot tree, I plucked off tiger-orange fruits, clearly bursting with juice. In fact several lay open on the ground, providing flies with a sumptuous brunch. I bit into one and a wet trickle ran down my chin. *Annoying*… Why did that remind me of Niko's juice-smeared mouth as he'd devoured half a fig?

Back indoors, I cracked on with the culinary task in hand. Ah, that was better, me kneading the scone dough, up and down, then around and around…. How pretty it looked with flecks of hard brown and squishy orange. Aaahhh… slowly my shoulders and brow relaxed and confused thoughts swapped places with happy images in my mind, such as a gently-breaking tide or colourful Greek salad.

I couldn't wait to see Grandma again. How she would loves these scones. Please let her get better... My vision blurred for a second. It was strange to think of the hardworking, no-nonsense Iris bed-ridden with people looking after her for a change.

'So, when are you going to replace my chocolate?' said Henrik, as we strolled into Taxos that evening, just before eight. The road was difficult to make out, due to the sunset. Like movie actors teasing paparazzi, stars glinted, now and again, in the sapphire sky. I breathed in cedarwood smells from the nearby forest.

He glanced down. I looked up. As he squeezed my fingers through the twilight, we both grinned. With the other hand I carried a basket, containing the scones with a tea-towel over the top. I felt like one of those American Stepford wives you see in TV series, who always welcome new neighbours with homemade delights. Or like Red Riding Hood in the woods, except without the cape.

'Although I guess I can write off the debt, seeing as you're such a hero,' Henrik continued. 'What happened Saturday – you saving that boy...'

I groaned. 'Please. I'm dreading tonight. Don't get me wrong, I appreciate the meal, but all this fuss – anyone else would have done the same.'

Henrik stopped and turned to face me. 'You really believe that? Remember when we went skiing last year? That man went off-piste and landed head-first on the ground, catching his helmet on a rock? Even though he declared himself fine, it was you who insisted he visit the resort's medical centre. He'd have been dead twelve hours later if it hadn't been for that.'

I shrugged.

'Then that time, shortly after we met, when a woman choked in that Chinese restaurant.'

I pulled his hand, to continue our journey towards the lights of Taxos. Hmm – fortunately I'd known how to employ the Heimlich manoeuvre, whilst everyone else panicked, apart from Henrik who'd calmed down her husband and kids.

Henrik looked sideways at me. 'Whilst other people are prepared to stand at the sidelines, watching disasters unfold, you get stuck in to change the course of events. No doubt that's why your career is such a success.' He cleared his throat which had broken a little. 'That's why you and I make such a good match. The easy way out is never an option. We do the right thing, even if that means making tough decisions that not everyone will like. In fact…' Henrik inhaled as if he had something important to say... was he about to propose? I steeled myself. You'd be mad to say no, Pippa, said a prim voice in my head.

'This Friday I have planned a very special day out for you and me. So don't arrange anything with your Taxos friends.'

I swallowed. So, Greta was right. No doubt he'd chosen an exquisite location for the proposal.

'And, er, also I forgot to mention...' he said, '...whilst you were showering – an urgent phone call came in. Tomorrow I have to go into Kos Town for a meeting and–'

'Henrik! We've only just arrived!'

'Sorry Pips… I promise, it won't take long.'

'So what's so important about this bit of business that it can't wait?' Suddenly his fingers seemed clammy and I loosened my grip.

'Oh, I won't bore you with the details…' He stared straight ahead. 'It's just some client who is anxious to close a big deal.'

'Which client?' I pushed, but all to no avail as at that moment shrieks of laughter greeted us at the village's edge. My heart flipped – it was just the shock, of course – at the sight of Niko with little Theo on his shoulder. He looked as comfortable as if he were the boy's actual dad, wearing a shirt as white as Greek yogurt, tucked into well-fitting jeans. With Leila, by his side, holding hands with a little girl. They looked like a family, happy and complete. On seeing us, Niko bent over and let Theo – who was carrying a football – slide onto the ground.

'*Ya sou*, Pippa…' His mouth twitched into a smile, the shirt showing off his caramel skin. He nodded at Henrik. 'We have come to greet you… Good food, good wine, good company – it awaits you in Taxos. Mind you…' He looked down at Theo and grinned. 'We almost didn't make it. At this time of night, with only a few locals and tourists around, the streets make a fine, empty football pitch.'

'I did my best to make them hurry,' said petite Leila and I couldn't stop smiling down at her amiable face. Nor could I stop gawping at her gorgeous dress. The colourful red and yellow floral pattern perfectly suited her skin. Nipped in at the waist, it accentuated her trim figure. Whilst I'd grown accustomed to and even liked my height, once again I just briefly wondered what it must be like to be a small, delicately-featured woman – and whether that aspect of her was what Niko found appealing.

'Lovely flower,' I said and pointed to the red-orange bloom with large petals, tucked behind her ear.

'Thank you. Our pomegranate trees have bloomed late this year.'

Theo looked up shyly and said something to Niko who shrugged. 'He asks if Henrik would go ahead with him, back to the wider part of the road, for a kick-around before we eat.'

A bubble of laughter tickled my throat. Henrik wasn't what I'd call child-friendly. I'd never forget his bulging eyes and wrinkled-up nose when we recently visited a friend who'd just had a baby. She'd insisted Henrik hold the tiny tot, who promptly screamed in his arms, filled its nappy and broke copious amounts of wind. Having said that, Henrik oozed charm, whether it be directed at toddlers, young adults or pensioners. Indeed, his love of football won the day and he ruffled Theo's hair before the two of them hurried away. Leila and the little girl laughed and ran after them.

Niko turned to me and took a step closer, fiddling with his leather bracelet. I doubted that a baby's dirty nappies would faze him. The sky was pitch black now, without the intrusive amber glow of city lights I was used to in London.

'Pippa – I am glad we are alone. We have something to discuss.'

I stared at the ground. 'Do we?'

'Yes.' He put a hand on my shoulder. 'The desire of Niko Sotiropoulos to make fuck with you.'

CHAPTER SIX

'*What did you say*?' I almost dropped my basket and shook off his hand as I looked up.

'That film. I watched it. You compared me to the Greek waiter. He said something like that to Shirley, about making f–'

'You watched Shirley Valentine?' I gasped. 'How… I mean… so quickly…'

'A shop in Kos Town stocks DVDs for tourists. It's not funny, that you think me like him. Pippa…' He threw his hands in the air. 'I have no agenda. Am serious. Unlike the waiter in film who was just looking for lightweight adventures.'

'At least he wasn't hiding a fiancée,' I muttered.

'Let me explain.'

His mocha eyes gazed earnestly into my face and tingles in all sorts of places pricked my skin.

'No! Let's just leave it – Henrik and I, we… are happy. Look, I kind of get it – life in dusty Taxos, especially after the recession, must be… well, I can't blame you for having a bit of fun with visiting tourists. Mind you, it stinks that you flirt with everyone behind Leila's back.' I started walking again. 'But don't badmouth Henrik to me.'

'And don't you badmouth Taxos – life here is as special as ever.'

My cheeks burned. He was right. For me, old-fashioned, unsullied Taxos was still idyllic, with its ramshackle character contrasting Kos Town's glossy glitz.

'As for Leila…' he continued. 'You really think so little of me?'

'What does my opinion matter?'

He swallowed. 'Everything.'

'Of course it does,' I said and pursed my lips, still cringing as I thought about Saturday's butterfly kisses.

'Look, about Henrik...'

'Niko, *please...*' My voice wavered. 'Can't we leave it? I don't know why you dislike him but he's a good man.'

Niko stared at me for a moment and took a step back. 'Sorry Pippa... I... I no mean to hurt your feelings. It's just...'

I raised an eyebrow. He sighed and nodded. Then with strides as wide as possible, I headed towards the shouts of Theo and Henrik, in the distance. With relief, I reached them and stood by Leila whilst the guys enjoyed a ten minute kick-around. Then we hurried to the taverna and wow! What a greeting awaited us with string music, laughter, flickering candles and savoury smells.

As we walked in, Mr Dellis, his wife and mother came over to give us tight hugs. I caught sight of a table at the back of the room, laden with… Wow again. Niko's family had prepared bowls of shiny olives, green and beige dips, fried calamari, *souvlaki* chicken kebabs and stuffed red peppers. Plus colourful salads dressed with glistening oil and lumps of squishy feta cheese.

I spied Sophia's famous spinach pie – in other words, comfort food at its best. My last holiday there, I'd been fretting about whether I'd chosen the right options for GCSE. Niko had fetched me a slice of this *Spanakopita* and sat with me, next to our favourite rock in Caretta Cove, whilst I'd relished every mouthful. A lump rose in my throat as I recalled him declaring the wrong choices would be just a small blip that would never hold back a girl like Pippa Pattinson.

Niko circled the room, kissing several women, family and friends…What had happened over the years to make him value an engagement so little – and to spurt out spiteful suspicions about people he hardly knew?

'Demetrios!' I said as the handsome potter came over and kissed me on either cheek. He stood back and grinned. I'd forgotten how he always wore a colourful cravat.

'*Ya sou*, Pippa. So, where are your muddy jeans and bare feet now?'

I grinned. 'Remember that vase I made? The hole at the top was so small all I could do was push in one stalk.'

Demetrios chuckled. 'Happy memories – you must come over before you leave. I make you a special vase to take back.'

'*Ya sou*, Pippa!' Pandora the baker came over and warmth radiated through me at the sight of her in catwalk tailored white trousers and a terracotta blouse. She hadn't changed a jot, apart from a few grey hairs in her stylish short cut and deep shadows under those ebony eyes. Plus now she wore black-rimmed glasses. I glanced at her perfectly varnished nails and... wedding finger. So she hadn't remarried. Pandora had lost her husband about ten years ago – flames had cornered him whilst he helped control a forest fire in a neighbouring village.

We hugged. 'I've brought cake tonight, Pippa, and trust you still like it as much?'

I patted my stomach. 'All these years, I've never eaten a sponge cake as good as yours, back in England.'

Pandora's skin flushed and she gave me another hug. Then she stood back. 'You've grown into a lovely young woman – and have important job in London, no?'

'It's no more important than baking heavenly food to earn a living – I can't wait to fill my plate from the buffet table.'

Pandora's cheeks flushed darker as Mr Dellis clapped his hands and a hush fell.

'Now that Niko and Miss Pat– I mean Pippa, are here...' he lifted up Theo, '...My sons talk of superheroes – Spiderman, Captain America. But they are fiction. In this room we have two real heroes, both bigger than The Hulk...'

Er. Okay. I think that was meant as a compliment.

'...who saved my boys from...' His voice trembled. 'Please, with your hands, thank them.'

As the room shook with claps and cheers, I glanced across the room at Niko and swallowed. Those deep mocha eyes met mine, a crease between the brows. It was as if time had rewound about ten years, to the day we alerted the neighbouring village to the forest fire that claimed Pandora's husband. After unsuccessfully trying to extinguish it with buckets of sand, we'd got back on our bikes and raised the alarm. Like many inhabitants of a small island, Taxos villagers were at the mercy of the elements. Some had called us heroes back then but we never felt it, because the fire's consequences had still been tragic, with the one death and several injured.

I looked back at Theo's parents and blinked hard. The little boy's mum had tears in her eyes.

'To celebrate their bravery, now we eat,' she said in a loud voice and opened her arms – cue another round of heartfelt hugs. Cosmo from the cycle shop pushed a shot of ouzo into my hand and squeezed my shoulder. I knocked it back before the catchy string music became louder and Cosmo took out his harmonica. Fashionable Pandora headed over with questions about where I'd bought my matching underwear, worn during the rescue. We chuckled that word about its stylishness had spread. On my return to England, I promised to send her some from M&S. Leila passed me a plate and Henrik slipped an arm around me as we headed towards the buffet table.

'Mmm. This spinach pie is still the best, Sophia,' I said, an hour or so later, after many conversations in Greeklish about where I learned to swim and my irrational fear of sharks. The combination of flavours and moistness made it a top quiche. The two of us sat at a table, whilst our men discussed the state of the Greek football team. Thanks to dating Henrik I now knew what constituted a good goal, although still faltered if asked to explain the offside rule.

'It was your favourite as a child, *Pippitsa*.' Sophia smiled before taking another bite. We both swayed from side-to-side, unable to sit still as Cosmo played a harmonica solo. 'Of course, you enjoy fancier food in London, no?' She eyed me up and down. 'I hope you eat enough, with your busy job.'

I squeezed her arm. 'It's a good thing I don't live with you, otherwise I'd be curvier than the most revered Ancient Greek goddess. In fact, this *is* the food of the gods.'

Sophia's heart-shaped face beamed. 'How kind – and you loved Grandma's puddings...' She stared at my cheeks. 'She would rub yogurt into that sunburnt skin.'

'Niko said the same,' I replied and chuckled. But just like in the taverna on Saturday, when I'd laughed with her son, a strange expression crossed Sophia's face.

'He... Leila... they seem like a well-matched couple.' I said and put down my fork. 'Have they been engaged long?'

'Over one year now. They told us just before Grandma fell ill.'

'Could I see her, tonight? Or is it too late? Will she be tired?'

'Of course. She is impatient to see *Pippitsa* too.' Sophia grinned. 'Did you bring scones?'

I nodded and stood up, my stomach twisting a little. How much would feisty Grandma have changed?

After fetching the basket from the buffet table, I followed Sophia up rickety stairs, just behind the bar. We came to a small kitchenette for the family and three bedrooms. The door around to the right belonged to Niko. I recalled the secret childhood tank containing two lizards, its floor lined with bark, plus a big piece of driftwood and bowl of water. A sign on his bedroom door had banned adults from entering his "private space". Sophia must have gone in now and again to change the bed and no doubt turned a blind eye to the lizards, as long as they were happy and well-fed.

We stopped by the door to the left of the tidy kitchenette and gently, Sophia knocked.

'I think your visit will do her good,' she murmured. Without waiting for an answer, Sophia opened the door and popped her head around to mumble something in Greek. I heard my name then the reply of a croaky female voice. Sophia straightened up and gave me a nod. I went in on my own and heard Niko's mum close the door before going back downstairs.

What a lovely room, with the simple whitewashed walls, quilted bedcover and colourful ceramic bowls. And what was that distinct grape-like smell? Of course, Grandma's signature perfume, made from irises, her namesake. Nostalgia wafted over me as I breathed in the floral aroma. Once again, I marvelled how some things never changed. Although, through the dim lamplight... I could avoid it no longer... I focussed on the wizened body of an elderly woman I hardly recognised. My throat ached. Gone were the full cheeks. Yet she still had those fiery cinnamon eyes that would glint when Niko and I got into trouble – and glow when I made her fresh scones or told a joke.

An arm that looked thin, despite the billowing blue nightie, stretched out. I hurried forward to grip her hand, blinking hard, forcing my mouth to upturn.

'Pippa! My little peach! You came!' Her eyes lit up. Eventually she let go and patted the bed as she pushed herself more upright. I sat down on the mosaic patterned red and brown bed quilt and put the basket on my lap. She gave a gap-toothed smile. 'You bring gifts?'

I parted the tea-towel and lifted out one of the scones. She took it and inhaled. 'Mmm, chocolate and...'

'Fresh apricots,' I said.

She handed it back. 'Tomorrow I shall breakfast like a king. *Efharisto*, dear Pippa. Now, hug old Grandma. Speak of your young man. Last winter I was too ill to meet him.' Her eyes twinkled. 'But I spotted on him out of my window, one day. He is like a very tall, very blonde Cary Grant – the movie star of my day...'

'Spying on young men? Grandma! You shock me!'

She smiled and for one nanosecond looked about sixteen. I willed my chin not to wobble at the wispiness of her hair and those hollow cheeks.

'...and so, that's how I met Henrik,' I said, about twenty minutes later, my fingers still holding hers tight.

Those cinnamon eyes studied me. 'He makes you happy, child?'

'Yes,' I said brightly. 'But, um, enough about me – I hear there is to be a wedding. Isn't Leila lovely?'

Grandma's face broke into another smile, reminiscent of the dancing grey-haired woman who'd taught me how to make honey soaked doughnuts, the last summer I visited

Taxos. 'Leila's family comes from my childhood village. Her grandmother and I were school friends. It is a perfect match. Their children will be much loved on both sides. Their union, it...' Her voice quietened. 'Without it, I don't know how I would have kept going, this year. So much has gone wrong... my health... poor business... Here in Taxos – in Greece. We see hard times. A wedding...' She tried to suppress a yawn. 'The joining of two families... is like a rainbow casting beauty across a stormy sky.'

I nodded. 'And... how are you doing?'

'Better than I expected, one year on – although I feel like such a burden to the family.'

'Pah – nonsense! They love you to bits and wouldn't begrudge a minute looking after you...'

She fingered the quilt cover. 'It's not just that – not all healthcare is free since things got bad in Greece. The taverna has money problems enough without Georgios and Sophia having to find extra to pay my bills. But enough about me,' she said, eyelids heavy now. 'You... you and Niko still get on well? Has time changed your friendship?'

'You are, um tired now,' I mumbled. 'I'll come back again to talk – and perhaps bake more scones.'

'Pippa? You are hiding something, no?'

'Grandma!' I said and forced a grin. 'You don't change, seeing intrigue where there is none!'

A small chuckle escaped her lips. 'I can tell it going to do me good to have you here. Everyone else treats me like a dandelion seed head that could be destroyed by just one puff of air. I am so glad you visit our island again. Always... you gave me... joy. Even the times when your cheeky face meant you and Niko had been bad.' Her lips twitched and I knew she was laughing inside.

Now that we were silent, chatter and music trickled up from the party below. I brushed strands of hair from her face, and hummed her favourite sleeping cuckoo song. The lines on her forehead smoothed out and her breathing became more even. Having neatened the bedclothes, I kissed her forehead, the scent of her grape-like perfume becoming stronger as I leant forward. After tip-toeing out of the room, I closed the squeaky wooden door behind me and my face crumpled for a moment. I hardly noticed someone come out of the kitchenette.

'Pippa? What you do up here? All okay?'

I looked up to see Niko wrapping a plaster around his finger. He shrugged. 'I was a little enthusiastic with the cheese knife.'

Heart pounding now, I followed him back into the kitchen and stared as he put away the first aid box. I struggled to control a balloon of anger inside my chest that was threatening to burst but oops – Epic Failure.

'You should have written or called,' I hissed.

Brow furrowed, Niko closed the cupboard and turned around. 'Huh?'

'Grandma. She's so... Things must have been... Why didn't you tell me? Do all those years of friendship with my family count for nothing? I mean, I know I've lost touch a bit, but Mum and Dad still–'

'Whoa, wait a minute – Henrik was here in January. He must have said something.'

'Yes, well, Henrik was only here briefly and probably didn't even see her and–'

'Look, Pippa, she wasn't diagnosed until after your parents left last summer and it... is hard thing to write in a Christmas card. And what would you have done? Left your busy London life? We haven't seen you for nine years.'

I opened my mouth.

'Pippa – that's no criticism... We're all busy. Lives change. You and me, we stopped writing to each other a long time ago. And I'm not much interested in the internet – that Facebook thing – when I could be outside in the sun.' He lifted his hands in the air. 'Sorry, okay. Perhaps I should have thought – made sure. Although...' He screwed up his forehead. 'Wait a minute... Mama mentioned it in a card to your mum for her birthday in March, no?'

I swallowed and thought hard for a second. March – when I'd been cramming for exams at work. I held my basket tighter. Thinking back now I recalled a telephone call – Mum saying something about Sophia being worried about Grandma. But... okay, I admit it, sometimes my mind wandered when on the phone. This year I'd been so wrapped up in my new job, my career, it was hard to switch off.

How could I have not been shaken out of my thoughts though, at the mention of the Big C? Had I really become so absorbed in stuff that – in comparison to this – didn't really matter, like projected profits, sales targets and staff expenditure?

Niko came towards me but I backed away.

'Okay.' My voice wobbled. 'Maybe I got it wrong. It's just... I hate seeing her like this. Sorry.' I sniffed, dying to ask if his family needed help paying Grandma's health bills.

'No need for sorry,' he said and gave a small smile. 'Although... If you want to make it up to me, just listen for two minutes to something I want to say about Henrik.'

I gasped. 'You don't know when to give up, do you?' After plonking the basket on the table, I swung around and headed for the stairs. Quickly I went down into the restaurant, cheerful voices blurred, due to loud music. Henrik, laughing with Georgios, caught my eye and winked. Sophia and old Mrs Dellis ate baklavas oozing with honey. Leila sat on the floor, next to a pile of

Nintendos – clearly confiscated – and with a group of children played a board game. Slowly my chest stopped heaving and I glanced out towards the patio, where Georgios was doing the Greek circle dance with guests.

He jerked his head, beckoning for me to join in. I beamed and gave the thumbs up. You know what? I intended to enjoy this holiday. Blocking all thoughts of Niko, I headed outside. In the corner, just in front of an olive tree, stood two men playing different-sized, pear-shaped string instruments – next to them sat an old woman, clapping. Georgios took his left arm away from Cosmo and made a gap for me. Fortunately, with my height, I was able to drape my arms across their shoulders, unlike the other women who made do with waists. I couldn't stop smiling as the music slowed for a moment and then got quicker and quicker, until I was almost out of breath. The footwork I'd learned during my childhood quickly came back – as did chef Georgios' signature aroma of herbs.

I admired the other women's colourful skirts decorated with rich floral patterns and laced headscarves. Gasps of breath escaped my lips as the circle moved quicker from side to side. By now we just held hands, at shoulder height, feet moving backwards and forwards and then around to the right... Finally the music stopped and we all clapped.

'No more... I need a drink...' I said.

'Bah, you youngsters have no sticking power,' said Georgios and chuckled. He took out a handkerchief and wiped his perspiring bald head.

I headed indoors, longing for an icy orange granita. However, a hand touched my shoulder. I turned around to see Niko. Before I could object, fingers curled around mine and led me outside to the front of the taverna and the street. I tugged my hand away as the humid night air enveloped my body. The moon shone brighter than a torch in a power cut. Stars peek-a-booed and a deliciously sweet scent wafted over from the white-flowered jasmine plants, either side of the taverna's entrance. Talk about a perfect romantic setting. I should have been out here hand-in-hand with Henrik... shouldn't I?

'Just hear me out,' he said.

'Look, oughtn't you get back inside to see Leila? Mind you... she looks perfectly happy playing with those children.'

His face lit up. 'Yes. Leila will be a wonderful mother.'

I nodded, knots in my stomach at the pride that crossed his face. Did he think I'd make a good mum?

I shook myself. 'Sophia was saying earlier that she helped her parents work the land and looked after neighbours' small kids – sounds like you'll both be happy staying in Taxos, like you always imagined...'

He shrugged, obviously still waiting for permission to talk about Henrik. I gave a big sigh.

'Look, just spit it out. But you've only got two minutes. Then I'm going back inside.'

Niko sat down at one of the nearby outdoor tables. I sat opposite him, my breathing back at its normal pace. The taverna's blinds were closed. The street was empty apart from a couple of stray cats and invisible chirping cicadas.

'No interrupt then. Please,' said Niko and took a deep breath. 'Henrik tells me he's going to Kos Town on business tomorrow.'

'Yes – to see a client for lunch and close some big deal.'

'That's what he said to me too – but looking decidedly suspicious. And despite my polite questions, would say no more.' Niko ran a hand through his black curls. 'So when he suddenly hurried out to the patio, to answer his phone, I innocently stood nearby.'

'You eavesdropped?'

'Yes. The dancing had not started then.' He pursed his lips. 'And it is a good thing I did. Henrik called the person on the line Stavros – so it is the mayor. They have this meeting tomorrow at one o'clock, in some English pub called The Flamingo Inn. I've seen it, not far from the famous Hippocrates Tree.' Niko stared at me. 'Henrik went on to say the word Caretta. Then mentioned ThinkBig, the name of his employer.'

'So? Look, how long's this going to–'

'He also said... ' Niko fiddled with his leather bracelet, '"Pippa must not find out." Something about you loving marine life...' His eyes widened. 'I'm convinced ThinkBig has bribed the mayor into helping them get permission to develop on the nature reserve, on the east side of the island – it is one of the few places in Kos where the endangered Caretta turtles still nest every twelve months. Experts think they are considering nesting here in Taxos again, in the cove – but that may not be for another year or two. Until then, every nesting site needs protection.'

My jaw fell open. 'There's no way Henrik would push for the decimation of a reserve. And corrupt or not, surely even the mayor wouldn't ever get permission?'

'You don't understand, Pippa – things have changed since the recession. New laws have been brought in that allow rich foreigners to invest in and develop protected land, as long as they replace it by building a reserve elsewhere. It happened three years ago on the southern tip of the island, near Kefalos. The beaches are perfect for surfing, so a holiday firm was allowed to take over that part of the beach and nearby land, at the expense of the turtles and peacocks. The nesting season was ruined and no turtles have been reported since, anywhere along that part of the coast.'

My chest tightened at the way Niko's eyes glistened – he loved sea life as much as me. But Henrik knew my views on protecting the natural world. I couldn't believe he'd be part of such a damaging programme. Yet an uneasy sensation rippled down my body, from head to toe. Henrik was ambitious, even ruthless when it came to business... Like the time one deal meant a forced purchase of several houses in a town up north. One elderly couple had appealed the decision but lost. Henrik seemed to have no qualms that ThinkBig had stolen many of their family's memories by knocking down their home – all he'd focussed on was that they'd been given a more than generous payment for their small bungalow

I stared at Niko... On the other hand, why would my childhood friend make this up? Nausea briefly hit the back of my throat at the thought of builders tearing apart the safe haven of those magnificent turtles. But I owed my loyalty to Henrik who, above all else, was always honest.

I tutted. 'This is what happens when people eavesdrop – you don't get the full story. I'm sure there's an explanation for all this that isn't sinister.'

'You should accompany him to Kos Town tomorrow, Pippa. Pretend to go shopping but really spy on him. This project needs to be stopped before it gets underway.'

I scraped back my chair and stood up. 'Are you completely mad? You may disrespect and deceive Leila behind her back, but my relationship with Henrik is based on openness and trust – you ought to try it sometime.'

'So, you told him about our butterfly kisses?'

'No... you see... they were your idea and... took me by surprise. What's more, I'm not engaged, whereas you... ' Urgh! How dare he smile? At least I'd already been having doubts about Henrik, whereas he'd committed to a future with his fiancée. Although a wave of discomfort washed over me, as if I'd been caught out.

'Pippa...'

I shook my head. 'You have insulted my boyfriend – and tried to lower my standards to yours, by saying I should spy. I don't understand all this trouble-stirring between me and Henrik.'

'But–'

'I don't know who you are any more. From now on, leave me alone!'

CHAPTER SEVEN

Long arms snaked around my body as I stood in front of the kitchen sink. Gentle kisses trailed a path up and down my neck. Hands covered in bubbles, I turned around to look up at those familiar slate eyes, crinkling at the corners. Henrik leant down but jerked away, laughing, when I put a dollop of soap suds on his nose.

'We'll be late for your lunchtime meeting, if you keep this up,' I said.

'Then stop looking so damn gorgeous,' he said huskily and firmly held my waist.

I smiled sheepishly until our lips met, and told myself that the irrational, crazy, all-encompassing, exciting sensations I'd felt when just millimetres from Niko's face, had simply been a blip. My love for Henrik was solid. Still a bit tingly. And I could rely on him not to deceive me. That magnetised feeling with my old Greek friend was clearly driven by nostalgia for our former friendship.

'Sure you won't get bored shopping, whilst I meet my client?' he said, after I pulled away to carry on washing up.

I shook my head and quickly turned back to the sink. Damn Niko for making his Greeklish accusations swirl around my head last night. On the way home from the taverna, I'd subtly questioned Henrik about his appointment, but he still said little and talked of meeting a client and not the mayor. Is it possible, that straight-up

Henrik would lie to me? Would decimate a nature reserve, despite having a girlfriend who loved and respected wildlife and had done for years? I emptied the washing-up bowl... No. I couldn't believe it. He probably just assumed I would get bored by hearing the details of his meeting. We were on holiday, after all.

Grumbling about having to put on a suit and tie in such hot weather, he left the lounge. I took the kitchen rubbish out to the bin that stood on the front porch. In the fresh air, I squinted for a moment, enjoying the warmth and sounds of a Greek summer morning – the honking of geese from a flock flying above and chug of a diesel-smelling engine as a battered car passed.

It took a while to spot the figure standing by the terracotta pots full of bubblegum-pink flowers. I sucked in my cheeks and shut the door behind me, forcing myself not to admire the cut of blue jeans and snug fit of the short-sleeved checked shirt – nor the casual, confident manner.

'What are you doing here?'

Niko removed a long blade of grass from his mouth and held out a plastic bag. 'Here – borrow Leila's big floppy red sunhat and matching shawl. Henrik no recognise you then. Stick them in a rucksack until you get to Kos Town.'

'Huh? Look, I told you–'

'Pippa. You think I've changed – but inside I'm still your loyal friend. And you may dress fancy, but will always be Tomboy to me – Tomboy who cannot resist a mystery and who fights for the good. I know you'll accompany Henrik today.'

'Have you gone mad? You and I... we are different people now. Honestly, aren't *I* the one who suffers from sunstroke? And you think a giant red hat is discreet? Forget "Pippa", you may as well call me Poppy.'

He shook the bag at me, but I simply put the rubbish into the bin, replaced the lid and folded my arms.

'Look... Pippa... You're angry – about Grandma. Plus I can tell you're sad about crumbling Taxos. And I think you're horrified about the idea of the Caretta turtles losing their home. Just like years ago when we found tourist boys abusing stray cats. You took photos and insisted we report them to the police. And remember feeding Grandma's fresh batch of bread to the baby seagulls we thought looked hungry? I know you still care about things like that.'

'Don't assume anything about me – especially that I believe your suspicions about ThinkBig.'

'I assume you want to know the truth – like me. Most of the times we got into trouble, when younger, was because we curious people, no? Like us staying out past midnight to find out why empty wine bottles kept appearing in Uncle Demetri's boat.'

I couldn't help returning his smile. We'd stumbled across an amorous local couple who couldn't find privacy anywhere else, at night.

'Not that it's any of your business, but I *am* going into Kos Town with Henrik – just to shop.'

Niko stared at me for a moment, then nodded. 'Still... you suffer from the sun – borrow Leila's hat. You won't find a bigger one anywhere.'

I gazed at him for a few seconds and took it. 'Okay. Thanks. But won't Leila need it? Today's due to be hotter than ever.'

'No – when I called around, she was ill in bed – some sort of, um, insect...'

'*Bug*, you mean...?'

'Yes. She doesn't look at all well and won't get up today. I will drop the hat and shawl back tomorrow.'

Weird that he wouldn't call around to check on her that evening, after work. But then, I thought later, as Henrik drove the thirty minute journey to Kos Town, Niko did live just a couple of streets away from Leila – if anything was wrong he could be there within minutes. Unlike my set-up, back in London, with no family or close friends within a twenty mile radius of our Notting Hill apartment. On the plus side, we had cinemas, sports centres, cosmopolitan restaurants and all the designer stores – although I kind of liked the random shops along the seafront of Kos Town.

After we'd parked, I kissed Henrik goodbye. He had to drop into the ThinkBig offices before his appointment. Firstly, I made my way to the harbour and hoped a stroll by the seafront would clear my head – help me decide just how much I trusted the man I might marry. Instead I just stood and admired the impossibly blue sky and swaying palm trees, well suited to those over-the-top glam music videos Mum watched, from the eighties.

Eventually, I left the bobbing fishing boats and headed for the shops and markets in the buzzing centre. Mmm, the aroma of squishy honey pastries and coffee smelt much better than sea salt and gutted mackerel. I enjoyed browsing through rails of clothes and ogled jars of shells, sponges and ceramic pots outside an array of gift shops. Boutiques overflowed with scarves, sandals and shawls, whilst souvenir shops sold blue and white painted pottery, fancy olive oils and herbs as well as bottles of jasmine perfume – all of which, my mother would have called "tat". Plus pushy waiters hovered outside restaurants, trying to attract tourists towards the enticing smells of oregano and garlic.

I couldn't be in a place more different to sleepy Taxos and disliked veering around puddles of sick left by drunk tourists who'd enjoyed Kos Town bars the night before.

Yet I couldn't stop staring at cash being exchanged at tills. This was how business should be during the summer months.

After treating myself to a pair of white roman sandals, I headed back to the seafront and studied the array of different styles of boats in the harbour. My gaze stretched to faraway yachts, their white sails erect, like the predatory fins of giant sharks (thanks again, Steven Spielberg). To my right, at the shore, stood the famous Castle of the Knights... I'd visited it several times as a child, to run amongst the ruins for just a few euros.

A distant clock chimed – half past one already. By now Henrik could be starting his main course. I'd already spotted The Flamingo Inn back in the town centre – it stood in between two other English pubs that had televisions on, blaring out sport. Was I really going to do this? Spy on the man about to ask me to become his wife?

Looking for inspiration, I pulled down my own beige sunhat and headed over to the famous Tree of Hippocrates, in a quiet square, opposite the entrance to the castle. A baby in a pram dropped its rattle and I hurried after the mum, to give it back, before returning to the tree. Despite screeching seagulls and chattering tourists, tranquillity washed over me as I gazed at its wide crown, held up by scaffolding. Like many tourist spots in Kos, there was no explanatory notice. I only knew its history because of visiting the island so often. Hundreds of years ago Hippocrates had supposedly taught his students underneath – to think that this man of priniciple, the Father of Medicine, had stood at this exact spot. No doubt this tree could tell many stories.

Hmm, like the one about the English woman, carrying a large red hat and debating whether to stalk her boyfriend. Aarghh! Henrik, too, was good man, but I felt a duty to the endangered turtles, with their huge heads, horny beaks and thick-skinned flippers. Other children used to throw pebbles at them and call them mutant Ninja turtles after the film. However Niko and I always appreciated their beauty – especially underwater where, despite their cumbersome shape, they cut through the currents like submarines.

If another nesting ground was decimated they might never recover. I gazed at the tree once more then opened my rucksack. Within minutes I'd swapped my hat for Leila's and, despite the suffocating heat, wrapped the red shawl around my shoulders. I did trust Henrik. At worst he was being forced to close some ill-conceived deal by the bosses at ThinkBig.

I smoothed down my linen trousers. Now it was almost two o'clock. Either way, it was best that I knew what was going on and could offer my boyfriend support. If I hurried, I'd just catch them having dessert. A wry smile crossed my face. I felt like a rather flamboyant Miss Marple.

Mentally thanking Hippocrates for pushing me in the right direction, I headed back into the town centre. Outdoor stalls with a rainbow of flower baskets contrasted the ancient brown buildings all around. The sign outside The Flamingo Inn, bearing a large pink bird, came into view, except so did... I paused outside an office. From the advertising photos in the window, I could tell it was an employment agency.

Was that *Leila* inside, being interviewed? I'd recognise that petite frame, the exotic flair for clothes and raven hair swept to the side anywhere. But she was supposed to be ill. Why would she lie to her fiancé? And why would Leila be looking for a job? Niko clearly thought their future was mapped out, working locally in Taxos.

I looked at my watch. Yes, well, so what – Niko's love life was nothing to do with me.

I darted behind the clothes rail of a nearby stall, but still peeked as she stood up and shook the hand of a lady behind the desk. Then she turned around. Hmm. Leila it definitely was. She left the agency, put on sunglasses and headed in the direction of the harbour. Aarggh! Why did I feel obliged to investigate? To see if she was up to something Niko didn't know about? It would serve him right for flirting behind her back...

I bit my lip. A small part of me, that I soon shot down, hoped that she was planning to move to another part of Kos. Perhaps with a new boyfriend, yes, and she'd get a job in a bar or restaurant. Maybe she'd been seeing someone else behind his back. My heart fluttered as I imagined her announcing her departure for a new life in a glitzier part of the island, because then Niko would be free to... to... *big sigh* I shook my head. What was I thinking of? She mustn't leave him – apart from anything else, it would hurt Georgios, Sophia and Grandma. In fact, I owed it to *them* to try to find out more. And this detective work would be nothing at all, in no way, to do with a ridiculous sense of loyalty to some boy I'd known a lifetime ago.

I cleared my throat, strode over to the agency and pushed open the glass door, prepared to make up some story about my "friend" – Leila – having lost her purse. However, the small plastic sign on the desk she'd been sitting at gave me all the information I required. "International Recruitment". Goodness. I hadn't seen that coming. Was Leila sneaking off abroad?

Quickly I left the office and stood outside again, perspiring not just because of the outside sun or shawl. Perhaps Leila's friendliness was all just an act. What if she'd seen the butterfly kisses last Saturday? Not that anything untoward had happened, but she was bound to have been aware of his flirting over the last few months, if I'd noticed within a matter of days. But where would she go? With her good English, Great Britain or the States? And to do what? As far as I knew, she had no formal training... I glanced at my watch again. Niko's problems would have to wait – at this rate I was about to miss out eavesdropping on Henrik's lunch date.

Hands up, no need to tell me I was a hypocrite as I snuck carefully through The Flamingo Inn's doors. But I'd only chided Niko for eavesdropping the night before as his aim had been to stir up trouble between me and Henrik – whereas I was acting shadily for the sake of endangered turtles. Pulling down the red hat, I surveyed the busy pub, filled with sunburnt holidaymakers, mahogany tables and a huge television to the right. Photos of Churchill, bulldogs and the Queen had been mounted on the walls. Plus to the left of the bar was a snooker table, just behind Henrik who sat with a generously built man with dyed curly black hair and a high forehead glistening with sweat.

Even sitting down, Henrik was easy to spot. In fact he looked way too big for the small circular table and wooden chair, like one of the giants out of his favourite TV series Game of Thrones. A waitress brought them coffees and she shot my boyfriend a flirtatious glance. Attention from other women used to make me proud, in the beginning, because I was his chosen one, but these days such behaviour didn't move me at all.

I hurried to sit on a tall stool at the bar nearby, my back to them, and ordered a mineral water from the landlord in a Union Jack T-shirt. A man, stinking of aftershave, stood next to me, in a black suit. He clicked his fingers at the landlord and I glanced sideways. Eek, it was Henrik's companion. He turned his head in my direction and gave me a smile full of yellow-stained teeth. He had beady eyes and a crooked nose. Without turning his head away he said, 'My usual cigar, Jim.' Then, 'you English?' to me.

Um... no I wasn't, just in case Henrik heard and recognised my voice.

'*Non, je suis française*,' I replied, thanks to my French GCSE, praying that he didn't speak that language.

'Ah, Paris, the city of love,' he said and leant close. Ew – stale retsina breath. Fortunately, at that moment, the landlord returned with a long, plastic-wrapped cigar. The man slid it into the top pocket of his coat and turned to go.

'That's six euros please, Stavros.'

Ah ha. So he was the mayor.

Stavros turned back to the landlord. 'So Jim... Tell me, how is your son looking forward to starting at his new school, in September? It's the best on the island. He was very lucky to get in there, no?'

'Er, yeah, he's well chuffed.' The landlord cleared his throat. 'Cheers for asking. Look, why don't you have that cigar on the house, mate, for, um, being one of my best customers?'

Stavros grinned, nodded to me and muttered *au revoir*.

Wow. Had I just witnessed proof of the mayor's corruption? It sounded as if he'd swung a favour for the landlord and expected freebie cigars and goodness knows what else, in return.

Nah, surely not – thanks to Niko, I'd become over-suspicious. No doubt "Jim" had just been grateful that someone as important as the mayor would take an interest in an expat's children. And if Stavros had helped Jim's son get into a smart school, well that was charitable, wasn't it? Not the action of someone who'd risk the future of endangered turtles.

'*Efharisto* for lunch, Henrik – us meeting has been productive, no?' I heard him say behind me. He must have sat down again.

'My pleasure, Stavros,' said Henrik. 'And it's me who should be thanking you.'

Sitting more upright, I strained to listen – just as a noisy couple collapsed onto the stools next to me and read the menu out loud. Would they have fish and chips? Pizza? Or double cheeseburger? I smiled as they oohed and aahed at the prospect of English food. Anyone would think they'd just suffered years of war food rationing.

Unfortunately, their loud voices meant I could only pick out odd snippets from the conversation behind me. Stavros said "It's been hurried through as a favour." Henrik replied – as Niko had mentioned – by saying that "Pippa must not know yet". I also heard "Taxos town hall", "send out the invitations Friday, in the post," and "shaped like a Caretta turtle – Pippa will like that."

A ball of nerves spun in my chest. No... I was imagining things... The two men couldn't mean... I listened hard again.

'Okay,' said Stavros. 'Saturday, midday, in the town hall. All paperwork done... No worry, Henrik. From what you tell me about her, I'm sure Pippa will approve of your proposal and it will all go to plan.'

Weakly, I beckoned to the landlord and ordered a straight ouzo. Henrik's mum had got it wrong. Her son wasn't hoping to get engaged. He was skipping that part and going straight for the wedding. That folder of "work" he'd brought over no doubt contained our birth certificates and all the paperwork... Wow. In four days' time I could be getting married. In Taxos town hall. With all the villagers as guests – and a Caretta turtle-shaped cake.

CHAPTER EIGHT

Did you know that the term Godzilla is a combination of the Japanese words for gorilla and whale? I liked to think "Bridezilla" would represent a cute monkey and graceful dolphin, seeing as my wedding was to be set on this beautiful, sunny island. Because, within the space of a few hours, all my previous ideas about my dream minimalist wedding day had disintegrated. Gone was the sophisticated white trouser suit – instead I wanted a full-length beach dress with intricate ruffles. And forget the small posy made up of white and cream roses – give me a giant bouquet of Greece's colourful wild flowers. Plus heart-shaped confetti, a four foot tall cake and cars draped with a mile of white ribbon.

Hmm. Was that how I should have reacted? Truth be told, I was in shock, now my potential future with Henrik seemed about to become real. I wanted to jump up and down, buy tens of bridal magazines and ring Mum, all bubbly and emotional, but just couldn't reach that level of excitement. Instead I went on automatic and logically made preparations. First and foremost, yes you've guessed it, this involved food, namely scones. Whilst I liked varying the traditional English cream tea recipe, with bright red jam, I've always thought nothing would suit a wedding better than that. Although to make them extra special, I'd mix edible gold glitter into the fruit conserve. What a fabulous centre piece on the buffet table they would make. Did they sell clotted cream in Greece?

As we drove back to Taxos later that afternoon, my stomach fizzed like a bath bomb. Everything now fell into place. My parents must have been staying somewhere secretly in Kos – I'd been surprised when they'd announced their visit to Canada anyway. Mum hadn't seen her sister for over ten years, so why now?

And take that folder of "ThinkBig paperwork" Henrik had brought on holiday – it probably contained all the documents we needed to get married abroad. In fact, this now explained why, a couple of weeks ago I couldn't find my birth certificate. Having finally decided to book driving lessons, I'd unsuccessfully hunted it out, in order to apply for my provisional licence. As for waiting until Saturday for the wedding, that made sense – a friend got married in Athens a few years ago and one of the regulations was that she had to live there for seven days before the ceremony could go ahead.

And of course, Henrik would propose this Friday, during lunch on the "special day out". After eating, he would no doubt take me on a shopping trip to buy the ring and dress. The invitations for locals wouldn't arrive until later that day either, in case anyone ruined my surprise. Super organised Henrik would have thought of everything. But then, as someone who excelled at arranging surprises, a wedding was the ultimate bash. He'd probably already picked out all essentials. All I'd need to do was turn up and approve his choices.

In a daze, as I'd left the pub, I headed for the nearest jewellers and spent a few minutes studying the exquisite wedding rings. Trouble was, the tingles I got came from admiring the craftsmanship of the jewellers, not from the prospect of spending the rest of my days with Henrik. So,

I gave myself a good talking to. Any man who went to such trouble to marry me must surely be The One. Pursing my lips, I tracked down a shop that sold edible gold glitter. I'd never meet a more suitable partner than Henrik, so I should get ready for the weekend, when we would exchange our vows.

'So, how did your lunch go, Henrik?' I said – since meeting up again, all we'd discussed was ThinkBig's more general plans to develop parts of the Aegean islands that bankrupt native builders couldn't afford.

He turned up the air-con and before returning to the steering wheel, his hand squeezed mine.

'You would have enjoyed it, Pippa – I had sticky toffee pudding, your favourite. And what a relief to drink English coffee again.'

'We've only been here four days!'

He grimaced. 'Four days of pouring sludge down my throat.'

'Nothing wrong with Greek coffee – Grandma Sotiropoulos reads the sediment like tea leaves, you know.'

'Did she predict your wonderful financial career when you were younger then? And your amazing boyfriend?'

We both laughed. Yet I thought for a moment...

'Funny you should say that – she did once say a man with foreign blood would capture my heart. Thanks to Greta, I'm guessing you'd fit the bill.' More proof perhaps, that Henrik was my Mr Right.

Of course, at the time of Grandma's prediction, newly fourteen year old me had pulled a face. The idea of even kissing any member of the opposite sex didn't appeal, (er okay, not unless he was Harry Potter, who I thought was really cool).

'Is that what I've done, Pippa?' he asked, softly. 'Captured your heart?'

The word “yes” should have easily slipped off my tongue, but for some reason my throat closed up. Thankfully a diversion took his attention, as a herd of goats wandered into our way. Henrik hooted the horn.

‘Blood and sand, it’s like living in the dark ages,’ he said and finally steered onto the road for Taxos.

I hardly heard his indignation, having turned back to watch the goat herder move the animals on, by walking amongst them and not at the front. As a young man, Georgios had herded goats. Apparently the secret was to make the animals think you were one of them. Dragging or shouting would never work. Georgios would spend weeks petting and feeding a new flock, to gain trust first. This was just another example of why Greek rural life rocked. Henrik knew me well by setting the wedding in Taxos and not Kos Town. Don’t get me wrong, I enjoyed a day of shopping and a night on the dance floor with cocktails as much as anyone – but my heart was in the village, not a soulless tourist spot.

Having said that, parts of Kos Town were beautiful and how lucky was Stavros working in its pretty Venetian town hall?

‘So, um, who did you meet exactly?’ I asked.

Henrik gazed firmly ahead. ‘A contractor. Cheap as chips. We might be able to offer him work.’

Despite my nerve-wracking discovery of an imminent proposal, I couldn’t help smiling. Honest Henrik had managed to force out a lie, so that the wedding day remained secret.

When we got back to the villa, I headed into the kitchen to take stock of our cupboards whilst he changed out of his stiff suit, to swiftly return in his lycra swimshorts – not the garish Hawaiian ones. He must have been planning some serious front crawl.

'Fancy joining me to do some lengths in the pool?' he said and walked over. I dropped my tea-towel on the unit as he bent down for a kiss. Tenderly, his arms draped around the back of my legs. With ease he lifted me onto the breakfast bar and nuzzled just beneath my ear. I used to like him doing that, but now it just felt like an annoying tickle.

'We're out of butter...' I said and cleared my throat, before breaking away. 'And milk. I'd better head into town before the supermarket closes.'

'You'd rather run errands than spend time here, kissing me?' His lips quirked into a smile as I laughed it off.

'Fine,' he said, 'but let me help you cool off before your dusty walk into Taxos.'

Henrik scooped me up and before I knew it, we'd gone onto the patio and passed the apricot tree, arriving poolside.

'Henrik! Don't you dare!' I said in a loud voice.

'Ask nicely,' he said and held tighter, a pretend fierce look on his face.

Wriggling like a hooked fish, I couldn't help laughing. 'For God's sake, we're in our twenties, not teens,' I yelled. Talk about out-of-character behaviour. Spontaneity and Henrik didn't often meet.

He swung me in his arms, backwards and forwards.

'No, Henrik, please don't do it. I'm begging you!' It was my turn to pretend now, so I'd put on a scared voice and screeched.

Uh oh. Too late. Picture me in the water, having resurfaced to shake my fist. Henrik jumped in after me and I swam over, trying to pull him under the water for a joke, enjoying a few seconds of pure fun. But I couldn't budge him one millimetre and his arms and legs flailed. And whose legs were those, in jeans? I shot up to the surface.

'What the... ? Get off him!' I hollered, before taking in a mouthful of chlorinated water. A man was in the pool, his caramel-skinned, strong-looking arm clamped around Henrik's neck. The checked shirt... curly black hair... '*Niko*? What the hell are you doing?'

'No worry, Pippa,' he spluttered. 'You're safe now. I heard screams.'

Henrik roared and after much effort, unwrapped Niko's arm from his throat, then span in the water and punched the Greek straight on the nose. Niko's face slammed to one side. When he looked back, eyes fiery, blood ran down from his nostrils and he raised his hand, about to deliver a return blow.

'Stop it, both of you!' I paddled my legs and arms furiously, until I bobbed in between them. 'Henrik was just messing about. He threw me in the pool for a joke.'

Both men gasped for breath.

'How did you get into our villa anyway, you moron,' spat Henrik.

'The front door isn't locked.' He scowled. 'I heard Pippa beg you to stop. Lots of screaming... that's unusual around here.' He swam to the side of the pool and pulled himself out. 'I thought...'

'What? That Henrik's a woman beater? How dare you!' I climbed out and picked up Henrik's towel.

The three of us grimaced for a few moments, whilst we caught our breath. 'Look... Henrik, you have your swim whilst I see Niko out.'

'He's lucky I don't call the police.' Henrik sneered.

I glared pointedly at Niko who duly stood up, slipped into his sandals and followed me inside, to the kitchen.

'What was that all about?' I said as he sat on one of the stools at the breakfast bar. Water dripped all over the laminate floor, but in this weather would soon dry.

'I was worried about you. I don't trust Henrik.'

Closing my lips firmly, so that an expletive didn't slip out, I passed him a square of kitchen roll for his nose.

'Then I suggest you keep out of our way, whilst we are here. This time your stupid allegations have gone too far. And I'm perfectly capable of looking after myself, thank you very much.'

'Against *Gigantes* Henrik?'

I flushed. 'What... you think I'd parade around here with a man who beat me?' I shook my head. 'And if it hadn't happened before, why would he start on a relaxing holiday?'

'I heard your fear and...' His hand went under his shirt and rubbed up and down, as he stared at the table top. I knew what he was thinking. That day, years ago... the jellyfish attack. His scar...

'The idea of you being hurt... I didn't think straight,' he muttered.

I avoided his eye. 'You don't need to worry about me. What were you doing out here, anyway?'

Niko pulled his hand back out into the open. 'I wanted to know about today. Henrik – he met Stavros no?'

My cheeks flushed as I ran the tap and filled a glass with water. I took a sip.

'Yes... But it's not what you think. I can't say any more at the moment. You'll just have to trust me – and the mayor and Henrik.'

Niko snorted. 'Trust, Stavros? No. And don't be so naïve – it has to be pretty big business for Henrik to interrupt his holiday.'

I put down the drink and my fists curled. 'Henrik is one of the most honest people I know. Just leave. I won't hear another word against him.'

He stood up. 'Pippa. Don't be foolish.'

'Foolish? To trust the most loyal, respectful man I know – who's actually arranging a secret wedding?' Shoot. I'd let out the secret, before Henrik had even had a chance to propose.

'What?' Niko's mouth fell open.

'That's what he and Stavros were meeting about – clearly they've become friends. They discussed the location, invitations and cake. No doubt the mayor has been helping Henrik wade through all the paperwork.'

Niko's shoulders slumped. 'You... Henrik... getting married?'

'Yes, he's going to ask me on Friday and I'd appreciate it if you'd keep it quiet. Henrik's gone to a lot of trouble to make this special. Not a word to anyone else, okay?'

His sandals made a squelching noise as he stepped forward. 'Look, Pippa, I still think you are making a mistake. Stavros no do anyone a favour without expecting something back. They must have made some deal. Open your eyes.'

'Perhaps you should open your eyes about Leila!' I snapped. Urgh. I hadn't meant to talk about his fiancée and her foreign job searching until I'd had time to word it carefully – or subtly quiz her. Annoying as Niko was, I didn't want to upset him. Yet he didn't seem bothered about hurting my feelings, when it came to Henrik.

'What do you mean?'

'Nothing... Look, ignore me I'm just being childish,' I mumbled and headed down the corridor to the front door. 'You should go now.'

I stopped as a hand squeezed my shoulder and turned me around.

'I always could tell when you lie. You hold your hands together.'

I glanced down at my fingers, all of them intertwined.

'So, Leila...?' He raised one eyebrow, drops of water still clinging to his face.

I sighed. 'She was in Kos Town today. I spotted her in an employment agency.' I stared at the floor. 'Leila sat at the international recruitment desk.'

'You're talking rubbish – she been in bed, ill.'

I met his gaze and swallowed. 'Sorry, but it was her. Perhaps, well, you know, she's as casual about the relationship as you.'

'Me? Casual about Leila?' His red cheeks turned purple. 'And you need glasses.'

'Did you actually see her this morning?' I asked.

'No, but–'

'Well, I did. Twenty kilometres from here. She lied to you about feeling sick. Sorry, but that's the truth.'

'You got close enough to speak to her?'

'No, but...'

'So. It's you who's mistaken.' His eyes sparked. 'You've got it wrong. Leila is marrying me – and staying in Taxos.' He took a step forwards. 'And I know you're close to Grandma but don't dare express doubts to her about my fiancée – she's so looking forward to our marriage. And since you've arrived, finally we're seeing signs of the old, cheerful Grandma. No one wants her recovery to go backwards.'

'You can't tell me what to do.' I scowled. 'Don't know why I bothered mentioning it. I should have just left you to find out the hard way.'

'I mean it!' he shouted and yanked open the front door, stepping onto the concrete path. 'Say nothing to no one!'

'Same to you about my wedding!' I hissed and slammed the door.

CHAPTER NINE

Something old? My gold dress watch.

New? Bought for the holiday, satin underwear.

Borrowed? Mum left her drop pearl earrings in the villa.

Something blue? My favourite eyeshadow.

Going through practicalities in my head, I kneaded the scone dough on the kitchen unit, having already mixed the edible gold glitter into the fresh strawberry conserve I'd bought from the Dellis'. I would assemble the scones last thing, before travelling to Taxos town hall for the wedding ceremony. I yawned. It was Friday and I'd got up early to prepare for the Big Day. It was nothing, absolutely zilch, nada, to do with keeping busy – keeping any doubtful thoughts at bay. No... I simply owed it to Henrik to make sure everything would run like clockwork. And I only had a few hours to myself before he whisked me off on my special outing.

At just after half past seven, I'd sat on the patio with a cup of rich coffee, watching the sun rise to the chorus of dawn birds. Streaks of Turkish delight pink ushered in the bright orange circle, as it rose, turning mysterious shadows into familiar friends. In practical mode, I'd tried to imagine the dress Henrik must have chosen. Maybe Mum had offered her opinion. I'd resisted ringing in case she accidentally let slip to Henrik that I knew.

A quick casual wedding for their daughter would suit my parents. It would fit with their overloaded schedule. Indeed they'd got married one lunch time, in a registry office, with two marketing canvassers, off the street, as witnesses.

I smiled at what my best friend Trudy would think to a surprise wedding. She'd got married last year and planned everything herself, down to the colour of the evening buffet napkins. Knowing she'd appreciate it, I'd even surprised her with personalised napkin rings for the top table. Whereas I – with my previous minimalist ideas when thinking about the possibility of marrying Henrik – had never been interested in thinking about details such as bridesmaids' shoes or buttonholes for guests. I didn't feel that need for control, which was because I am an extremely laid back person, no doubt.

I kneaded the dough harder. It had no link to the fact that I didn't feel as passionately about my marriage to Henrik as I should. There. I'd said it (in my head at least). This whole wedding business did seem rather matter-of-fact. Was that okay? Shouldn't I feel more excited or be upset that my friends from England wouldn't get an invite? I picked up the rolling pin. Grand affairs with doves and calico teal marquee tents were only for my romance novels, right? Whereas Henrik and I were a pragmatic, unsentimental couple. This must explain why there were no flutters of anticipation in my stomach.

Since his meeting with Stavros on Tuesday, we'd played the perfect holidaymakers by eating out, visiting places of interest and lounging on the beach. Henrik dropped no clues about the weekend ahead and I had to admire his cool. Fortunately Niko kept away. I didn't even see him yesterday when I went into Taxos to take Grandma a batch of her favourite honey and dried fig scones. The apricot and chocolate ones had already gone.

'You need building up, Grandma,' I'd said and breathed in her grape-like smelling perfume. 'Although you look really well today...' It was great to see her out of bed, cross-stitching in a chair.

'Happy to oblige, my little peach.' She took the plate that I'd carried upstairs. As she bit into the scone, I sat on her bed. 'Mmm... So, you have fun on your holiday?' she said, between mouthfuls. 'See much of Niko and Leila?'

Fortunately for her irritating grandson, I agreed that shedding doubts on Leila's intentions would only hurt Iris, so I just waffled about me and Henrik being busy, then mentioned our visit, on Wednesday, to the ruins of the Asklepion healing temple.

'This Henrik sounds like a good man – you have lots in common?'

'Yes.' I ran my hand across the red and brown mosaic patterned bed quilt. 'We are both ambitious and share the same life-goals.'

She lifted her chin. 'Like having children?'

'Eventually.'

She'd taken my hand and squeezed it tight. 'Remember how you always said you'd never send your little ones to boarding school.'

I'd nodded.

'I am glad you've found a man who shares your principles. Is important, no?' Grandma stared at me hard, as my cheeks flushed. I had the feeling she was finally getting back to being the savvy woman of old.

'Um, yes. Of course,' I'd said, with a cheerful tone. 'And he's loyal, caring...' I went on to mention the surprise day out arranged for me today, hard as it was to keep Henrik's intended marriage proposal secret. And perhaps it was just as well, as later that day, after we'd had brunch and Henrik started up the engine of the Range Rover, he still hadn't come clean and revealed the day's plans.

Could I have been wrong? What if he and Stavros had been talking about something else? I concentrated for a moment. No – it all made sense. Henrik combining a holiday with a wedding fitted perfectly with his spendthrift nature. However, to my surprise we didn't head north towards Kos Town, but turned onto the highway leading south-west and a ball of stress inside me deflated for one second as if I'd imagined this whole proposal thing. I swallowed, admitting to myself that this probably meant I wasn't ready to say "yes".

'Tyrionitsa?' I mumbled as we turned off the main road, to head towards this village. Over the years I'd visited this quaint little place a few times. A similar size to Taxos, it had a stunning beach. Uncle Christos would take me and Niko there to collect shells – and what an array of beautiful colours and sizes. I found spotted cones, speckled periwinkles and curvy whelks, all washed up onto the finest sand. I grinned to myself. With string, Niko made me a bikini top, cheekily using a small pair of scallop shells. He got a handful of wet sea grass down his top, for that.

As we neared, I squinted at a big board saying "Welcome to Tyrionitsa". It was in the shape of a mermaid. Ah yes – the legend of the kind-hearted mythical creature, who had supposedly swum nearby and granted wishes to children with her magic comb. A local potter would tell us those legendary tales, whilst making ornaments out of shells. I still had one, back at the flat – it was a seagull with a cone shell for a beak and periwinkles for eyes. All of his goods represented animals or plants and weren't like the gaudy souvenirs you could pick up in Kos Town.

Like Taxos, Tyrionitsa was practically untouched by tourism, so why had the council erected that cartoonish board?

'Wow!' I leant forward as the sea came into view, my turmoil about Henrik and Niko and Henrik and – you get the picture – forgotten. But I wasn't admiring the frothy white break of the waves or speeding yachts in the distance. My jaw dropped instead at the nearby sight of an ugly building. A huge concrete rectangle, it had a neon sign at the front bearing a picture of skittles and a bowling ball. Next to it was a square shaped construction with a sign saying "Disco Tyrionitsa".

'Impressive, isn't it?' said Henrik and a grin spread across his face. 'Have you ever been here?'

'Yes, but... I hardly recognise it, now.'

My jaw remained open as we drove into the town. Gone were the higgledy-piggledy blue and white houses and restaurants I remembered. Instead groups of young tourists milled in and out of glitzy burger bars. I wound down my window, to hear grinding pop music waft in from a swanky pub. Next to that stood an American style ice cream parlour and further along, a glass-fronted slot machine arcade. Finally we reached the beach. Oh my. Groups of youngsters clapped and cheered as one of many speed boats zoomed off, a paraglider attached to the back, rising fast into the air. Ice cream wrappers and beer bottles littered the sand. An old Greek lady, head to toe in black, shuffled past the queue, looking as if *she* were the visiting foreigner.

Henrik turned the car into a parking area to the right and stopped next to a coach. Day trippers were getting out. I put on my sunhat and dark glasses. As I opened my door and jumped down to the tarmac, a little girl pointed and asked if she'd see the famous mermaid. I followed her finger to a sign on the beach with an arrow faced to the right, saying "Mermaid Cove".

Huh? A cove in Tyrionitsa? That wasn't right. Legends said that the mermaid came to land where the jetty is built, on the main frontline of the shore.

Our car bleeped as Henrik locked the doors. He came around to where I stood and took my hand. Why on earth would he bring me here to propose? Thanks to its soulless makeover, Tyrionitsa had lost all its romance. Henrik led me up the high street.

'Great to see this place buzzing, isn't it?' he said. 'What do you fancy for lunch? A burger? Hot dog? I know, why don't we just share a really big ice cream sundae? I'm still full after that huge brunch.'

Before I could express an opinion, we'd walked into the American ice cream parlour and sat down. It provided a welcome refuge from the afternoon sun. A woman dressed in a pencil skirt and short-sleeved blouse roller-skated (I repeat, roller-skated) over to us and Henrik ordered the triple chocolate fudge any day sundae. The streamlined tables had gilt edges and photos of American movie stars, from the fifties, covered the walls. In the corner a juke box played Elvis Presley.

I was just about to feign indignation that he'd ordered for me, when I understood. Of course – he could hardly hide a ring box in his flimsy T-shirt or shorts' pocket. Henrik must have come to Tyrionitsa earlier in the week to drop off the ring which, no doubt, would be served in the ice cream he'd ordered. My mouth went dry as the moment I'd worried about for weeks was just a few minutes away.

Okay, so the table wasn't candlelit, with sophisticated glasses of champagne, but the parlour was fun. In fact a little bit too fun for Henrik... I studied his face. This whole trip was bizarre.

'So...' I smiled and took off my hat and glasses. 'What are we doing here? Of all the places to visit in Kos, what's special about Tyrionitsa – especially now?'

'Especially now?' His brow furrowed.

A group of young English men sitting near us laughed as one of them ran to the toilets, gagging, with dried vomit already down his shirt.

'It's hardly the picturesque fishing village I remember, with a carpet of pretty shells on the beach and traditional smells of garlic and oregano wafting down avenues.' I pulled a face. 'And did you see that tacky souvenir shop we passed outside?' Through the window I'd seen what looked like mass-produced shell mermaid ornaments, covered in pink and blue glitter.

A muscle in Henrik's face twitched as the waitress skated over and put the massive sundae between us, with two spoons.

'Wow. That's enormous,' I said and stared at the dessert glass which held squares of fudge cake wedged between generous scoops of ice cream. On top lay rivers of dark brown sauce, sprinkled with white, dark and milk chocolate shavings.

Bearing what I hoped was a bright, cheery expression, I gazed at Henrik, then the sundae, trying to spot a diamond ring. Perhaps it would be wrapped in plastic. Or hidden at the bottom and we had to scoff the whole dessert before finding it. My stomach scrunched but tough luck, I told it – I'll never meet a more suitable man than Henrik. Plus Niko has proposed to another and in any case, me and him? How could that work? No... marrying my Dutch boyfriend made sense. Urgh! This indecision was so unlike me. Any moment I could be faced with a ring, yet I still couldn't swear what my answer would be.

'You don't approve of the village's renovation?' he asked and picked up a spoon. 'Surely your business mind sees the value. Tourists now visit Tyrionitsa. That brings in money. Puts food on the table in these challenging times... Picturesque views don't fill empty stomachs, nor placate bank managers waiting for loans to be repaid.'

I looked through the window. 'But all its character has gone... What about Greek heritage?'

Henrik snorted. 'Oh come on, Pips, it's not like you to be naïve... You know most people come to Greece for the weather, cheap booze and great beaches. They don't give a stuff about whether the souvenirs are made here or in Taiwan.'

I dug my spoon into a moist square of cake. My head knew Henrik might be right but my heart ached for the Tyrionitsa from my memories. Eventually I shrugged.

'Well, I guess people have had to do what it takes and move forward to survive the economic downturn.'

'Exactly,' said Henrik and his eyes shone. 'And talking of moving forward, I've brought you here today for a very exciting reason...'

This was it. I swallowed my mouthful, put down the spoon and wiped my lips with a napkin. I leant forward, noting the slight flush in Henrik's cheeks and for a moment I felt a tiny surge of how I used to feel about him. He was a good man. He'd make a good husband. Mum and Dad would be pleased.

'I've brought you here today,' he said, 'because...'

Oh, God... suddenly I felt sick. Deep breaths. Yes. Henrik was perfect. Me deciding to stay with him was in no way a knee-jerk reaction to discovering how much Niko has changed. More deep breaths. A proposal from such an honest, hardworking, caring man didn't come along every day.

I forced a wide smile. 'Because...?'

Henrik took my hand. 'Dear Pippa... tomorrow at midday, in the town hall in Taxos...'

Here we go...

'...will you help me reveal ThinkBig's next big project to the residents?'

Huh?

His grin widened. 'Rundown, struggling Taxos is set to become the next dynamic, euro-rich Tyrionitsa!'

I stared at him. Blinked several times. Opened my mouth but no words came out.

'I brought you here today to show you how ThinkBig can breathe new life into your favourite Greek village. My meeting last Tuesday wasn't really with a customer. I met up with Stavros, the mayor of Kos Town. I put the wheels in motion last January when I met up with him – we're going to turn little Taxos into one of the most profitable, tourist-driven areas of the island, just like Tyrionitsa which is a success story of foreign investment.'

I don't know what shocked me more – the lack of marriage proposal or horrific proposal for the destruction of Taxos.

'Isn't it brilliant?' said Henrik, slightly less buoyant. 'You don't have to worry about your friends – next summer their tills won't stop ringing with a constant influx of new trade.'

'ThinkBig... developing Taxos?'

Henrik cleared his throat. 'Yes. Permission is going through to approve a quad bike track on the land behind the church. In the centre we'll construct one nightclub and encourage locals to buy the franchise for fast-food restaurants – otherwise we've a list of investors who'll come up with the money and employees themselves. Plus a cocktail bar will be built in Caretta Cove, which will be the booking centre for all-day boat parties and drinking games. They'll take place just off the shore.'

'But... what about the fishing and sponge-diving? It'll be ruined. And experts believe the endangered Caretta turtle might finally be considering the cove in Taxos again, as a nesting site.'

Henrik snorted. 'I've read those reports and the marine people have no solid proof. Pippa! Your Taxos friends are barely scraping a living... you've now seen it for yourself. As soon as I came here in January, I knew Taxos would benefit from this type of project.' He swallowed a mouthful of ice cream. 'I can just picture Niko hosting parties, out at sea... There is no reason why anyone in the village should be worse off.' He ate another mouthful. 'And we thought signs in the shape of the Caretta turtle could be the theme for the village – like mermaids are here.'

I swallowed. Stupid me. I thought Stavros and he had been talking about the shape of a wedding cake.

My eyes narrowed as I thought back to their conversation that I'd overheard in The Flamingo Inn. The words "hurried through as a favour" popped into my head – no wonder Henrik hadn't wanted me to look in that folder of paperwork he'd brought over to Greece with him.

'So you only decided this in January...' That explained why he'd come back from that trip all excited. He'd clearly struck the deal then, as all the extra phone calls he took at home started from his return. 'How come the permission has gone through so quickly?' I asked, the words sounding shaky.

Henrik shuffled in his seat. 'Um... Stavros helped pave the way...' His face broke into a smile again. 'But you can see the advantages, can't you? This development will turn the town around. You don't need to work in a bank to work out how little profit the locals are turning over at the moment. Their tourist trade is zilch and locals can't support the economy on their own...'

'I know – on paper this is the answer to their problems but...' I shuddered. 'Those all-day boat parties... I saw a documentary about them last year. Within the space of a few months these changes would destroy Taxos' history – the look of the shoreline... the old buildings which for years have withstood bad weather and forest fires... and as for the authentic, gentle ambience...'

Henrik shook his head. 'I can't believe I'm hearing this. You're a businesswoman. You know ambience doesn't feed hungry mouths – doesn't secure a future. The residents are lucky that out of all the locations on Kos, ThinkBig has picked Taxos.'

I stood up. 'Sorry Henrik – I need some fresh air.' Without looking at him I went out of the ice cream parlour and sat down on a bench outside.

A few moments later Henrik sat next to me, his long legs stretched out in front. He squeezed my arm. 'I thought you'd be more excited.'

'So this was the special day out – to visit Tyrionitsa, as a snapshot of the future Taxos?'

His fingers intertwined with mine. 'Yes. I've seen the concern on your face at the ramshackle sight of Georgios and Sophia's restaurant. I thought you'd be pleased, and as a bank executive approve of and support this project.'

Pleased? No. Instead a ball of something unpleasant spun in my chest.

'And when are the residents going to be told?' I said, in even tones.

He cleared his throat. 'They should receive their invitations today for the meeting, tomorrow, in Taxos town hall. We don't give details, just say to turn up for exciting information about the village's future.'

And I'd assumed they were wedding invitations.

'If you thought I'd consider ThinkBig some sort of saviour, why have you held off so long telling me? All these months you've known, yet I've found out the day before everyone else? In fact why keep it such a secret from me and everyone, right until the very last minute? Clearly you knew this decision won't go down well.'

His cheeks flushed. ‘No one likes change. But eventually the positives will win them over. I... I didn’t want to bother you with all this – you’ve had such a challenging year. And you needed to see Taxos firsthand, to understand just how much this project will benefit the area.’

‘Liar!’ My eyes tingled. Wow. That’s not a word I ever thought I’d use to describe Henrik. ‘You knew I’d hate the thought of beloved Taxos being turned into one of those playgrounds for binge-drinking, sex-seeking tourists. You’ve told me right at the last minute, so I don’t have time to mention the plans to my friends before your presentation which, no doubt, will be heavily persuasive...’ My voice wobbled. ‘I fell in love with your honesty, Henrik.’ I turned to look at him. That was the one quality that had stood up to my doubts about marrying him. ‘But it seems you aren’t that upfront after all.’

‘That’s absurd,’ he said, in a measured voice. ‘I realise the news must have been a shock, but your business logic should have kicked in by now. Taxos is home to people who’ve lost their jobs – seen their retirement savings decimated just to get through each day. How do you think your beloved Greek village would look in five years from now, without the financial support of ThinkBig?’

Yes, my head knew he was right – but still my heart grieved for the Taxos I might lose. I gazed up and down Tyrionitsa’s high street. It had no personality and could have been anywhere in the Mediterranean.

I got to my feet. ‘Absurd or not, I can’t support your scheme. Surely the locals have recourse to an appeal?’

His mouth twitched. ‘Of course, but what would be the point? A few down-on-their-luck villagers against the might of ThinkBig and a mayor?’

‘An underhand mayor, if rumour is to be believed.’

He stood up too, towering over me. 'Business works in a different way, over here – especially since the collapse of the Greek economy.'

Niko's words about Stavros's shiny white Range Rover sprang to my mind – the same model, no doubt, as the ThinkBig company car Henrik had been driving.

'So you've bribed the authorities, been working in cahoots with one of the most corrupt officials... you've gone behind my friends' backs... you've lied to me.' I put on my sunhat. 'Who are you, Henrik? Not the upstanding, clean-cut man I thought I'd come on holiday with.' I walked in the direction of the beach. Easily he caught up and grabbed my arm.

'Pippa. Think it through. It's for the best – and if you stand by my side it will give your Taxos friends confidence in the project...'

'I'd rather support the building of a nuclear reactor nearby.'

'Look, come on, get in the car. Let's talk about this sensibly,' he said in a tight voice.

'No. I'll make my own way back to the villa,' I snapped and ran towards the sand.

CHAPTER TEN

'Fancy some sex with an alligator, love?'

I lifted up the brim of my hat to see the grinning face of a sunburnt man, in the queue for paragliding. He held out a drink, layered dark red and green.

'Melon and raspberry liqueur with Jagermeister – it's hot stuff, honey.'

'No thanks,' I said, wondering what the other cocktails were called, as every young person in the queue held a rainbow-coloured drink in a plastic beaker. I hurried along towards the so-called Mermaid Cove where artificial caves had been carved out of the cliff. Small children lined up to go in. On nearby rocks sat ceramic mermaids. A young Greek man, in some kind of holiday resort uniform, explained to a small English girl that they were real mermaids, turned to stone centuries ago by a curse.

At a relaxed pace now and glad that Henrik had given up the chase, I headed along the beach, determined to walk back to Taxos on my own. Litter was strewn across the sand, including beer bottles, takeaway wrappers and rubber.... Ew. You'd rather not know. A pebble slipped into my sandal and I sat down on some rocks, near a Greek mum with two children. I undid my shoe and the small stone slid out. I smiled at the daughter who was building a sandcastle.

'*Kalos*,' I said and held up my thumb, remembering that was the word for good. The mother smiled and removed her sunglasses. I took off mine too.

'You no going up in the sky on those boats or drinking cocktails?' she said.

I grimaced. 'No. I didn't realise Tyrionitsa had changed so much. I knew it a long time ago.'

The light left her face for a moment, dark eyebrows furrowing together.

'Is not Tyrionitsa any more – not the village I grew up in.'

I put my sandal back on. 'But you earn more money now?'

'Pah! Euros not everything. Yes, our bar makes good business at night – but the customers... When we used to run our little taverna, people no sick on the floor nor ...' her face flushed, '... nor made sex in the toilets with strangers.'

I shook my head and we sat quietly, watching a distant paraglider. A sense of doom weighed me down, due to ThinkBig's plans for Taxos. I shifted uncomfortably on the rock as I realised this upset me more than the lack of marriage proposal. Couldn't Henrik see the village as a living, breathing entity, made up of individuals' lives and dreams – instead of just acreage to knock down and tackily rebuild? What would Georgios and Sophia say? And Grandma? My mouth dried. Dear Iris – how would this affect her health? Niko had said my presence seemed to have perked her up, even though I'd just been back in Greece a few days – this news from Henrik could undo all that progress.

I shuddered at the thought of what ThinkBig would do to Caretta Cove... Probably stick imitation turtles everywhere and tell children they were just hibernating. They'd flatten little landmarks in the village where generations of families had made memories. Like the peach tree near the village's main post box – Georgios would often mention how he'd first kissed Sophia underneath it. And Grandma would point out a huge rock on the outskirts of town, from which one of her brothers supposedly spotted German troops, prior to the Battle of Kos during the Second World War.

I chewed my thumbnail, imagining gaudy neon signs lighting up Taxos at night, instead of the glow of candlelight from restaurants and stars; imagining shrieks of young tourists falling out of nightclubs, as opposed to the gentle cheers from local and visiting families playing boules. The aroma of garlic and oregano would disappear due to the strong stench of burgers and hotdogs. Fishbowls of cocktails guzzled by riotous groups, through straws, would be the norm, instead of a few ouzos shared over backgammon and cards.

After what seemed like hours, I stood up. The family next to me had gone. I looked to my left. The queue for the paragliding was small now. I brushed sand off my dress, before turning northwards. The beach was wide and the cliff not too steep to climb, if the tide came in. I would continue my walk to Taxos. I'd done it once as a child, with Niko's uncle.

My watch said half past six and the sun had started to descend. It would be almost dark by the time I got back – and quiet, compared to Tyrionitsa. I swallowed. Henrik no doubt had good intentions – the entrepreneurial side of me could see why ThinkBig thought they were doing the Greeks a favour. However, a ball of fire swelled in my chest. He'd kept these plans secret for months, so must have known that people – I – would object. Well, stuff him... At that precise moment I didn't care whether he was scouring Tyrionitsa for me or flying back to England.

An hour later, twilight had fallen. The chirp of cicadas and gently breaking tide accompanied me back to Taxos. Powdery sand, like the finest scone mix, slipped in between my toes as I walked bare foot. The outline of the cliff gently disappeared as darkness fell. Ahead I could see the amber lights from Taxos, indicating tavernas and homes – so beautiful. Despite all my love-stuff ups and downs, I wouldn't have changed being back in dear Taxos for anything. A bat swooped over my head and I headed into the waves as I kept on walking. If only I had my swimming costume, I could wash away the perspiration of another humid evening. I stopped for a moment as catchy Greek guitar music wafted over from the village.

My eyes squinted as I saw the fig tree and... was someone sitting underneath? I cleared my throat and walked forward, sunhat in one hand, sandals in the other, handbag over my shoulder. A man with curly hair and a checked shirt sat on the sand, knees bent up, head in his hands.

'Niko? Is that you?'

He met my gaze. Moonlight lit up a downturned mouth and drooping eyes.

'Pippa... *Ya sou*... Why are you walking here?'

I sighed and sat down next to him. Where to begin? His voice sounded flat. Perhaps he was worrying about Leila – what I'd said about her seeking employment abroad. I'd got my special day out with Henrik so wrong, thinking he was about to seal our future together... Perhaps I'd been wrong about Leila too, and the woman I saw in Kos Town wasn't her.

'Look, Niko... About Leila... perhaps I made a mistake. Just forget what I said. You'd know, right, if she wasn't happy in Taxos and wanted to move abroad? After all, you two are engaged.'

Weird... his face didn't brighten. Must have been something else bothering him. Grandma, perhaps? Yet she was better by the day...

'Thanks...' He stared at me, then picked up a flat pebble. Niko stood up, strolled to the water's edge and threw it hard so that it skimmed across the surface.

'Two bounces? Not bad,' I said, now by his side, squinting through the poor light. I picked up a pebble. Mine bounced off the tranquil surface three times.

Niko chuckled. 'You always were better than me at skimming stones.'

'That must niggle, seeing as you are the one who taught me...' We grinned at each other, just like old times.

He picked up another pebble. 'So... talking of me being engaged, how was your day?' he asked, without looking at me. 'Did Henrik finally reveal all about his surprise wedding and ask you to marry him?'

'Um...' Damn – my voice broke. My eyes felt wet. Niko dropped his stone and turned to face me.

'Pippa? What's the matter?'

I sniffed. 'He didn't, you see...'

A curious look crossed his face before he leant forward to hug me. As our bodies touched, that magnetised feeling washed over my body again. Breathing quicker, my skin prickled as his hands ran up and down my back. Images of us kissing sidled into my mind.

'Sorry you're sad, Pippa,' he said eventually, and stood back. 'You... you must really love him. Maybe he'll ask another time.'

'No... yes... I mean...' I wiped an eye. 'I'm not really upset because of that.'

Niko's mouth seemed to quirk up for a moment and then he shook his head. 'So, what's the problem?'

How could I tell him that the place he'd grown up in was about to be destroyed? The two of us walked back to the fig tree and sat down.

'I made glittery scones you know. For the surprise wedding ceremony I thought Henrik had planned for tomorrow.'

'That's what's bothering you?' he said gently and squeezed my arm. 'Then I'll eat them. Bring the scones over tomorrow. A bit of glitter – that will put an even bigger smile on Grandma's face.'

To my surprise I burst out laughing. 'No... I'm not that much of a romantic... a waste of glittery scones hasn't upset me, but thanks all the same.' I gave a wry smile. 'But... it's not that, you see... Henrik took me to Tyrionitsa.'

Niko snorted. 'That spiritless place?' He banged his chest with his fist. 'No heart there, any more. Big corporations... They destroyed everything it once was.' He glanced sideways at me. 'Why Henrik take you there? Tyrionitsa must be the least scenic place on the whole of the island.'

I stared at him, feeling my eyes fill with liquid, holding it close like a dam, ready to burst. 'You know he works for ThinkBig, a development company?'

Not dropping his gaze from my face, Niko nodded.

'You were right about Stavros. He's pushed through permission for ThinkBig to... to...'

'What?'

'... to turn Taxos into the next Tyrionitsa,' I blurted out.

Blood filled Niko's cheeks and he gasped, before insisting I must have got it wrong. So I repeated everything Henrik had said. Niko got to his feet. He paced up and down, arms flailing in the air.

'Not possible! Taxos... people love this village. Our grandparents... our grandchildren in the future... Taxos is our heritage. You knew about this, Pippa?' He shook a finger in my direction.

Finally the dam burst and a tear trickled down my face.

His eyes glistened. 'No... you've got heart... This is as much a shock to you.' He turned and walked quickly in the direction of the village. 'I'll wake up everyone!' he said. 'We'll fight this development!'

I got up and ran after him. With both my hands I dragged him backwards. 'Niko! Use your brain. Think this through. A knee-jerk reaction won't get Taxos anywhere.'

He turned to face me and pulled away his arm.

'I'm not a brain-person like you, but a simple fisherman. My fists, my angry voice, they are the weapons I use.'

'Henrik has brains. Doesn't make him a clever person,' I said. 'Anyone can see that, long-term, it's a sense of community, of belonging, that holds a country together. Although...'

'There is an "although"?' spat Niko.

I shrugged. 'Henrik is a good man. People have to eat. Buy clothes. Put aside for their retirement... All he can see is the short-term financial benefits. With my mathematician head on, I understand. He sees how you and your fellow villagers struggle... To him a quad bike track, nightclub, bars... It is the obvious answer. He won't put nostalgia or the future of some turtle before economic factors.' I shrugged. 'Taxos fits the bill perfectly for being reinvented. Henrik is great at his job. In theory, he was a whizz to close this deal.'

'Sounds like you are on his side.'

'No... I mean... during my walk back, tonight, I calmed down and thought it through. I understand his reasons, that's all.'

Niko threw his arms up in the air. 'So, what do we do? This meeting tomorrow...'

'Hmm, at midday, in the town hall. Invitations should have arrived today.'

Niko nodded. 'Now you mention it, Papa talked of a letter from the council, talking of an "exciting" planning meeting tomorrow. We just thought it referred to some modernisation of the roads that has been talked about for months now.' He shook his head. 'We need to warn everyone.'

I went back to the fig tree to collect my hat and handbag, before slipping back into my sandals. We walked towards the harbour, finally sitting down together on a large rock. It smelt of seaweed and salt. I inhaled, relishing the pollution-free air.

'Not yet. Let's think through a plan first. If we tell the village without offering a way out, they may think it's a hopeless cause to begin with. Why don't we let Henrik say his piece then invite locals to the taverna afterwards?'

'Henrik has been planning this since January?'

I nodded, as my chest squeezed. Part of me felt disloyal to Henrik giving away details – but then he had hidden this from me on purpose, for the last six months.

'Okay. Our taverna will be an open house tomorrow then, after the meeting. Now I go back – tell my parents about the plan. But first I'll walk you back to the villa.'

'No need.'

'But still.'

'Okay... if it makes you feel better.'

'And when you get in, eat one of those glittery scones. Pippa Pattinson doesn't need a man to feel special and enjoy a bit of sparkle.'

My chest tingled. 'Thanks, Niko.'

'What for?'

'For not saying "I told you so". You suspected Stavros and Henrik were up to something. I should have listened, but–'

'You love him, no? Love isn't logical.'

'I thought I loved him, but recently... I mean... of course. Yes. Henrik and I – we're a good match. Like you and Leila.'

That curious look crossed Niko's face again, that I'd seen earlier and before I knew it, we were standing inches in front of each other.

'Yes... naturally. I... respect her a lot,' he whispered.

My heart raced. Weird that he would say respect and not love. Our hands found each other and his thumbs gently rubbed my palms. Oh God, forget all my reservations about how much he'd changed – I longed to press my lips against his. I bet they were so soft and warm and sweet. But Henrik and I were still officially together, and then there was Leila of course and Grandma's excitement about her grandson's wedding... How could we kiss? How could I be that selfish and put my needs above a whole family's?

Niko broke his gaze, gave a sigh and just gave me another hug. My head swirled. The way he behaved around me was so confusing, one moment touching me like a tender lover, but in the next breath joking around like just a good mate.

'No problem,' he murmured. 'I understand why you stuck up for Henrik.'

Kaleidoscopic magic fairy dust flickered in front of my eyes, at this brief but overwhelming closeness, just like the time we'd laid close for butterfly kisses. A hot glow surged down my back, where his hands had touched and felt unfamiliar yet comfortable... dangerous yet safe...

He jerked his head towards the village and I nodded. Side-by-side, we headed back to the high street. I longed to hold his hand and feel his arm against mine. It was as if some uncontrollable physical force pulled us towards each other, regardless of circumstances. But consequences mattered and had so far managed to keep us from crossing an unacceptable line.

'What happened to those carefree days of our youth,' I muttered.

Niko stopped and his mouth upturned. 'Come on, old woman – let's stop off at the taverna first. I make you a special coffee.'

'*Old woman*?' I said, as the sexy sensations between us had morphed into the banter of old. 'Forget it, young man – and I'll make my own way home.'

'I don't think so,' he grinned and ducked down to stand up again, with me over his shoulder.

I screamed and beat his back with my hands. Strong Niko would do this to me when we were youngsters, even though he was shorter. How the fishermen, who saw this on a regular basis, would laugh because they knew exactly how I'd get Niko back – by mercilessly exploiting a particular tickle spot I'd identified, under his left arm.

'Niko. Put me down!'

Which he did immediately as suddenly bright lights shone our way and a Greek voice bellowed out. Once on terra firma I looked up to find... Oh my God. Two policemen had handcuffed Niko and read him some kind of rights.

CHAPTER ELEVEN

'Niko? Arrested for abduction?' Henrik snorted as he did up his tie and grinned.

'It's not funny,' I said, voice tight. He was getting to the town hall early, to go over the presentation with Stavros. 'There was no need to call the police to search for me. I'm surprised they agreed, considering I'd only "gone missing" for a few hours. They totally overreacted to Niko and me just–'

'Just doing what?' Henrik raised an eyebrow. 'You profess to be deeply upset about the transformation of Taxos, yet in a matter of hours after hearing the news, you're larking around on the beach. Anyway, what's the big deal – they dropped all charges.' Henrik poured me an orange juice. I sat at the breakfast bar and sighed. Our arguments had gone around in circles when I'd returned to the villa, last night.

'Niko and I... we, um, go back a long way. Banter always got us through tough situations when we were small.' Like when I'd just started a new boarding school and was dreading going back. Niko refused to let me mooch.

Henrik pursed his lips. 'Don't expect every villager to see this proposal as a "tough situation". If Stavros' experience is anything to go by, many Greeks have accepted that drastic action is needed to save the local and national economies.' He reached in the fridge for eggs and flour. 'Look...' His voice softened. 'I hate us arguing... how about I make pancakes?'

'Would that be a guilty conscience cooking?'

I tied my dressing gown more tightly around my waist. Henrik sat down next to me and those slate eyes crinkled. He'd always looked great in a starched shirt, with his oat hair slicked back. I'd never met a man so well-groomed, but just lately I'd found it irritating. Organised. Neat. Successful. Charming. An answer for everything... It may sound churlish to complain, but sometimes it was hard dating someone whose flaws were either non-existent or hidden. It set the standards way too high for more laid back, imperfect me, who didn't iron her underwear (he did), slouched in onesies at weekends and left the kitchen tap running on a recent weekend away (thankfully without the sink plug left in).

'Pips... don't be like this... It's nothing personal and you know it makes sense. ThinkBig are investing in Taxos' future. Like it or not, things can't go on as they have been.'

'That's true,' I said. 'But can't ThinkBig come up with a plan that doesn't tear the heart out of the place?'

Henrik took my hand. 'That heart stopped beating a long time ago – youngsters have moved away to cities, older people have been driven to working the land. Things haven't stayed the same in Taxos since you last visited, like you romantically imagine, Pippa – they've gone backwards. Life here needs to start moving forwards again.'

Urgh, and that was the annoying thing – the logical part of me knew that Henrik was right. Yes, compared to my last trip here, nine years ago, everything that was thriving about Taxos had declined.

Gently Henrik squeezed my fingers. 'Stand by me today, Pippa. Your support would make all the difference.'

I pulled my hand away. 'Sorry. Just can't. ThinkBig's proposal is too drastic.' I gave a hopeful smile. 'Why don't you stand by me instead, and try to dilute your employer's plans?'

'Dilute?' Henrik shook his head and stood up. He knocked back his orange juice. 'I don't know what's happened to you this last week, Pippa, but where's that savvy executive gone? Back home you have no qualms about turning down much-wanted loan applications or declaring family businesses bankrupt... Whereas here you are letting sentimentality affect your common sense.'

When he left the villa, without saying goodbye, I rang Mum and Dad. They were surprised to hear of ThinkBig's plans but thought it also the only way forwards. They even gleefully discussed how the development would increase the value of their villa.

What was wrong with me? Why couldn't the sensible mathematician in me talk my romantic side around? The trouble was, when I thought of Taxos, I still dreamed of running a little afternoon teashop and enjoying a traditional family life. With a sigh, I turned off my phone and headed to the shower. A brisk walk into Taxos would clear my head. I'd grab a coffee at Taxos Taverna before the meeting, and then walk to the town hall with Niko's family.

'*Ya sou*, Pippa!' called the postman, as I strode down the dusty road, an hour or so later. I smiled as he slowed his bike. How Niko and I had played jokes on him, in the past, stashing heavy rocks at the bottom of his bag. 'You go to this meeting later?'

I took off my sunglasses. 'Wouldn't miss it for anything. Did you have lots of invitations to post yesterday?'

'Oh, yes. I'm exhausted. Lots of parcels, too. It was Theo Dellis' birthday. And the Kostas' thirtieth wedding anniversary.'

Postie always had let slip what was in everyone's mail.

'Plus an official envelope for Leila... I think it contained a passport. She and Niko must be planning a honeymoon.'

Huh? I nodded politely, as he continued to explain why yesterday's mailbag had been such hard work.

Leila? Applying for a passport? The hairs stood up on the back of my neck. That would fit with her looking for international employment – there was no way the couple could afford a honeymoon. However, Niko had enough on his mind at the moment, without me mentioning my suspicions again. A flame of desire licked the inside of my chest. If Leila *was* leaving, then surely there was nothing wrong with me... with me and Niko...

My thoughts were interrupted as Postie said goodbye. I stood up straighter, back in a rational place, and made myself think sensible thoughts, like... like how good it was to at least see the mail service was booming. Wiping my handkerchief across my perspiring brow, I gazed up into the sky as a squawking seagull swooped and dived. Eventually I moved on and before I knew it I was outside Taxos Taverna.

'*Pippitsa*!' Sophia straightened up in front of one of the outdoor tables, a dripping dishcloth in her hand. 'Come in for coffee.' She glanced at her watch. 'We have an hour until the meeting, no?'

I followed her inside. Georgios, Niko, his Uncle Christos and cousin Stefan, plus Leila and Grandma sat round one of the tables. They stopped talking. Niko jumped to his feet and came over, guiding me by the elbow to the window.

'Don't tell them about the police last night,' he mumbled. 'They're upset enough at the idea of Taxos becoming the next Tyrionitsa.' Warmth shot up my arm from where his fingers curled around my bare flesh. Those feelings I had, last night, when we hugged... I avoided his eyes. God, why did I feel so shy?

'Pippa, look at me,' he murmured, as if understanding. Our eyes met and a genuine, caring smile lit up his eyes. 'Last night... you are special – magical, glittery, like your scones. And this isn't bullshit like the waiter in Shirley Valentine.' His breath teased my face and I longed to feel the soft warmth of his mouth. His pupils dilated and my pulse quickened, but we said nothing, nor moved a centimetre, as if we were both scared of what might happen. Was I imagining this chemistry or did Niko, too, find it a struggle not to brush his lips against mine?

I glanced away and caught Grandma's eye. Could she see us clearly without her glasses on? Immediately I backed away from Niko, not wanting her to suspect any shenanigans between me and her grandson. Not that there were any. I mean, we'd done nothing wrong.

'It is good to see you downstairs, Grandma,' I said in a bright voice and went over to kiss her cheek. 'Love that floral shawl.'

'I make it myself.' She smiled, her face becoming a mass of wrinkles, thanks to a lifetime enjoying sun and cigarettes. 'Sit down next to me, my little peach.'

'Grandma is feeling better, all right,' said Georgios, 'bossing us all around.' His lips pushed upwards, into a smile, but his eyes looked dull and he stared at a letter on the table – no doubt his invitation to the meeting.

Sophia placed a coffee in front of me.

'I just want you all to know...' My throat felt dry. 'I knew nothing about ThinkBig's plans until yesterday.'

Georgios nodded. 'Niko explained.'

'To think, we offered Henrik our hospitality back in January,' spat Uncle Christos. His face flushed purple. 'Sorry, Pippa, but am angry.'

Georgios held up his hand before running it over his perspiring bald head. 'Henrik is a good man. We don't agree with his plans but no doubt he thinks he's doing the best.'

I gave a big sigh. 'That's just it, Georgios – he does honestly believe this is the only option for Taxos. And whilst I can't agree with my boyfriend, I won't insult him. Part of me understands why he wants to press ahead with the quad bike track and nightclubs.'

'You're a loyal girl,' said Grandma and patted my hand.

An uneasy sensation twisted my insides.

'So that's it? We just give in?' said Sophia and picked up a square of moist baklava from a plate.

'Not at all. We... we just need to come up with an alternative plan.' I gazed around the table. 'I mean, let's be honest... things *can't* continue as they have been.' I glanced at Niko. 'The accident in the sea, with the Dellis' boys... that should be the wake-up call you all need.'

'What you mean?' said Christos, who fiddled with amber rosary beads.

'Old Mrs Dellis was worn out looking after her grandchildren, which is why she fell asleep. But what choice did she have, with both parents working just to put food in their mouths? What will happen next? A fatal farm accident due to exhaustion? Divorce rates climbing because of stress? Whilst ThinkBig's plans will impact this community, so will doing nothing.'

Georgios smiled. 'And now we see why you have a successful job in London.'

I blushed. 'Not saying I have all the answers, just... Let's try to take control – come up with our own solution. Try to fight this big corporation.'

'Can we, really?' said Christos, shoulders slumped and calm now.

'Pippa's right,' said Leila. 'Between us we can surely offer Taxos a different future?'

I studied her face – perhaps Leila's real answer was to ditch Niko, move abroad and build a stronger future there. At that thought, rightly or wrongly, my heart gave a little leap.

Grandma put down her cup. 'Taxos still standing after the earthquake of 1933, after the Battle of Kos and numerous forest fires.... We survive this as well.'

'Yes, don't you worry Grandma,' said Niko.

'Worry? That's a grandma's job,' she said and smiled. 'But I'm not made of puff pastry. Fighting for something makes me feel strong – makes me feel alive again. I'm okay.'

Niko and Leila exchanged happy looks.

'In any case,' said Grandma and lifted her cup. 'I've read the coffee sediment... it says the sea will save Taxos.'

'The sea?' chorused everyone. But Grandma had picked up her sewing again, cheeks pink, eyes sparkling, giving me a flash of the feisty woman she used to be.

We were still trying to work out exactly how a vast amount of saltwater could save the village when seated in the town hall, waiting for Stavros and Henrik to take the stage. Grandma had stayed at home, although just before we'd left the taverna, I took her into the garden and we reminisced over old times. We left her sitting in the sun, a healthy caramel colour already darkening on her cheeks.

Most of the villagers seemed to have turned up before us and I shifted uncomfortably in my seat as Kos' mayor worked his way around the room, muttering to villagers under his breath. I'd gone up the front to greet Henrik but his reply was icy when I turned down a chance to sit on the stage.

'Go join your Greek friends, then,' he'd said. 'Just remember, you are doing them no favours by rejecting this proposal.'

I still had to disagree when Henrik began his PowerPoint presentation, Stavros chipping in to speak Greek. Like a Mexican wave spreading around a stadium, people's faces turned from interest to horror within minutes.

'Friends, this is the chance of a lifetime for Taxos,' said Henrik. 'Out of all the villages on this wonderful island, ThinkBig has chosen yours.'

Expressions of dismay deepened as Henrik presented sketches of how the village would look, with the new, characterless concrete buildings and snorts of disbelief filled the room when he showed photos of Mermaid Cove in Tyrionitsa and how ThinkBig hoped to transform Caretta Cove into a cute turtle-themed area for children.

'The Caretta turtle will be the emblem for Taxos...' said Henrik, glancing around the room, '...which is appropriate as without this development, *your* very existence is endangered as well.'

A hush fell over the room.

'No doubt Stavros can translate the expression "ghost town" for me...' he said.

The mayor nodded and uttered two words.

Henrik lifted his hands. 'Several ghost towns have sprung up across the Greek islands. Families can no longer afford to live in the villages they grew up in, due to people leaving for work elsewhere, due to lack of local investment... Picture Taxos abandoned, overgrown... doesn't that make ThingBig's images of its future more appealing?'

People looked uncertain, whilst beady-eyed Stavros took over talking in Greek and managed to smooth out some of the deep lines on their foreheads. In fact they leant forwards when he helped translate the finer details. How the villagers would be offered decent prices for their properties, in the area where the land needed to be flattened. How these prices would not be repeated though, if any of those residents initially obstructed ThinkBig's plans. Plus he talked of the franchises to takeaways and bars that had proven successful elsewhere in Greece – Henrik promised, again, that ThinkBig would offer an interest-free loan scheme to inhabitants keen to start up one of these businesses. Plus he reiterated that all jobs would be offered first to locals, be that positions in the nightclubs or showing children around Caretta Cove.

'We won't keep you any longer,' Henrik finally announced. 'I realise it's a lot to take in. Just to say that ThinkBig and I are excited about securing your future. Don't hesitate to approach me or Stavros with any questions.'

Niko stood up. 'Perhaps I could ask a question right now, in front of everyone?' He didn't wait for an answer. 'Why has this been rushed through, leaving us hardly time to think; to come up with an alternative solution?' He fired out some Greek at the locals, no doubt translating what he'd asked.

Henrik fixed a bright smile on his face. 'Alternative solution? But why would anyone oppose such a win–win project? Unless you have a thought-through business plan you'd like to present, with financial backing, that will guarantee jobs in Taxos for generations to come?'

Niko's fists curled.

'I thought not.' Henrik shrugged. 'There is no sinister motive here. Foreign investment is keeping this country afloat. And now, dear friends, if you head towards the back of the hall we've put on burgers and hotdogs to give you a taste of the fast food tourists to Taxos will enjoy. I have handouts of design plans and the proposed construction schedule, plus application forms for the various franchises.' His face became serious. 'I know that for many of you this concept will come as a shock. ThinkBig is here to help you through the transformation. And I'm available twenty-four seven, to listen to your concerns.'

Wow. Henrik was good – although these days, that Dutch charisma irked. Was the empathy that etched his face genuine, as he toured the room? As he shook hands and nodded as pensioners chatted in Greeklish about the good old days? Henrik handed out drinks, ruffled the hair of children and oozed charm when approached by women. He patted shoulders, attempted to speak the local lingo and shook hands – whereas Stavros circulated the room, speaking quietly under his breath.... Niko, Georgios and I watched the mayor's every move.

'What game is he playing?' I muttered under my breath. We found out when cycle shop owner Cosmo came over. He spoke quickly to Georgios and Niko in Greek. The two men's eyes widened. Then Pandora, the baker, came over, having just spoken to Stavros and said something to Cosmo – he nodded. Tears in her eyes, she looked at me.

'Say it is a joke, Pippa. All the memories I have of my husband, here – they'll be gone if ThinkBig have their way.' She glanced around the room. 'Why more people no upset?'

I gave her a hug. 'So, what is Stavros saying?

Georgios' chest heaved. 'We should have known better than to think he'd play fairly... He going around offering... how you say in English...'

'Tax breaks,' said Niko, with a grimace. 'He says villagers and especially local businessmen who make no fuss... Stavros will work it so they pay less tax.'

'That's corruption of the highest order!' I said. 'All this talk of financial help – it makes people forget the bigger picture.'

'Enough of this!' muttered Niko. He jerked his head towards Sophia, Leila, Uncle Christos and his cousin Stefan – they all came over. 'Spread the word – there is a meeting today at Taxos Taverna, six o'clock.'

'Say there will be free coffee and scones.' I said.

'Huh?' Niko shrugged.

'People like free food and will think better on a full stomach of solid home-cooked food as opposed to ThinkBig's plastic, takeaway snacks – every little helps. Now let's hurry back. We only have a few hours to come up with a plan to present to the rest of the village.'

Someone tapped on my shoulder. I turned around and looked up. Henrik. I shook my head.

'I can't believe you're so deeply involved with that jerk, Stavros. His game is hardly above board.'

His shoulders moved up and down. 'I don't know what you mean.'

'Illegal tax breaks?'

'I've said nothing about that.'

'Well you clearly bribed Stavros to rush through building plans... I've seen his new car...' A loud sigh escaped my lips. 'Henrik? What's happening to you? Where's the honourable man I've always admired?'

His mouth tightened. 'This deal needs to be closed for the good of everyone – there is honour in that.'

I shook my head. 'I'll be late back tonight.'

'Why? Planning a mutiny?' Henrik straightened his tie. 'No worries. I'm staying over in Kos Town. Stavros and I are going out to celebrate. Today's gone well.'

My eyes tingled. How had it come to this? I stood watching him leave the town hall.

'*Pippitsa*?' said Sophia gently. 'You okay?'

I nodded.

'Come,' she said. 'Let us report back to Grandma. We talk. You make scones.' She raised one eyebrow. 'And on the way you can tell me how one of our friends spotted you and Niko being stopped by police on the beach last night.'

CHAPTER TWELVE

Because they must have popped some party pills from the Kos nightclub scene and were hallucinating.

That was the answer I wanted to give. But Sophia deserved more than a witticism. I wondered if she suspected my true feelings for her son. When we were younger, she was almost as astute as Grandma when it came to children's mischief. Like the time Niko and I returned home from an afternoon playing, covered in grease, and made up some story about trying to mend his bike. She saw through our cover story straight away, as a few days earlier she'd banned us from going on part of the beach near a fuel spill. We'd set our hearts on giving the oil-covered dead birds a proper burial.

Sophia took my arm and directed me to a palm tree outside Pandora's bakery. We sat down underneath, on a shady bench, me breathing in yummy, honey pastry smells.

'We can catch the others up,' she said. 'First you, me, talk... Last night... you and Niko...' She let out a sigh. '*Pippitsa*, what going on? The police – do I need to be worried? I haven't asked Niko as he has been so fired up today about ThinkBig's plans.'

'No!' I forced a laugh, cheeks hot as I watched a green caterpillar crawl, in undulating waves, across my foot, instead of looking at her. 'Henrik and I – we had an argument. I went off on my own and he overreacted by reporting me missing to the police. That's all the officers wanted to talk about.'

Sophia exhaled.

'We didn't think it necessary to tell you all,' I continued and met her gaze. 'Not with everything else going on.'

She nodded. 'Thank goodness that's all it was... Because if Niko was in trouble... with all this ThinkBig trouble as well...' Her eyes looked shiny as she sniffed. 'All I want is for him and Leila to get married, settle down, have a family. The idea of a wedding between them has been the one positive thing that has got us all through the recent difficult months. Soon winter is coming. We all need this cheerful celebration as much as the young couple. Especially Grandma...' Her voice cracked. 'For her it has almost meant the difference between life and death.'

I had the feeling now my eyes were shiny.

'You won't let him take things too far with this plan against ThinkBig, will you Pippa? Niko can be fiery... I don't want him to risk his future by doing something against the law. You care for him, very much, that is obvious.'

I swallowed. If only she knew.

'From the first moment you arrived, last weekend, Niko... his smile is brighter, I've noticed. Times have been hard and you've been like a lighthouse beacon – to us all. Grandma too... Your visit has been a tonic in many ways, and I'm grateful. And sure you understand how important it is that he and Leila stay together.'

Oh God. Unintended guilt-tripping or what? No emotion flicked across her face but I wondered... Did she suspect something between me and her son? Our eyes locked and I smiled at the familiar, warm, caring heart-shaped face. In that moment I realised that indulgent daydreams of me and Niko getting together were nothing but that. His marriage to Leila meant everything to his family and so much for the health of Grandma. Perhaps I'd overestimated his feelings for me; maybe he didn't sense that magnetic attraction. But just to be sure there was no misunderstanding, I'd have to make it clear to him that my life was back in London, living my executive lifestyle.

I forced a smile. 'And this trip has done me good too.'

'And Henrik?' She patted my hand. 'You see a future with him? Living the busy life in London? You imagine having his children? Growing old together?'

'I don't know.' There. I'd said it out loud.

She gasped. 'But–'

'Today's made me realise that the doubts I've been having...' My voice wavered. 'Perhaps I should have acted on them weeks ago. Henrik's honesty was the thing I most admired about him – but now that's gone. There's no sparkle to fall back on.' I shook myself. 'Listen to me, Sophia. I sound like a romance writer.' We smiled and ever-polite, she said nothing. Unlike Grandma, Sophia would never pry!

Me feeling as if an anchor was attached to my chest, we continued our journey back to the taverna. On arriving, I avoided Niko and went straight into the kitchen. It was large and spotlessly clean, with metal work surfaces running the length of the room and gleaming silver equipment hanging from the walls I had scones to make – scones for filling the bellies of locals with the desire to fight for their way of life.

Sophia helped me find the ingredients and our chat had now returned to the meeting and the underhand mayor. What a relief it was to get kneading some dough. A relief that was, until Leila offered to help me. My feelings would be easier to cope with, if she wasn't so likeable.

'You think our stomachs look like this after having children?' she said, with a glint in her eye, as she pummelled the stretchy flour and butter mixture.

I couldn't help grinning. 'Yes. But it would be worth it.' I cleared my throat... 'You and Niko – ThinkBig's plans must have especially upset you, as you see your future in this village, don't you?'

Leila didn't meet my gaze but carried on kneading. 'It would take a biblical storm to tear Niko away from this place.'

'And you?' I said brightly.

Cheeks pinking, Leila shrugged. 'I... Travel could be exciting, but... but my place, it is here, by Niko.'

My stomach twisted. She didn't sound sure. Wow. Perhaps my suspicions had a concrete base. But I didn't push her further. It was none of my business. Niko had his life to sort out and I had mine. My stomach twisted tighter – starting with me making it clear to Niko that there was nothing romantic between us. Then by finally discussing my doubts about our relationship, with Henrik when he returned from Kos Town tomorrow morning. I gazed at Leila. Was she really planning an escape from downtrodden Greece, behind Niko's back?

She sprinkled more flour onto the dough and I tapped my foot in time with her humming. Unlike me, she cleared up whilst we worked... I liked Leila. She'd be good for Niko. A great daughter-in-law. A wonderful addition to any family.

'Grandma says, can you make those roasted pepper scones with feta cheese in the middle, from your last stay here?'

'Of course,' I said. 'Plus I thought we could try some tzatziki ones, with cucumber and garlic blended into the dough.'

'How about olive and halloumi cheese? The black specks look so pretty,' she said and popped an olive into her mouth.

I snacked on a handful of walnuts. 'At this rate our stomachs won't need babies inside them to look wobbly.'

We both laughed. I fetched us both an orange granita, whilst Leila started to cut out circles of dough. A couple of hours later, she put her hands on her hips. 'So, let's scribble down all the choices, see if we have enough. They smell delicious.'

Leila passed me a pen and paper and scanning the work surfaces, I made a list.

Roasted pepper and feta cheese

Olive and halloumi

Tzatziki

Honey and walnuts

Lemon filled with cream cheese

Cinnamon and syrup

Glittery jam and cream

'Those with cream and cheese in the middle better go in the fridge.' I said. 'The list looks pretty impressive.' I passed it to Leila. 'What do you think?'

'I feel hungry already.'

'Let's hope they act as fuel to drive the villagers' forwards in their appeal against ThinkBig's proposal. Everyone seemed complacent at lunchtime – especially when Stavros mentioned incentive payments and tax breaks.' I sniffed. 'Well, two can play at that game. In some small way, our baking might help win around the locals. Good homemade food kept the nation going through the Second World War. On a smaller scale, perhaps scones can contribute to us triumphing in this battle.'

Leila smiled. 'Although our enemy is more good-looking and oozes charm.'

'Yes, I think some of the local women fell for *Gigantes* Henrik.'

'Imagine if they'd seen him in a military uniform.'

'Leila!' With real warmth, I shot her a smile.

Niko came in. 'Brilliant! These scones look fit for gods.' He consulted his watch. 'Four o'clock. We have two hours left to finish coming up with a plan. You two join us now? My parents and some of the business people drink coffee.'

We nodded, put the scones in the fridge and washed our hands.

'Is Grandma downstairs?' I said.

Niko chuckled. 'Just try to stop her... Our mission to save Taxos seems to have fired her up – in a good way.'

Leila and I followed him into the taverna's dining room and Sophia poured me a large coffee as I sat down, next to Georgios. He was fiddling with one end of his big, black moustache.

'What have you concluded?' I asked and looked around at Uncle Christos, baker Pandora, Cosmo and the potter, Demetrios.

'The village pulls together,' said Georgios. 'We all refuse any corporate pay-off. With all our strength, we fight these plans.'

'So, in practical terms, that means...?' I raised an eyebrow.

Demetrios shrugged. 'We try to think of a characteristic only Taxos has, to make us different. Then work to demonstrate that.'

'Good idea,' I said. 'We call that a USP – a Unique Selling Point... So what have you come up with so far?'

'It hurts to say it,' said Pandora, 'but we agree with ThinkBig – it is Caretta Cove. The fact that turtles used to nest there and might do once more.'

'So perhaps we need to attract your older tourist, more interested in nature,' I said.

Demetrios nodded. 'I could make ceramic turtles to sell.'

I stared at him for a moment. 'Why not go one step further and offer pottery classes, for children and adults? Or you could make ceramic turtles and people pay to paint them and come back later during their holiday to collect them, once they've been in the kiln.'

'I like that,' said Demetrios. 'And have plenty of clay in stock, so for a while it would cost me little.'

'And I saw a programme about Japanese bakeries, once – they love pastries in animal shapes. Pandora, you could make turtle cakes.'

'But these all small ideas, no?' Cosmo sighed. 'We need something big, Pippa, to compete with your Henrik. And we need your help, your business know-how – what can we achieve in two weeks, before you go back to England?'

My chest glowed at them placing so much importance on me.

'Well, we can't achieve the impossible,' I said and gave a wry smile. 'There isn't long enough to magically transform Taxos into a booming economy. But we can set out business plans and list our objections. Plus, start to put those ideas into practice, to show that we are deadly serious.' I sipped my coffee. 'We just need to prove that perhaps there is another way, to move Taxos' financial situation forwards. So, for starters, let's put all of our tourist plans together in a leaflet. We can circulate them around the island and ask travel agencies in Kos to put up signs in their windows, advertising our concept. Let's really see what solid business seeds we can sow, in the next couple of weeks.'

'Something big can come out of lots of small ideas, pooled together,' said Grandma.

I nodded encouragingly. 'Why concentrate on turtles? What other animals or plants here would appeal to tourists?' I screwed up my forehead. 'Demetrios, I remember, when I was little, seeing lots of pottery lizards in your workshop.'

He loosened his bright green cravat. 'Yes, up near the wetlands, at the back of Caretta Cove, live many geckos, frogs and lizards. They are easy to spot. Some are protected by Greek law.'

'So that would make them of more interest to wildlife lovers... And Niko mentioned you've made cat bowls with your pets' names on – tourists would love that. You could personalise them and just add some Greek-themed pattern, like a mosaic or olives.'

'Don't forget Georgios knows a lot about birds,' said Grandma.

His eyes lit up... 'Yes, we have some beauties. Demetrios could make models of flamingos... the yellow and orange bee-eater... and in the evenings I know good spots to watch eagles and buzzards.'

I thought for a moment. 'Georgios – you could offer guided birdwatching tours.'

'Great idea,' said Niko and I tried to ignore his adorable, lopsided smile. 'And Cosmo,' he continued, 'why don't you allocate some bikes for hiring – you could take visitors on a cycle ride to Taxos' prettiest spots, like... like the top of the cliff, with its clear view of the Turkish mainland.'

Cosmo nodded. 'Or the meadows, near the church.'

'Yes, they are carpeted with the prettiest wild flowers throughout the year,' said Leila. 'Like poppies and wild orchids... ah, bicycles are so much nicer than smelly, noisy quad bikes.'

'So, we have wildlife tours, pottery and cakes to buy and ceramic workshops...' I remembered what Henrik had said about Niko hosting boat parties and thought of a less X-rated version. 'Niko, you and some of the other fishermen could offer trips out on your boats. It could include – ooh, a barbecue on the beach, when you return, to cook what you've caught.'

'Great idea!' said Sophia. 'Taxos Taverna would provide the crockery, drinks and salads.'

'And I could offer baking classes, yes?' suggested Pandora and straightened her black-rimmed glasses. 'The occasional tourist we have always asks me how I make the pastry layers for baklava.'

Grandma clapped her hands. 'Pandora, you must.' She glanced at me. 'Whereas you, my little peach, know exactly what this village needs to help attract the Americans and English.'

'I do?'

She gave a gap-toothed smile. 'Remember your dream, when you were little? Of opening a little teashop?'

My stomach fluttered. 'Yes, but...'

'No buts.' Grandma folded her arms. 'We could set up in the half of this taverna we don't use. All nationalities love cake. I seen all the scones you just made – with Greek flavours to appeal to locals. Plus you could do traditional ones for tourists and help us run it – offer tea or coffee. It would make our village different – wildlife trips and scones. A more reserved, but enjoyable holiday experience.'

I glanced around at the faces and one by one they nodded. Wow. Was I really going to live out my fantasy, even if it was just for a couple of weeks?'

'I could make you a simple sign in no time,' said Cousin Stefan. 'Leila can help me spell "teashop"'. He grinned.

'Really?' My heart thumped and I felt a big smile cross my face. 'Wow... yes... so...' I rubbed my hands. 'We have our plan and now must convince the other villagers to get on board.'

'So glad you are going to work here, at the taverna, and help us run a teashop – it is your fantasy come true,' said Niko , just before the villagers were due to arrive. We were taking the scones out of the fridge, and piling them onto plates.

I took a deep breath. Oh God. May as well get it over with. The sooner I let him know where he stood, the better. I felt sick.

'Look, um Niko, don't take this the wrong way,' I said, mouth dry, as I turned to face him, 'but can I just clarify something, seeing as we are going to be spending a lot more time together?'

His brow furrowed.

'You... me... I wouldn't want you to think... We are grown adults – last night was irresponsible, us fooling around. When those police turned up...'

'Pippa? What talk is this? Last night, it was great... And we were only having fun.'

My chest tightened. This was hard, but I'd worked out exactly how to put him off.

'Fun?' I said and shrugged, 'I suppose so. But, I'd rather spend my remaining time on the island thinking about what really gets me passionate, and that's business. Profits and losses; earning this village a living. You and I, we'll have no time for casual foolishness, over the next couple of weeks.'

'You don't want to spend time together... but I thought... us... our relationship...' He took my hands in his and I fought the urge to place them on my waist; to wrap my arms around his broad shoulders, lean forwards and press my lips against his.

'What relationship?' I said and forced a laugh. 'We haven't seen each other for nine years. It's a challenge for me to try and dig Taxos out of recession, which I'll enjoy, but after that my London life awaits.'

'A challenge? Is that all? Pippa? Who is this talking? I know that Taxos is more to you than just a project.' He squeezed my fingers. 'Why these harsh words? They cloud your face; hide your beauty which is as stunning as the mountain mist...'

I laughed louder. Niko backed away as if I'd slapped his cheek. Bile at the back of my throat, I carried on speaking, every ounce of me willing my voice not to tremble. Sometimes it was hard, so hard, to do the right thing.

'Niko, stop saying such nonsense, for goodness' sake! I'm... I'm flattered, of course, but these days we have so little in common for any sort of deep friendship. You're a simple fisherman. You said so yourself.' My chest ached. 'I'm an ambitious executive.'

'So what?'

'I think you'll make Leila a great husband, be a wonderful father and have continued success at catching fish but...'

He gave a long, drawn-out whistle. 'I get it. You think I'm not intelligent enough – not exciting enough for your mind?' A muscle flinched in his cheek.

I shrugged, willing my eyes not to spurt tears. 'What's the big deal about us spending time together? You...' Damn it, my voice wavered. 'You are committed to Leila, right?'

He opened his mouth then closed it, nodded and shifted from one foot to the other.

'See? Then you shouldn't be spending valuable free time with another woman – particularly one who has the job of sorting out the mess Taxos has got itself into.'

Hand shaking, I turned away and piled up the olive scones on one plate. 'Sorry Niko, but there is only so much chat about sardines and sponge-diving I can take. And I must bore you with high-falutin' talk of accounts and investments. The trouble is...' My chest could tighten no further, as I turned back to see his crumpled face. Oh God. This last lie was really going to hurt. 'My life has moved on whereas yours has stalled.'

CHAPTER THIRTEEN

'Ooh... Ahh... Just a little higher... Mmm, that's going to hit the spot...'

Er, no, I hadn't made a three hundred and sixty degree turn on my position with Niko, in order to enjoy a romantic massage. It was a couple of hours into the meeting with locals, and during a break Georgios was instructing me on how to construct one of his favourite lemon scones.

'Just another dollop of cream cheese, in the middle, so that it is the skyscraper of cakes,' he said. 'But no tell Sophia – she worries about my ancestral level.'

Inwardly I almost smiled. Bless Georgios. Never again would I say *cholesterol* without laughing.

He gazed around. We were in the kitchen, refilling plates. Most of the scones had gone. He wiped his perspiring forehead.

'So Pippa – how do you judge the mood of the villagers? Are they up for a fight?

The only fight I could think of at the moment, was between me and Niko.

Sophia came in at that moment, took Georgios' lemon creation and shot him a stern look. I handed the last of the glittery scones to her.

'They sound positive.' I eventually said. 'Now ThinkBig's plans have sunk in, most people seem angry and up for a battle, determined that Taxos won't end up like Tyrionitsa.'

Sophia nodded. 'People are coming up with lots of ideas and see the tax breaks for what they are: shallow bribes. I was worried earlier today – thought everyone felt there was no point in opposing this big corporation and being tempted by the talk of pay-offs. I should have trusted in the villagers. The Dellis' say they'll make part of their land into an animal zoo for children to visit – they have rabbits, a pig and sheep, and friendly goats the visitors can milk. They shall work on it tonight. Mr Dellis' brother, the fireman, can lend some equipment to do a controlled burn of some of the land. Then they can build fencing on the flat ground. Mrs Dellis also suggested they set up a little farm shop, as well, selling their homemade goats' cheese.'

Georgios nodded. 'And the postman's wife makes jewellery as a hobby – tries to sell it at the market in Kos Town from time to time. Demetrios offered her a permanent table in the pottery. Tomorrow she will spend the day working on a new collection, based on the local animals and flowers.'

'Although the Vesteros family still want to accept ThinkBig's offer on their property,' said Sophia, 'which stands where the quad bike track would be built.'

'Yes. A few villagers spoke keenly of the tax breaks but...' I shrugged... 'I've spoken to lots of people and most are willing to give our ideas their best shot, over the next couple of weeks. They like the sound of attracting people here because of the wildlife and more traditional activities. Then just before I leave perhaps we can reassess – decide if our plans really could save the village.'

'Also they like the idea of the teashop.' Sophia smiled. 'Those roasted pepper scones disappeared within minutes.'

My stomach tingled at the prospect of helping my friends set up their teashop tomorrow.

We went back into the taverna. Villagers had spilled out onto the front road. I surveyed the room. Niko sat in the far corner, near the patio, drinking retsina. He caught my eye and turned away as quickly as he could.

I winced, handed my plate of scones to Leila and took a deep breath. As I clapped my hands, a hush fell.

'*Efharisto*, again, for coming,' I said. 'I am glad most of you are keen to save the Taxos we know and love.'

Did that sarcastic laugh come from Niko?

An unfamiliar Greek voice shouted out from the back of the crowd and I looked to Georgios whose cheeks flushed.

'He says is a pity your Dutch boyfriend isn't more traditional.'

I bit my lip. 'Henrik is a successful real estate developer and feels he's doing the best from a financial view. But we have a chance to offer an alternative.' I glanced at Demetrios. 'When will you be able to start offering pottery workshops?'

He loosened his cravat and smiled. 'As soon as. I have the clay.'

'Same with my baking lessons,' said Pandora.

'We need about two days to build pens for our small animal farm – our neighbours have offered to help,' said Mrs Dellis.

'I only need tomorrow to plan the cycle route for my tours, and put together some maps,' said Cosmo, slipping his harmonica into his jeans' pocket.

'The fishing trips can be slotted in early afternoon, during my usual siesta,' said Niko, in a loud slurred voice. 'Tourists don't seem to mind the hot sun. That mean when getting back it'll be time for a barbecue dinner.'

'And *Pippitsa* – tomorrow we set up your afternoon teashop,' said Georgios. 'You spend the day cooking. We spend the day with soapy water and mops.'

'I can have your shop sign made by tomorrow night,' said Cousin Stefan.

A woman shouted something out in Greek.

'Good idea!' said Sophia and everyone nodded. She turned to me. 'We should start up a petition – I can help with that. We have friends in neighbouring villages who will doubtless support us.'

I beamed. 'Great... So, all that leaves is to put together that leaflet listing all our services with prices. Perhaps Leila could help me translate the Greek to English.'

'Of course, Pippa.' Leila shot me one of her friendly smiles.

'Then some of us can head into Kos Town and distribute them in shops and travel agencies...' I turned to Postie. 'Do you think the post office would let us use its printer, at a discounted rate?'

His brow furrowed so Leila translated.

'For sure,' he said.

'We also need to put together some paperwork,' I said. 'Listing our objections and–'

'Count me out,' said a voice from the back. 'I no risk upsetting ThinkBig. My family come first – I need the franchise of one of those takeaways.'

A couple of voices murmured in agreement and a tall, thin man at the back, with a ponytail, just crossed his arms and listened.

'I understand. You feel ThinkBig offers the only way out of this recession – but at what price? Pride in your job? Happiness in where you live? The modest tradition of your way of life lost, in favour of the reckless lifestyle of binge-drinking young tourists?' I gazed around at everyone.

'What you care?' said another voice. 'You go home soon, back to England.'

Niko sneered at me, as if he'd like to add "Hear, hear".

'And I shall leave my heart here,' I said quietly. 'Taxos is special. More than anything, I want to preserve that.'

Shaking his head, Niko got up and went onto the back patio. Luckily no one else seemed to notice.

Georgios spoke to the villagers in Greek as if he were translating what I said and some people's faces softened.

In fact, one person clapped and within seconds the sound of applause and stamping feet filled the room. Retsina was drunk, the remaining scones were scoffed and people punched the air whilst making fighting talk. Then, to the tired strains of Cosmo's harmonica, the yawning villagers returned to their beds. Several of us left behind started planning out leaflets and posters.

We agreed to keep in touch during the week and perhaps Friday night have a community barbecue on the beach, to take stock of the progress made. Sophia kept us supplied with coffee. Grandma hugged us all, before heading to bed. Niko disappeared – perhaps for a bracing sea walk so that he could sober up. Finally, at gone one in the morning, when I could write no more, I helped wash and clear the last plates and cups, before preparing to walk the fifteen minutes home.

'I accompany you back,' said Demetrios.

'No you won't,' said a voice from the doorway.

I glanced over. Henrik? 'I thought you were sleeping over in Kos Town.'

He said nothing but looked around the tables, littered with pens and paper.

'So, this is the headquarters of Operation Reject ThinkBig's Once-in-a-lifetime Offer?'

'Henrik, look...'

'It's okay. I understand.' His eyes crinkled as he smiled. 'I'll wait for you outside.'

I grabbed my handbag and sunhat, before kissing everyone goodbye.

'We see you tomorrow morning, *Pippitsa*?' said Sophia and gave a wide yawn.

I winked. 'Yes. Bright and early. Chin up, everyone. We'll give this our best shot.'

I headed out towards Henrik but didn't take his hand. We walked in silence, up Taxos' central high street, past The Fish House and Pandora's bakery. It was another typically humid August night, accompanied by the chirp of cicadas and mew of a passing tabby cat. In the distance an owl hooted and a welcome breeze lifted my hair. Henrik looked fashion-catalogue perfect, as usual, with his long legs in tailored beige chinos and a short-sleeved linen shirt just tight enough to hint at his pecs. He'd slicked back his thick hair and a holiday tan made his slate eyes seem paler – and more appealing – than ever. And quickly I extinguished the thought that Nico's exotic mocha eyes, ruffled hair and casual clothes were far sexier.

I glanced away as we headed towards the dusty road, wondering why this man beside me, impressive on the inside and out, wasn't enough. We cut through the wooded area and I relished nature's cedar pine scent – no celebrity or fashion designer could come up with a fragrance to beat that.

'Why did you come back to Taxos tonight?' I said and looked up at him.

Henrik gave a wry smile. 'We're on holiday. I didn't want to spend my last Saturday night here with some pompous mayor who spends the evening eyeing up short-skirted tourists. He just got more and more drunk, sneering about the Taxos villagers, saying they'd be utterly stupid to reject my company's "generous offer".' He shrugged. 'I may agree, but I don't look down on your friends...' He cleared his throat. 'In fact, clearly the villagers are going to try to fight off the project. I kind of respect that.'

'Yes and... I'm helping them. Sorry, Henrik, but I simply can't approve ThinkBig's plans.'

Then a not uncomfortable silence fell as we strolled along the dusty path, away from the village. Eventually we reached the villa – thankfully without a single mosquito bite. I went in, turned on the lights and kicked off my sandals. We both sat down on the sofa. Henrik took my hand.

'I owe you an apology, Pippa – for keeping ThinkBig's proposition from you all these months. And... I get what you are trying to do for the village. Like me, you are fighting for what you consider to be right. That's why I love you.'

Blimey. Henrik didn't often use the L word.

'In fact...' He slid onto the floor, and whilst on one knee slipped a hand beneath a cushion. Out came a royal blue velvet box.

Oh no. No, no, no... Don't do this, Henrik. Not now that I've finally made up my mind we have no future together.

'Pippa... You not supporting me yesterday, at the town hall meeting, in a perverse way made me more sure than ever, that you are The One. You are independent... courageous... morally admirable... everything I aspire to be.' His voice wavered. 'Marry me, Pippa. We make a great team – have the same life-goals.'

He opened a box to reveal a ring only Henrik could have chosen. Beautiful in its simplicity, its practicality, it was a slim silver band with three small diamonds embedded in the metal.

'Henrik... no...'

My vision went blurry as tears threatened – a sensation I was not used to, back in England. But first of all, today, I'd had to reject Niko against my true feelings, and now I was going to have to turn down a man I truly cared for.

He half-smiled and took the ring out of the box. 'Just try it on, Pippa... for me,' he whispered.

I swallowed. It slipped on. A perfect fit.

'I... I've sensed in recent weeks a distance between us,' he said, and sat back up on the sofa. 'So if you need time, that's okay. But there is no question in my mind. We fit, Pippa – as well as your finger and that ring. We are both ambitious, and follow our heads. As a couple we could achieve great things. Just look at your Mum and Dad.'

I smiled at him, really wanting to feel a rush of excitement surge through my veins, willing me to throw my arms around his neck and shout to the world that this man was mine.

However, all I could think of was the words Niko had used to describe me, like "mountain mist". Whereas Henrik's declaration of love used business-speak like "team" and "goals". And as for us being like Mum and Dad... No. Returning to Taxos had only confirmed what I'd secretly thought all these years – that boarding school and jet-setting through the world without getting to know your very own neighbours... That wasn't for me or my potential children.

Henrik stood up. 'Look. Let's go to bed. It's almost two and we've both got a big day tomorrow.'

On automatic, I nodded as he bent down to brush his lips against mine. But his touch, which lit no flames, sent a different kind of guilty jolt through me. I couldn't do this. I, for one, had to be honest. Henrik deserved that. Urgh! A conscience was a troublesome thing.

'Look... There's something you don't know: last night, on the beach, and since we've arrived...' Deep breaths. 'I... I've got... I've had feelings for Niko.'

CHAPTER FOURTEEN

With a roar, Henrik fled out of the villa and sprinted into Taxos, convinced that Niko must have made a move on me. By the time I'd caught up, with a torch, sandals rubbing against my heels, he was hammering on the door of the Sotiropoulos' taverna. I grabbed his arm, hissing that he'd upset Grandma, but Henrik easily held me at a distance with one hand, whilst continuing to knock with the other. Finally Niko answered. Henrik let go of me, dragged him onto the road and punched him in the face. Niko went flying and landed, face down, in the dust, blood streaming from his mouth.

Ooh, wasn't that just like a scene from one of my romantic sagas? *sigh*. Sorry for the deception, but yes, I made it up. Instead, back at the villa, last night, Henrik's eyes had widened for a moment and he pursed his lips. Then he calmly announced it was no surprise – Niko and I were good friends, we "had history" and yesterday I was upset about the news concerning Taxos. That was bound to have confused my mind. That once back in London, everything about Taxos and Niko would be forgotten. He kissed my cheek – said it didn't change how he felt, that we'd talk about it the next day.

But then Henrik had never been the jealous sort – nor one for hot arguments, which was good, right? Aarggh, no! Just occasionally a woman wanted proof that a man would fight for her. Like those scenes from Bridget Jones's Diary, when Hugh Grant and Colin Firth shatter glass and tumble into a fountain.

Didn't it rile Henrik at all that my lips and another man's had almost danced the rumba? Where was his passion for me? A passion Niko had no trouble demonstrating with his misty mountain and orange sunset words...

Sigh again. Must bury that thought; must be grateful that Henrik was so sane; so level-headed – so stereotypically cool and clinically Dutch and not an impulsive, hot-blooded Mediterraneono (yes, made-up word). Perhaps he was right – I'd lost all sense in Greece and once back home, it would seem like nothing more than a dream. With another sigh I glanced at the pillow next to me. Henrik wasn't there. The air smelt of tea tree shampoo, as I fought my way out of the mosquito net. He must have already left. Yawning again, I strolled into the kitchen and noticed a note.

Meet me back here tonight. I'll cook dinner. Henrik.

Next to it sat the blue velvet box. I opened it and slid the understated ring onto my finger again. At that moment the front door bell went. Hoping I looked half-decent in my shorts and T-shirt pyjama set, I smoothed down my hair before heading down the corridor by the bedrooms. I pulled open the front door.

'Niko!' Was it the morning sun making me feel hot, or something else?

'*Ya sou*, Pippa.' He met my eye, mouth straight, no teasing light radiating from those mocha eyes. 'May I come in?' he asked and cleared his throat. His gaze fell onto my hand – the ring – and colour rose into his cheeks.

'It's not what you think,' I rambled. 'Nothing's been agreed. I'm just–'

'Whatever,' he interrupted. 'Is none of my business.'

I stood to one side so that he could come into the villa, and shut the door behind us. We headed into the kitchen and sat up the breakfast bar.

'Coffee?'

He shook his head, expression not changing whilst I slipped off the ring and put it back in the box.

'Henrik no here?'

'He's spending the day in Kos Town, having lunch with the quad bike track designers. Then drinks with Stavros later.'

'No doubt he owes our island's mayor many favours.' Niko wrinkled his nose. 'Anyway, I no here about Henrik. Just to say... I appreciate your honesty yesterday. You right. I lucky man with Leila. Seeing you this last week had thrown me off balance. You and I, we no longer know each other and Taxos' future is all that matters.'

'Oh... um... agreed. That's exactly how I feel.' It is. Even though my hand longed to touch his; even though he looked crazy sexy in that casual shirt and jeans.

'Although I question your motives...' A frown crossed his face. 'You say your heart is in Taxos, but yesterday sounded as if rescuing it from financial ruin was nothing but an interesting project.'

I fiddled with the ring box. 'Look...'

'No matter. I don't care about that. As long as we defeat ThinkBig. That is all I care about – along with my family and Leila.'

'Niko...' Please, upturn those soft lips, make those deep, rich eyes dance with laughter.

He held up his palm. 'Save it. Right, Papa sent me here to say he and Mama are cleaning the unused side of our taverna from head to toe this morning, so there no point in coming over.'

'Don't shoosh me, Niko. There's no need to be rude.'

'Well, clearly you don't want me to be friendly. Which is it, Pippa? You can't have it both ways.'

What could I say?

'So, to continue, Postie has just visited – he has permission to open up today, so that we can all use the printer. This morning you go there, with Leila – help carry on the work we did last night, putting together the leaflet. Cosmo will join you to complete maps of the cycling routes and the village. Then Pandora, Demetrios, the Dellis' and everyone else offering a service will give you a short paragraph for Leila to translate, along with prices. Leila already has the information needed for my boat trips and Papa's birdwatching walks.'

'Fine. That means later today we can print everything out and first thing tomorrow some of us can go into Kos Town to spread the word.' I avoided his eye, returning his clipped tones.

'Yes. Demetrios has already designed a pattern for the front of the leaflet, in gold and red. And you could start on your menu, today. Mama thought we could ask Pandora to supply the teashop with traditional Greek pastries – that way we no steal her trade.'

I stood up and filled the kettle. 'You must have all got up early to think this through.' I glanced at the clock. 'It's only half past eight.'

'This is our life at risk, Pippa. It's not just a challenging project to us. We have no time to waste as you and your expertise, to help us, are only here for two weeks.' Niko stood up. 'I need to start hunting out barbecue equipment and making signs that look a least a bit professional.' Expressionless, he gazed at me. 'I go. Let's both strive to at least be civil.'

Before I knew it, he was gone and I sipped my coffee, hoping it would salve my aching chest. But that ache had no physical cause – it had roots in the feeling that I'd lost something special.

I felt no better, hours later, when I headed to the taverna following a morning putting the leaflet together. We'd decided to head it "*Taxos – the hidden treasure of Kos. Discover the wonders of the real Greek way of life*". Leila had helped me understand the villagers' scribblings. We kept the amount of information short and punchy, including photos where possible.

Sophia and Georgios waved. They sat at a table, outside, both drinking orange granitas. Sophia wore a scarf around her hair and Georgios' head glistened with sweat. His normally white shirt had dust marks across it and a mop leaned against Sophia's chair.

'*Ya sou*, Pippa! Let me get you a drink,' said Georgios and swatted away a fly as he stood up. I took off my hat and glasses, glad to sit under the shade of the table's parasol. I took the first leaflet printed out of my handbag and held it open for Sophia.

'Here we have a list of attractions in Taxos,' I said. 'The pottery workshop and the baker's pastries plus cooking classes... There are details of the days out cycling or birdwatching – everything we've discussed.' We smiled at each other. 'Looks impressive, doesn't it?'

Sophia glanced at the leaflet again. 'I like the red and gold colour, and calling Taxos the hidden treasure of Kos. Hey, look Georgios!'

He returned with my granita and, whilst I gratefully downed mouthfuls of icy drink, Georgios held the leaflet at a distance and studied each paragraph.

'Is very, very good,' he said finally, and patted my arm. 'You've all worked hard. I like the simple layout – not too much information, clear prices and everything in Greek or English...' He waved the leaflet. 'Will these be ready to drop off in Kos Town tomorrow?'

'Yes, and hopefully, from Tuesday, a little business should start to roll in. As you can see, we've included phone numbers. I gave the taverna's for the teashop, your birdwatching tours and Niko's boat trips – I hope that is all right.'

He gazed at the leaflet again, particularly the paragraph describing the teashop. 'What is this?'

Sophia leant over to read it too and grinned.

'Grandma wanted to do her bit...' I gave a sheepish smile. 'So I suggested she be on hand in the teashop to read guests' coffee sediment. Tourists love that sort of stuff.'

Georgios burst out laughing. 'No wonder she was up early today with us, insisting on taking our empty cups into the kitchen. She was getting some practise in!'

'You a good girl, *Pippitsa*,' said Sophia, softly. 'Grandma whistling this morning – we no heard her do that for months.'

'Did someone mention my name?' Grandma appeared at the doorway and everyone chuckled.

I passed her my granita glass. 'Can you read ice as well?'

Eyes laughing, she shook her finger. 'No, but I can pour it over cheeky girls' heads.'

Grandma was still threatening to slip ice cubes down my neck, half an hour later, when I messed up her tidy kitchen by pulling out ingredients. It was time to assemble a menu for Taxos Teashop. I could have jumped up and down as the reality of me living my dream sunk in.

Anyone for Earl Grey and cucumber sandwiches? Time to be serious, though. I needed to plan the menu with military precision so that it appealed both to the villagers and potential tourists. Right... definite options would be the most favourite scones from the meeting yesterday. Plus Grandma liked those honey and dried fig ones and cherry scones always went down well... Furiously, I jotted flavours down. Plus Sophia mentioned she would collect some of Pandora's baklava and chocolate walnut tart... I surveyed the list. None of the ingredients were very expensive and I wouldn't make whole batches of each flavour until I got an idea of how many might sell, per day. We could open up to locals tomorrow afternoon after my trip to Kos Town, seeing as the place was now clean. Stefan was dropping the sign off later and Georgios and Sophia's computer printer was good enough, just to print off a few basic menus. So, in preparation for tomorrow, I'd just make a few scones that the Greek villagers might like.

Humming, I sieved flour into a bowl and rubbed in a small amount of butter. My shoulders relaxed and my breathing rate fell. As always, making scones helped empty my mind of worries and focus it, instead, on textures and flavours. When the mixture turned to small squidgy crumbs between my fingers, I divided it into four. Into one quarter I added a pinch of salt, quartered olives and a little oregano. In the other a cupful of chopped roasted red pepper, leftover from yesterday, with a pinch of paprika. Into the third quarter, honey and chopped dried figs and into the final lot, sugar, grated lemon rind and lemon juice... Then I kneaded each separately.

Mmm, how divine to breathe in the contrasting aromas of citrus, meaty pepper and pungent black olives. My mouth upturned as I watched the dough's blank canvas change into four different pictures. I used Sophia's small pie cutters to divide the four lumps of dough further, into perfect rounds. I glazed the savoury ones with beaten egg and the sweet ones with milk.

Aahhh, imagine doing this every day of your life. Although I wasn't naive enough to think it wouldn't ever become routine...

I'd need an extra challenge, such as... I don't know, perhaps creating an online shop. I'd also have a scone of the month and run competitions for local children to create a new recipe that they'd come in and bake. Plus I'd produce gift vouchers for locals to give as presents, a bit like Afternoon Tea at The Ritz, just with cheaper crockery, Greek music and sunshine thrown in.

I swallowed. Yes, I was lucky, not many people ever got near living their dream, but it was going to be hard, handing the teashop over completely to its owners in two weeks and leaving to return to my banking job in London.

Banking. Mathematics. Studying. Exams. This had been my life, up until now. If the opportunity came along to give it all up permanently and live here, could I really sacrifice everything I'd achieved career-wise? A chirpy voice inside me immediately answered yes. It listed all the reasons, including how well I'd been sleeping in Taxos and how I hadn't suffered a single stress headache. Plus back in London I'd inwardly groan as my alarm clock woke me up each day, whereas here in dear Kos I gladly woke to birds and jumped out of bed.

Shoulders aching from kneading, scrubbing and sweeping up, I strolled home late that afternoon, having agreed with Leila that she and I would take the leaflets into Kos Town early the next morning. Indefatigable Sophia had just set out to tour Taxos with the petition. Whistling, I breathed in the cedar pine aroma of the wooded forest with relish. An old man walking a donkey approached, as I came to the dusty road leading to the villa. I was carrying a small basket of scones back to the villa, for Henrik and me, and offered him one. Then two young boys cycled past and shouting something to each other, before laughing and stopping. I grinned as they greedily took one each. If Taxos lost the appeal, this road would be filled with unsteady tourists on mopeds, the engines of quad bikes revving in the far distance. I quickened my pace. That wasn't going to happen. The leaflet showed how much Taxos had to offer without some tacky, fancy development.

I turned my key in the lock and the aroma of... mmm, garlic and fish welcomed me. Henrik came into the hallway, still in his shirt but with his tie off and shirt sleeves rolled up.

'Something smells delicious,' I said and smiled. 'It's so humid, you should have got changed. I'm gasping for a glass of water.' Henrik mumbled something as I headed into the kitchen and put the basket down on the breakfast bar.

I stopped dead and stared at the sofa as someone stood up. Huh? What was smarmy Stavros with his dyed curly hair and generous waistline doing here?

'A pleasure to meet you, Pippa,' he said and came over to give my hand a wet kiss – urgh, those yellow-stained teeth. 'Henrik kindly invited me to dinner, so that you and I could chat. No point delaying so let me be straight, and explain to you everything that is wrong and dangerous with your birdwatching and cycle tour plans to save the Taxos.'

'Um, what birdwatching?' I said, innocently.

He smiled. 'Pippa, dear lady, Kos is a very small island.'

Damn. Somehow he must have found out about all our ideas and the leaflets.

Stavros stretched out his legs and put his arms behind his head. I forced my gaze to avoid the sweat patches on his shirt.

'What do you mean, dangerous?' I said.

'For tourists and villagers – the former face injury, the second a stint in jail.'

My brow furrowed.

'Take these boat trips and the cycle rides...' he began. 'I assume lifejackets and helmets will be provided, plus those in charge have insurance, no? Plus are up-to-date with first aid as well? And added paperwork will be needed for those premises offering pottery and baking classes...'

Damn – he really did know what we were up to.

'Of course. I made sure the villagers drew up a list of permissions and licences to apply for. I'm handing it into the council tomorrow morning, when I'm in Kos Town.'

Stavros chuckled. 'I suspected as much. With an astute businesswoman on their side, the villagers will do well. But...' he shrugged, '...oh dear, the council is a busy place at the moment. I might have to suggest that such applications are buried for a while, to give priority to more important work.'

I gasped. 'You can't do that!'

He smirked.

'This will mean that all of your little projects provide nothing but a health and safety nightmare scenario.'

My lips pursed. 'Everyone involved is an experienced, safety-conscious adult. I'm sure nothing will happen. '

Stavros puffed out his chest. 'Sorry, but it would be irresponsible of me if I didn't inform the necessary authorities.'

'And perhaps it would be irresponsible of me not to report your suggested illegal tax breaks,' I said in a tight voice.

Stavros burst out laughing. 'Dear girl, I have a strong network of friends throughout the whole of Kos – most of the people you'd speak to owe me favours. They would not listen to a random tourist.'

'Stavros is right, Pips,' said Henrik. 'Think it through – you wouldn't want the villagers to get into trouble.'

I forced a smile. 'Sounds as if you are both running scared... What's the matter? Has it suddenly hit home that community spirit might defeat corporate greed?'

Stavros guffawed again and wiped a tear from his eye. 'You live in a dream world, Miss Pattinson. Full of unrealistic ideals.'

I stared at the pompous mayor for a moment. 'Look Stavros, what's it going to take for you to leave off the villagers, for just two weeks?'

'Do you really believe they stand a chance against us?' He shook his head. 'From what Henrik says, you are a savvy businesswoman who must realise there is no hope for Taxos without ThinkBig's investment. I'm amazed you haven't got on board with his proposal.'

'I'm a human first and foremost and nothing compares to their passion,' I snapped. 'And if you are so convinced they'll fail to defeat ThinkBig's plans, why do the next two weeks matter? At least if the villagers make some attempt to save their way of life, the final outcome will be easier for them to cope with. These people are my friends – I don't want them to feel any more miserable about this than necessary.'

'I have a proposition,' said Henrik, perched on the edge of the sofa. 'Stavros doesn't bury the necessary paperwork – in fact he hurries it through. In return, when all of your little ideas have come to nothing, before returning to England, Pippa, you promise to stand by ThinkBig and Stavros; you persuade the villagers to sign on the dotted line without further fuss.'

'Pah! Hardly seems like a fair exchange!' said the mayor.

Henrik shrugged. 'You'd be surprised – the most successful developments are where you have the enthusiasm and support of locals. Think of your reputation, Stavros – if you end the villagers' fight before they've even had a chance to prove themselves, you'll always be the villain – whereas this way you'll appear like some gracious saviour who they respect. You can't put a price on that.'

'So you mean, play nicely,' he said and gave a smile that didn't come from his eyes, 'Okay. Agreed. I will turn a blind eye to any indiscretions until the paperwork is in place – a process I will speed up – in return for your support, Pippa, before you go home.'

He held out his arm and I forced my hand to shake his and then Henrik's. What did I have to lose? If the appeal was lost, ThinkBig's proposition, however ghastly, probably was the best – the only – way forward.

'I guess I should have realised Stavros would have found out about all our plans, eventually,' I said to Henrik later, in bed.

He nodded. 'Sorry about dinner, by the way – I wasn't expecting Stavros to come by. But when he started talking about how the locals could get into trouble, I thought you should know.' He gave a small smile. 'I'm not a monster – I like Georgios and Sophia. And Leila's pretty cool.'

'You won't tell her that I... what I said about Niko?'

'Niko?' Henrik's smile dropped. 'Nothing to tell, is there?'

I shook my head.

'So, about my proposal, the ring...'

'I don't know, Henrik. There's so much going on and–'

Ever the gentleman, he nodded, broad shoulders dipping down.

'How about I... I give you a reply before we go back home?'

'Really? Yes, sounds great.' His face lit up.

So, I just had less than two weeks to save Taxos and decide my romantic future with Henrik, once and for all. No pressure then.

CHAPTER FIFTEEN

Pressure is all about force applied to a certain area and can often result in some sort of explosion... like when your moisturiser bottle congeals over, so you squeeze it dead hard and a huge gloop of cream fires out. Er, why am I talking physics? Because I'm glad to say that, unexpectedly the next few days were actually relaxed. Yes, the villagers worked hard and no one less than dear Sophia – by Friday she'd collected over one thousand signatures on her petition. Even Niko helped by keeping away from me where possible. Plus Henrik respected my desire to help the villagers and spent his time swimming or busying himself at ThinkBig's offices – and didn't keep mentioning his marriage proposal. What's more, Stavros kept to his word and hurried through the paperwork for the locals.

To be precise, on Monday Leila and I circulated the leaflets in Kos Town. Most of the travel agencies were kind enough to put up our A4 sized poster in their windows. A couple said Taxos would definitely fill the gap in the market for tourists seeking more than hangovers and wet T-shirts – although the biggest one laughed in our faces. 'Visitors won't give a toss about viewing wildlife without free cocktails,' he declared. I spied Leila admiring new luggage and then chatted over a baklava and coffee. She made me laugh, listened to me talk about London and spoke of her fondness for Grandma. Whether she was planning to travel or not, Leila was a kind-hearted person and helped me keep my resolve to stay away from Niko, because I couldn't bear the thought of upsetting her.

When I returned to Taxos that afternoon – oh... my... God. Cousin Stefan had put up the wooden sign on the unused side of Sotiropoulos' taverna.

'*Pippa's Pantry*?' I said, in a choked voice and studied the illustrations of cakes and shells, either side of the words, courtesy of Demetrios. 'Niko told you?' Perhaps he wasn't so cross with me after all.

'No, Leila mentioned it,' said Stefan. 'Niko talked about it to her once – said another possible name was "Shiver me Sandwiches"?'

I caught Stefan's eye and we smiled. 'But what about when I've gone back to England... if the teashop stays in business, the title won't make sense.'

'Georgios and Sophia said you will always be in their hearts and say this is their way of showing it.'

My eyes blinked quickly for a few seconds.

Apparently a couple of the locals had already come by for some takeaway scones. Georgios told us that the Dellis' animal pen was halfway complete, and Cosmo had cleaned up and serviced some old bikes for his tours. Pandora had made her first batch of turtle cakes, whilst Demetrios already had some ceramic animals in his kiln. I made a quick visit to the pottery to thank him for the drawings on my sign and couldn't help buying an adorable turtle brooch that Postie's wife had quickly put together.

Henrik met me back at the villa that night, for dinner. Neither of us spoke much about our day – but we enjoyed an evening dip in the pool and a bottle of red wine.

'Let's not forget we're on holiday, Pips,' Henrik murmured, after a few glasses. He ran a hand down my cheek and we agreed to have a night out in Kos Town, the following day. After which I fell soundly asleep on the sofa. Monday was an excellent start to the week.

Whereas Tuesday offered more challenges, accompanied by lots of finger drumming and prayers for business to come in. The leaflets were out there – all we could do was wait for the phone to ring. A couple of locals came to the teashop, (squee, Taxos had a teashop!) for a coffee and scone. I loved taking customers' orders and seeing the looks on their faces when they bit into the food. Two small children ordered the glittery jam scones and I also put crayons and paper out for them. An elderly couple visited and gave me a hearty thumbs up for the roasted pepper and feta cheese ones. In the background I decided to play a CD of traditional Greek string music.

However, the phone in the taverna was decidedly quiet. We became over-excited at one point when it rang – all for nothing as it was just the hospital changing one of Grandma's appointments. She came in from outside to answer the call herself. How great it was to see her out of bed and enjoying the August sun.

But a little despair did set in, when teatime arrived with no bookings for Georgios' wildlife tours, nor Niko's fishing trips and barbecues.

'No worry,' Grandma said. 'This morning's coffee sediment said all will be well.'

And sure enough, as the sun set the sound of a harmonica floated through the doorway and Cosmo appeared with Demetrios (cherry cravat today), and Pandora who'd dyed her short hair a rich shade of chestnut. All three beamed– a group of six were booked in for a cycle tour the next day, and Demetrios and Pandora each had tourists arriving too – a family who wanted to paint ceramics and a group of young women keen to learn Greek baking skills.

That afternoon I made more scones, as Cosmo, Demetrios and Pandora had promised to spread word of Pippa's Pantry. Old Mrs Dellis visited, eyes all sparkly, to say that thanks to many neighbours' help, the pet farm's pens were built.

In the evening I met Henrik in Kos Town, as agreed, for dinner and we feasted on fried whitebait, drizzled with an amazing lemon sauce. We drank cocktails and danced, me blocking out the fact that in just over a week I had to make a decision about our relationship.

On Wednesday... Hurrah! Bright and early the phone rang! (Okay, so I had a slight hangover, but a couple of painkillers and the walk into Taxos cleared my head). A hotel owner had seen our poster and said several older guests would love a day in Taxos. He rang later with exact numbers – fifteen for Thursday! They wanted to do the birdwatching walk, visit the pottery, have afternoon tea in my shop, plus buy cheese from the Dellis' farm. Then a group of young men rang up, interested in the fishing trip and barbecue for the next day. And Demetrios stopped by to say he had more bookings for later in the week. During the day some Germans, who'd picked up a leaflet, spontaneously caught the bus here and Cosmo took half of them on a cycle ride, up to the cliff.

They loved the magnificent view of Turkey, apparently marvelling over the wild orchids, and then came back to mine for honey and fig scones. The rest of their group had gone on the birdwatching walk and been thrilled to catch sight of some bee-eaters and buzzards. I quizzed them about their stay in Kos and they said they'd be happy to sign any petition; that variety was the key to a good holiday, and whilst they loved the beach life, Taxos offered a different angle on their vacation. I also promised to make a little girl a special apple strudel – her favourite – if they called again the following week. Plus they were keen to come back to the pottery, and make personalised bowls for their pets.

Sophia kept an eye on the teashop whilst I visited Pandora. Her cookery class had gone very well. She'd pre-prepared handouts so that people had could take home all the details of what they'd learnt during her lessons. Plus the young women apparently visited the pottery afterwards, and painted various ceramics which they'd pick up next week. I then visited the Dellis family who'd sold several rounds of cheese, and had huge fun teaching an English couple how to milk their goats.

On Thursday, Henrik and I made an effort to have breakfast together. I made a tomato and oregano omelette, whilst he picked apricots and mixed them with yogurt. The unwritten rule continued to hold fast, that we didn't discuss the detail of our day – after all, we were on opposite sides. But he ironed me a blouse, saying I looked tired. Plus I packed him a fresh lunch, when he said he'd be working all day, at his desk, tying up the details for a small hotel development on the other side of the island.

But Thursday did dampen our spirits a little, as the group of young men weren't impressed with Niko's fishing trip. They moaned about the lack of alcohol and were disappointed with the size of fish. They'd expected big rods and didn't understand the skill in handline fishing. Fortunately no-nonsense Uncle Christos turned up just in time, when they became aggressive and demanded their money back. They seemed determined not to enjoy the barbecue either and complained that they weren't allowed to smash the plates afterwards, as they'd seen Greeks do in the movies.

On the bright side, the hotel group loved Georgios' birdwatching walk, where an eagle kindly made an appearance. They also spoke enthusiastically of the ceramic turtles they'd painted at the pottery. I was rushed off my feet at the teashop, and ran out of the cherry and Greek yogurt filled scones. As for Grandma, the tourists couldn't get enough of her reading their coffee sediment – even if she did predict one broken arm, two divorces and three affairs.

In the evening, a downhearted Niko sat outside on the patio, alone. My heart squeezed as I noted the downturned mouth and drooping shoulders. I went out to join him.

'Those passengers were fools and not representative of the type of tourist Taxos is bound to attract,' I said.

He stood, still staring ahead, out to sea. 'I don't need your sympathy, Pippa. And what do you really care? This is a financial experiment for you, no? To see if your expertise can really make a difference.'

I gasped and grabbed his arm. He met my gaze. 'You're taking this too far,' I said, voice wobbling. 'Just because... because we've fallen out, there's no need to make out I am some sort of heartless robot.'

'Your words, not mine,' he said and turned back.

Vision blurred, I went back into the taverna. One good thing – the hurt I felt at *his* words made me realise Henrik and me really were over. My feelings for Niko – love, hate, whatever, were driven by passion. I just didn't feel that for Henrik and if I'm honest, doubted I ever really had. So my answer was "No" and I would tell him, as soon as.

As soon as meant Friday, the next day. Bright and early I got up and drank coffee. Henrik came out of the bathroom, towel wrapped around his waist. He came over to the breakfast bar and trailed his hand down my back. I was already dressed in shorts and a light, long-sleeved cotton blouse. Despite my protests, Sophia had insisted I was the perfect person to help Niko out on a fishing trip he had booked today, to boost his confidence after yesterday's disaster. Sophia and Grandma would look after the teashop. Little did she know me and her son were hardly talking.

'Make sure you apply enough sunscreen,' Henrik said. 'We don't want you fainting again.'

I didn't answer and took another mouthful of coffee.

His brow furrowed. 'What's the matter?'

My glance moved to the velvet blue box on the table. 'I... I don't need to wait until next week to give you an answer.'

Henrik sat down and slid the box across the table, to my cup. 'Pippa?'

My lip wobbled. Deep breaths. 'I'm so sorry, Henrik, but it's no.'

His throat expanded briefly, as he swallowed. Those slate eyes glistened. The very core of me twisted tight. This was exactly what I'd wanted to avoid, by coming on holiday alone, so that I could come to a decision before Henrik popped the question. Nothing hurt like rejection, but now I had no choice.

'What's brought this on?' he said in a rough voice. 'Why suddenly so sure?'

Now I swallowed, unable to double the blow by telling him it really was because of the feelings I had for Niko, that seemed so real. Don't get me wrong, I knew soon I'd be back in England and that this idyllic life in Taxos... my friendship with Niko... would be no more than a memory. But the depth of feeling for my childhood friend crystallised the fact that Henrik really wasn't the man for me.

Ironic, isn't it, because in so many practical ways my Dutch Titan was perfect. But romantic magic was important, right? I didn't want to settle for a marriage of convenience – even if that convenience was successful and dynamic. And if that sparkle never arrived in my life, at least I'd not be constantly questioning myself. That wouldn't be fair to Henrik or me. I had work... good friends and family... a life blessed with many positives. Marriage had to be with the right man or not at all and I could cope with that.

'I've had doubts for a while, and Taxos has given me some perspective. The last few days away from you has given me space to think.'

Henrik stared at the box. 'Have I done something wrong? Because I can work on it...' He took my hand and turned to face me. 'Pips – us... I thought things were going great? We're the ideal couple, aren't we? Can't you picture the amazing penthouse we'll own one day, on the Thames, and our kids in posh straw hats and blazers as we wave them off for an amazing term at a top school? Us both promoted at work? The fantastic holidays we'll take in the Caribbean?'

My eyes felt wet. 'No...' I whispered. 'I don't need all that. Mum and Dad sent me to boarding school whereas all I wanted was a normal life, like Georgios and Sophia gave Niko...'

Henrik let go of my hand and snorted. 'Has this got anything to do with that deadbeat jerk? Because he wouldn't make you happy. Living in a village on a sunny island... as the recession has proved, that's just an unhappy dream based on a place where, in reality, rioters burn down banks and no one can afford to pay their tax.'

'Look, Henrik... Niko is engaged to Leila anyway and...'

'*Anyway*? That makes it sound as if you'd consider him otherwise.' Henrik stood up, the high stool scraping the floor. 'Niko has no life-plan. And I've seen the way he's drooled over you, ever since we've arrived.

'Drooled?'

Henrik snorted. 'Yes – despite having a fiancée who deserves more respect.' He curled a fist. 'The man's an imbecile, sticking around in this dusty dump all this time, ignoring the question of how he'd properly provide for a wife and kids. Where's his ambition? His discipline? His work ethic?' Henrik shook his head. 'Whatever feelings you think you've got for him is based on the stuff of teenage fairy tales and belongs in one of those bloody silly romance books you read. For goodness' sake, Pippa, grow up.'

Ouch. 'I'd say he and his cousin work damn hard, fishing and sponge-diving every day.'

Henrik snorted again. 'Apart from in the winter, when they no doubt lounge around drinking retsina and playing cards...' He threw his arms in the air. 'Can't you see that intellectually he'd bore you within a week?'

My cheeks felt hot – he'd used the very argument I made up to put off Niko. But it wasn't true. I could spend a lifetime talking to Niko about the things that mattered, like family, friends, fishing, baking...

Henrik snatched the ring from the table and marched back to the bedroom. In a puff of aftershave, he came back into the kitchen minutes later, and poured himself a juice.

'Look, don't go like this...' I put my hand on his arm, now dressed in a sharp suit, but he shook it off.

'You're no better than my father,' he snarled. 'He led Mum on for years. Apparently he'd never loved her, but "made do with second best."'

'I'm nothing like him!'

'Have you been stringing me along all this time? Don't you love me?' he asked, in a high pitch. 'You'd throw everything away for some girlish dream of a holiday romance?'

Wow. Finally Henrik showed a bit of passion. My legs wobbled. He deserved the truth and a proper reason for ending our relationship, but I didn't want to deepen the bruise to his ego. How could I spell out that sometimes, kissing him, I felt like a gadget carrying out some pre-programmed task expected of me?

I shook my head. 'Look, things between you and me... they haven't felt right for a while. Not for a lifelong commitment. But of course I thought I loved you in the beginning – I would have never moved in with you, otherwise.'

A muscle flinched in his cheek, as he strode over to the sofa and picked up his briefcase.

'Perhaps we should see what Leila makes of all this?' he spat before heading towards the front door. 'Has she any idea of how her new friend Pippa feels about her fiancé?'

'No, Henrik! Don't!' I frantically called and hurried after him.

CHAPTER SIXTEEN

Grandma... Sorry to tell you this, but it's best that I break the news: Henrik believes I have really strong feelings for Niko. He told Leila who got upset and has fled abroad. The wedding is off.

The old woman clutched her heart, face pale, lips wobbling, and fell to the ground...

I shuddered, not even liking to imagine that fictional scene (yes, of course, I made it up – clue? I wouldn't dare refer to feisty Iris as an *old* woman).

With a sigh, I piled scones on to cake plates and covered them with domed glass lids. After leaving the villa early, shortly after furious Henrik, I'd headed straight for Pippa's Pantry (LOVED saying that). The fresh cedar pine smell of the woods had helped clear my head, plus baking batches of olive and halloumi, lemon and cream cheese, and honey and fig scones slowed down my heartbeat, and smoothed out my brow. How good it felt – kind of safe – to rub butter into flour and then knead the dough. Plus cooking kept me busy until Niko got back. As usual, he'd gone fishing with his cousin, before he'd return and we'd take out a group of four tourists who'd booked in yesterday afternoon.

'*Ya sou*, my little peach – can I help?' said Grandma and she came into the room wearing a red, orange and gold-trimmed blouse.

'Wow – you look beautiful!'

Cue her gap-toothed smile. '*Efharisto*, Pippa. I feel good – stronger than I have for a while. Which means...' Grandma came over to me, took my arm and sat me down at one of the small, round mahogany tables. The room smelt of bleach. Sophia had already mopped away any overnight dust before I arrived this morning.

'...you can tell me, what is the problem? You are sad, no?' Her fingers stayed curled around my arm. 'Although you look a tiny bit more relaxed than when you first arrived a couple of hours ago.'

I'm fine,' I said brightly. 'Just tired – I didn't sleep well.'

Grandma made a kind of "tsk" sound and lifted her hand to shake her finger.

'Pippa! Not you, please! I sick of people tip-toeing around me as if I a cracked plate that is about to shatter. This last week or two I feel much stronger. Now come on – tell me. Or I shall fret.'

I wiped my hands across my apron and put my elbow on the table. Resting my chin in my hands, I looked at her. I couldn't tell her about my fairy dust feelings for Niko, nor my suspicions about Leila wanting to travel abroad.

'It's me and Henrik. That's all. We've split up.'

'Ah...' Grandma nodded her head and ran her hand over my ponytail. 'Poor little peach – how that must hurt. But is for the best – I can tell.'

I sat upright and raised my eyebrows.

'Ever since you two arrived and I've seen you together...' Grandma shrugged. 'Something hasn't been right.'

'What? How did you know?'

Grandma fiddled with her wedding ring. 'From the first day I met my husband, the whole world seemed different – like... like a diamond that had been polished and suddenly flashed light. My mama would laugh – could always tell when I'd met him, because she said my eyes would twinkle like waves reflecting the sun or stars lighting up the sky; like frost glittering on tree branches, or the wings of fireflies... But in you, I no see that twinkle, when you're with Henrik – and that twinkle is essential, to keep the love alive.'

A lump rose in my throat – trust Grandma to notice that. Had she observed anything strange about Niko or Leila, as well?

'Pippa?' called a male voice and I jumped up to pull off my apron. Grandma looked up and an odd expression crossed her face, before she smiled. Niko slouched into the room and pointed at his watch. 'We must grab a quick lunch – I've already made it,' he said, in a flat voice, whilst walking over to plant a kiss on Iris' cheek. 'You really don't need to come on the trip though, Pippa. We haven't much time. The passengers will meet me on the beach at two.'

'Of course she must go. For moral support,' said Grandma.

'Yes, of course,' I said weakly, not wanting Grandma to suspect anything was wrong. 'Do you know anything about today's passengers?'

'Like yesterday, all English young men. But they sounded keen to catch fish, and this time I warned them my business is new and explained about our plan to save Taxos.' He shrugged. 'Perhaps I should have explained to those men yesterday.'

'Sounds like it wouldn't have made a difference – so what did they say?'

'They aren't concerned and wished us well with our goal.'

'At least not all visitors are trouble-makers.'

'Only little peaches,' said Grandma and I forced a laugh, ignoring Niko's expression which suggested Iris was absolutely right.

'Grandma seems better every day,' I said and sat down opposite Niko, in the taverna, warm rays from the sun hitting my back from the open patio doors.

Niko just grunted, so with a sigh, I turned to my plate. A smile crossed my face as my eyes feasted on the food and I breathed in... Whatever Henrik thought, sometimes nothing beat the simple things in life, like this feast made up of pitta bread, mozzarella cheese and tomato salad, shiny black olives and a bowl of creamy hummus. God, it felt good to be back in Greece.

When we'd finished, having exchanged not one word, I fetched two honey and fig scones, then halved and spread them with creamy Greek yogurt. My hand brushed his as I put down his plate. Blood filled his cheeks. Tingles ran up my arm. Abruptly he pulled away his arm. Sophia brought over two coffees and ordered Niko to change his clothes, before meeting the tourists. I applied sun cream to my face, arms and legs, plus borrowed a cap from Georgios, in case my sunhat flew off into the sea-breeze. I wore my sunglasses and took a rucksack filled with six water bottles for us and the passengers. Niko and I headed down to the beach, leaving the rest of his family to man the taverna and teashop. He carried a big bag, containing six handlines and, lures, whatever they were, along with an icebox to bring back the catch.

'Is everyone in the village coming to the beach barbecue tonight, that we all talked about on Saturday, to discuss the progress we've made?' I said, giving conversation another attempt.

'Yes – my guests' barbecue will finish around seven – the villagers will arrive after that. Cosmo, Demetrios, Pandora, the Dellis'... Lots of people I've spoken to will be coming, plus they've invited friends from other towns – so Mama will pass around the petition.'

'How are we catering for everyone?'

'Cousin Stefan and I did well this morning – a lot of fish is on ice. Everyone knows to bring their own meat and each household will pack a salad and drinks. Pandora is bringing bread from her bakery and between us we should have enough grill plates.' We walked onto the sand. 'It reminds me of the big barbecues we used to have to celebrate Easter – lots of lamb chops and ouzo and dancing... before times got hard.'

I squeezed his arm but he shook it off.

'Niko, please... don't be like this. Let's try to enjoy the days I've got left.'

He glared at me. 'How? I am not clever enough for you? And apologies in advance – I realise this fishing trip will be very boring for an intellectual like you.'

I opened my mouth but what could I say in my defence? I shut it again, praying the afternoon would go by at top speed. If I was him, I'd feel exactly the same.

He stopped by his boat and we stepped into it. Niko showed me a handline and how you fitted it with a weight and "lure" – the lure was the pretty, feathery thing you tied on the end, which caused noise and bubbles to attract fish. Niko explained why the length of the line was important, and the speed of the boat. He'd also packed pairs of heavy duty gloves for people to handle the fish and line when they pulled in the catch – plus a bottle of *Tsipouro*, a strong Greek brandy.

'I wouldn't have thought that was the best drink, out on a boat, in the hot afternoon sun,' I said.

He unscrewed the lid and let me smell. Ew. I pulled a face.

'You're in luck, then – it isn't for the humans.' He screwed the lid back on. 'When catching single, big fish the kindest way to kill them is to pour a little alcohol into the gills. They pass out and the brain dies.'

Phew! I never enjoyed watching fish slowly suffocate to death. In fact the first question one of the men asked, when they boarded, was if he could throw his catch back.

As the motor chugged and we headed out to sea, I was impressed with Niko's spiel. He insisted we all wore lifejackets and squinting in the sun, he described how to avoid the most common accidents. Passengers were to keep seated at all times. He also asked if anyone couldn't swim, so he'd know who to look out for if we overturned. Plus he listed a few tips on how to cope with sea-sickness, including heading for the stern of the boat, and keeping low where there is the least movement.

'That's beautiful!' I said, pulling down my cap, as one of the beaming men, in Hawaiian shorts, pulled a large fish onto the boat. It had yellow and green stripes – the next was red and white, caught by the passenger who wanted to throw his back. So, wearing gloves, Niko gently removed the hook and obliged. My chest burned when I thought how Henrik had genuinely implied Niko was stupid. My Greek friend made the handline fishing look easy, but having talked me through it, I knew just how much of the detail Niko had prepared. And indeed, during the two hour journey, we caught two grey mullets, three sea bream and one sea bass. The passengers were thrilled and with each success cheered and punched the air.

At one point, a wave made me slip and fall backwards against Niko. His hands grabbed my shoulders and he steadied me until the water calmed down. Slowly his fingers ran down my arms and held me firmly by my waist. My pulse sped up and a sudden thirst dried my throat. When I finally gained my balance, I removed his hands with mine and turned around.

'Thank you,' I muttered, feeling breathless.

'Just doing my job,' he replied, mocha eyes intense, blood in his cheeks. For a second his hands held mine back and then abruptly, he bent down and showed us how to pour alcohol into the gills and afterwards I placed the fish in the ice box. Later, whilst Niko drove, I was happy to take photos of the beginner fishermen, with their mobile phones, and handed out water bottles. Glad to have brought my sun lotion, I reapplied another layer, and passed it to one of the men who'd fallen asleep on the beach the day before.

'A well mint day – *efharisto*,' said the man in the Hawaiian shorts, with a thick Mancunian accent, as the sun set. He and his friends had learned how to gut the fish and grill them on the barbecue, whilst they finished off the Greek brandy. Sophia had brought over salad and bread and a camping table and chairs. Niko shook the man's hand and nodded to the rest who gave the thumbs up. A wide smile spread across his face and they left, declaring they would recommend the trip to their friends.

I sat down next to Niko on the sand, and for a few moments we watched the luminous tangerine sun sink beneath the horizon.

'You were amazing today,' I said. 'Really skilled.'

'No need to sound so surprised,' he said. 'Where's Leila?' He stood up. As villagers flocked onto the beach, carrying beach bags, rugs and cooking equipment, she headed straight over to us, violet coloured skirt swaying, black blouse showing off her gold earrings, red lips and exotic curls, all topped off with a yellow flower behind her ear.

'How happy you look,' he said and stroked her arm, as if no one else was there. 'Is Grandma coming tonight?'

Her face broke into a smile. 'Yes, I just can't believe how she continues to improve, every hour of every day.'

They spoke briefly in Greek before hugging each other tight. I coughed, got to my feet and headed over to Sophia, a slice of pain cutting through my chest. Was it wrong that I still wanted Niko's arms to wrap around *me*? Clearly my arrival in Kos had simply unsettled him for a while, and now his strong feelings for Leila were back on track.

'*Pippitsa*? You okay? Is Henrik coming?' said Sophia and stopped walking.

I gave a wry smile. 'No. This morning... didn't Grandma tell you? We split up.'

'Oh, dearest... sorry to hear that. You okay?'

I nodded. 'But please, only you two know. I'd prefer it to stay that way.'

I couldn't face a barrage of questions from everyone and what was the point of telling Niko now?

Sophia put down her bags and patted my arm. 'Of course. Now help me with this rug.' I took one end and between us we lay it on the sand. 'How did the fishing trip go? Better than yesterday?'

'Niko was brilliant and the passengers loved every minute – said they'd spread the word amongst their friends.' I put my sun cap and glasses into my rucksack and placed it on the rug. 'The way he handled the fish... with such respect. I'd never heard of killing them with alcohol.'

Sophia passed me a ripe fig. 'Because he's a fisherman, you expect him not to care?'

I bit into the fruit and wiped sticky juice from my chin. 'No. I remember when we went crabbing as youngsters – how he'd insist we gently return them to the sea, not carelessly lob them back like other children. And when Ajax died...'

We looked at each other and nodded. Niko had worked day and night for a week, trying to tempt the dog with tasty titbits. And talking of tasty titbits, a couple of hours later, I sat on that rug, in the dark, scoffing lamb kebabs with the most delicious crusty bread. Leila insisted she and Niko join me on there, too, whilst Georgios, Sophia and Grandma borrowed deckchairs from friends.

'So...' I said to the crowd, when most of the food was eaten, and the smell of wood smoke replaced the aroma of barbecuing meat. 'This week – how confident do we feel that our new ventures could eventually support the village?' I gazed around. Thanks to small fires dotted along the sand, I picked out familiar faces. 'Demetrios?'

Demetrios finished chewing and wiped a hand down his striped shirt. 'We're only a few days in, but so far I'm impressed. The pet-bowl painting went down well, as did the clay turtles – and the jewellery. Over the winter I can build up a supply of prettily painted ceramics ready to buy and I have new ideas... During those quiet months I could offer training sessions to people around the island, who want to learn pottery. Plus hold lessons for small groups of school children.'

'Excellent.' I scanned the crowd again. 'Cosmo?'

He took a swig of cloudy ouzo and grinned. 'Cycle tours good and on these clear August days a view of Turkey is going down well. I need to find more to say though about things of interest as we pass by. The old graveyard up on the cliffs, for example – I have no idea who is buried there. Plus need to brush up my nature knowledge.' He looked at Georgios. 'Perhaps my friend from Taxos Taverna can help with that.'

Georgios nodded and twisted one end of his moustache as Mrs Dellis spoke up. 'Early days for us, but children visiting our pet farm this week have had fun. Adults too laughed a lot, trying to milk our friendly goats – and sales of cheese were good. Over the winter I will experiment with new recipes and stock up.' She shrugged. 'It has given me the confidence to try to sell it to shops in Kos Town.'

'Brill! That would provide income all year round,' I said. 'Pandora – what about you?'

But a noise distracted me – cross Greek voices and loud derisory snorts.

'This is all very heart-warming, but a waste of time,' slurred an English voice. I swallowed as Henrik staggered into view. He pointed a finger at me and from nowhere, Niko stood by my side. 'Don't trust a word this woman says... Pippa doesn't care – not about anyone.' He gave a hollow laugh. 'Your "Pippitsa" has already agreed this feeble attempt to save yourselves will fail and when it does she'll stand swiftly by my and Stavros' side.'

CHAPTER SEVENTEEN

The crowd took a simultaneous intake of breath.

'It's not true!' I said. 'I mean, yes I agreed to stand by them, but only because–'

'Because you don't believe in us, Pippa?' shouted a voice.

'No... No! I can't think that,' said Pandora and folded her arms.

'Of course she believes in us,' said Grandma.

'Absolutely I do, but Henrik and Stavros... I was put in a difficult position.'

Henrik laughed again and leant on a stranger's shoulder. Wow. I'd only ever seen him this out of control once before – when his Dad didn't bother turning up for his twenty-fifth birthday. He drank a whole bottle of champagne, and several gins, all by himself. Fitting, isn't it, that Dutchmen are supposedly tight-fisted, but are so tall they have to spend loads on alcohol if they want to get drunk?

'But do you have honest doubts?' said Demetrios and loosened his mustard cravat. 'I mean... lovely Pippa you would tell us – is this help all partly for show? Is your heart with ThinkBig?'

'No! Don't even consider, for one second, that my heart is anywhere but with this village.' My chest tightened at the sight of the doubting faces.

'The truth is, Henrik and Kos Town mayor, Stavros, bribed me into an agreement.'

I looked down at a movement by my side – Niko's fists had curled into balls. I swallowed. Even he didn't believe me.

'Bribe – that a rather strong word, be careful what you say,' said a smarmy voice and out of the crowd appeared Stavros. 'Henrik and I heard about this meeting – in fact whispers have wafted our way all week about the success of your plans here in Taxos. And look at Miss Pattinson, fooling you all into thinking you stood a chance, when she knows as much as anyone that you fight a losing battle.'

'What is he talking about, Pippa?' said Georgios.

'Nothing – he's just trying to scare you,' I mumbled back.

'So it's not true that, ultimately, you will stand by ThinkBig?' he asked and ran a hand over his bald head.

I surveyed the beach and nothing moved apart from a few gulls gratefully pecking up crumbs. My throat ached. 'I had no choice – unless I agreed to stand by them if our plan fails...'

Stavros snorted. 'You mean *when*!'

'*If*,' I repeated in a firm voice and gazed around the crowd. 'They were going to make it impossible for you to even try to save the village from the developers, unless I said I would be on their side, in the end.'

'What you mean?' asked Mr Dellis, youngest son asleep in his arms.

'Stavros threatened to delay approval of the paperwork for all the extra permissions and licences we needed.'

Niko turned to face me. 'Do you really believe our appeal can win?'

'I... To be honest, I didn't know at the time. But I reckoned you'd all feel better about your village's future if you knew you'd put up a fight, and that was enough for me to give it a go.' I shrugged. 'And if we do fail, then I will have no choice but to stand by ThinkBig in any case because, as we've all agreed, Taxos can't continue as it is. So I didn't feel agreeing this with them betrayed the village in any way. Believe me, I detest the idea of quad bikes and nightclubs, and will do everything I can do in the time I have left here, to push our case forwards. But I see ThinkBig's development as a very last but necessary resort. Otherwise people will have to leave the village to earn a living. Taxos will, indeed, become a ghost town.' I straightened up. 'We can still win this. I feel much more positive, now we've started to instigate our various ideas.'

'Yes, carry on this little game, if you wish,' said Stavros to the crowd. 'I'm impressed. Honestly. So much so, I'm staying here in the Vesteros' hotel to keep an eye on things. However, you are only putting off the inevitable – and by then I might have sold some of the franchises to outsiders.'

He disappeared into the back of the crowd. Minutes later, I spotted him on a sand dune talking to a very thin man, who, from his outline, I could tell had a ponytail and the collar of his shirt upturned. I'd seen him before at one of the meetings – perhaps he'd been a spy.

'Why would the Vesteros family let him stay?' muttered Sophia.

'They live on the outskirts near the proposed quad bike track, don't they, and were one of the first to be interested in ThinkBig's offer. We can't really blame them.'

'So what next?' called out Pandora.

'Think sensibly and think big,' said Henrik and sniggered. He staggered over to me and I looked up, wrinkling my nose at the stench of ouzo. 'Almost lost your fan club then, didn't you, Little Miss Protector?'

Niko's fists curled tighter and I realised that drunk Henrik was the cause.

'Be quiet!' said a female voice. The crowd hardly seemed to hear. 'Quiet!' she repeated in a harsher tone and people hushed as Grandma got up from her deckchair and came over to me. Under any other circumstances it would have been humorous to see her standing next to my giant boyf... ex-boyfriend. Grandma had never been blessed with height and had shrunk a centimetre or two since my last holiday here.

'We are not afraid of you, big man,' she said and folded her arms. 'You turn up here, falling sideways like an inexperienced eighteen-year-old tourist. You show no respect. You laugh at our tradition.'

'Now wait a minute...' he slurred.

'Shut up, you overgrown beanstalk!' hissed Niko, eyes on fire.

Henrik sniggered again. Grandma turned to the villagers.

'Of course we won't give up. Yes, we face obstacles...' She said something – probably a translation of this – in Greek. Then it was back to English. 'Honourable Pippa is right – without putting up a fight we would feel twice as bad. One step at a time we do this. That's how we've survived the last few years.'

Georgios translated this time.

'By paying one bill at a time... providing one meal... buying one pair of shoes – we take it day by day,' she continued and shook a finger. 'And you know what? I think Stavros is here because he's really worried. Word must have spread that Taxos is offering good tourist services. He wouldn't bother coming to this meeting if we were no threat.'

Georgios translated again.

'Taxos people are strong,' she said and shook her small fist. 'The developers are weak – they rely on their money, whereas we count on loyalty, friendship and community spirit.'

Top lip curled, Henrik shook his head. Oh bugger. Under his breath he muttered "Honourable?" and "Loyal?" Then he glared at me.

'Henrik,' I whispered. 'Please... if I ever meant anything to you, don't mention how I felt – how I thought I felt about Niko. Leila doesn't deserve it and Grandma... any negative fallout from that could kill her.'

'She looks pretty feisty to me,' he whispered back. 'Bet she was a right goer in her youth.'

I stood back and wrinkled my nose in disgust. Henrik's cheeks flushed and a sheepish look crossed his face – which meant he was just on the verge of apologising. However...

'I heard that!' snarled Niko and lunged forwards. Within seconds, both were writhing on the sand.

'Stop this!' I tried to pull them apart, but arms and legs flailed in all directions and before I knew it someone's limb had hit me full-force in the chest.

I flew back several feet and landed in the sand, gasping for breath, afraid I might never take another.

'Pippa!' shouted Henrik and Niko together. Fight forgotten, they ran over. Leila bent down and calmly counted to ten, trying to get my chest to match the rhythm of her words.

'Help,' I said in a strangulated voice, tears running down my face. I held a hand to my chest. 'Can't breathe...' Terrified, I looked up as villagers crowded around.

Henrik stood up. 'Doctor!' he shouted, in a panicked voice that suddenly sounded sober.

Niko took my hand and stared straight into my eyes. His chin trembled as he brushed hair out of my face. During the fall, my ponytail must have come undone. 'You'll be okay, Pippa,' he said, a break in his voice. 'The air just knocked out of your lungs. Like a returning tide, it will come back. Don't be afraid. Just focus on me. In and out... in and out... Getting better?'

'Ow... it hurts...' Heaving, I gratefully refilled with air.

'Take your time,' he said and held both my hands tight.

I stared into his face, at that moment not wanting to be with anyone else in the world. And eventually, my breathing regained its normal pace, and somehow I stood up. 'Just go, Henrik.'

'Yes, this is your fault,' spat Niko.

'We'll fight harder than ever against ThinkBig now,' muttered someone from the crowd.

'No one wants some long-legged drunken hooligan to decide our village's future!' shouted someone else.

Henrik looked at me, but I turned away, and bent over slowly, hoping my chest would ache less.

When I eventually stretched up again, Henrik had disappeared and several villagers came over to give me a hug.

'We believe you on our side, Pippa – we no give up our fight,' said little Theo Dellis.

I smiled down. 'Thank you, sweetheart – that means a lot.'

'Let's meet tomorrow morning at Taxos Taverna, to take stock,' shouted out Niko.

Little Theo said something to his dad in Greek.

Mr Dellis smiled. 'Will there be scones?'

'Yes,' I managed a laugh. 'How about chocolate wholemeal ones with... I know, orange-flavoured yogurt filling? Fighters need wholesome food to keep up their strength.'

Theo seemed to understand the word "chocolate" and gave a toothy grin.

'And you need a good night's sleep, *Pippitsa*,' said Sophia as the crowd dispersed. 'Tonight you no go home to the villa. Henrik – he's in a volatile mood.'

'My, um, boyfriend,' I said, noticing Niko nearby, 'would never hurt me – he doesn't even like to kill spiders.'

'Still... you need good food and rest after that accident – and it will be easier to bake scones if you wake up at the taverna. I'm sure Leila could fetch some clothes from her house for you to borrow...' She smiled. 'Except for her trousers. They would be far too short.'

I nodded and winced as I bent over to pick up my rucksack. Georgios and Sophia folded the rug. Leila hugged me and headed home with her parents, to collect some outfits. I walked towards the sea, slipped off my pumps and paddled in the water. I couldn't believe Henrik's behaviour, and as for that slimy slug, Stavros...

My eyes tingled, though, as only one (admittedly over-dramatic) thought had occupied my head since flying through the air, backwards. What if I died and had never told Niko how I really felt? Oh the irony, because now that I had survived and had all the time in the world, declaring my passion for him was the last thing I could do.

Someone appeared at my side and I glanced across at the caramel skin and mocha eyes – the sturdy frame and caress-able shoulders. We stared out to sea and all the drama must have caused a tear to slide down my cheek. It was nothing to do with the fact that, for a few precious moments, Niko seemed to have lost his hostility towards me.

'I do love Taxos, Niko, believe me,' I said.

'I know,' he said. Ooh. This was good. He'd stopped using grunts with me, instead of words. For a while we sat staring at the sea. It was as if time had turned back and we were kids, waiting for something magical to happen, like Pegasus flying over the waves. Yet as adults, I had only one magical wish – for us to slide our arms around each other and kiss for eternity.

'How is your chest now?' he asked, eventually.

'Okay, thanks.' For a nanosecond, I tingled from head to toe as I imagined him kissing it better.

'Good. We don't need another person ill in the taverna,' he said, gruffly.

'How did Grandma's final tests go yesterday?'

A big smile spread across his face and his shoulders relaxed. 'We only just found out – the hospital rang a couple of hours ago. It is better than we could have ever hoped. She is still clear and must only go back every six months. Apparently the doctors are thrilled with her progress.'

'Wow...' My eyes tingled. 'That's great news. She kept that quiet.'

'You know Grandma – she doesn't like a fuss.'

He took my hand and all of a sudden my world lit up. 'Pippa... did you mean it? About me being stupid? Because if not... You and Henrik... Me and Leila, we were thinking...'

Wow. It was as if Grandma's good prognosis had made him prepared to forgive my horrible comments. 'If anything happened to you, Pippa...'

'I know. Me too.'

He looked at me and I could tell that even though that sentence didn't make sense, somehow it did.

'As I was saying, now that Grandma's better, me and Leila... I'd like to ask you...' He faltered and stopped for a second. For the first time since I'd arrived in Taxos, his face looked like a young boy's, all the worries of Greek and family life erased. For one moment he looked about to raise my fingers to his lips. What on earth was he going to ask? Did he want us to be witnesses at his wedding? Surely not? He opened his mouth to continue, but instead a different voice shouting his name filled the silence. Cue frantic footsteps on the sand. Cousin Stefan appeared, out of breath.

'Come quickly,' he gasped and held Niko's arm. 'It's Grandma... she's collapsed!'

CHAPTER EIGHTEEN

'Drink this tea and eat this scone immediately,' I said to Grandma in a mock stern voice.

She looked sheepish, out on the patio of the taverna, her cheeks full of colour after a good night's sleep.

'Little peach, I only fainted. Dehydration. Silly of me after weeks in bed – I should have known to drink more. And yesterday evening was so humid.'

'Plus I saw you enjoy a crafty retsina,' I said and raised one eyebrow. 'Don't get carried away, just because the doctors say you're in great health.'

We looked at each other and laughed as the wind got up. It was the perfect day to get an island tan – unless, like me, gales made you burn even more.

'Seriously, though, you had us all worried last night...' my voice broke. 'Niko and Leila were in bits. It was such a shock, because everyone says you've really picked up over the last few weeks. And after the doctors gave you the all-clear...'

'I still feel better than I have for over a year – but, ach, I've always had low blood pressure and even as a girl, people always said I never drank enough.' Grandma bit into the chocolate orange scone, from the batch I'd made for Theo Dellis. The villagers had just started to arrive for the meeting, some nursing headaches after the action-packed barbecue last night.

'Mmm. Mmmmmm,' she said.

I grinned. Nothing on this earth felt better than people enjoying your cooking, (er, okay, perhaps I can think of just one other thing, but scone appreciation came a definite second). 'Do you like the filling – yogurt infused with fresh orange juice?'

'Don't make me talk,' she said, 'because that means I have to stop eating.'

I grinned again and went back into the taverna. Demetrios greeted me and, avoiding her plate, I gave Pandora a hug.

'Love those shoes,' I said, staring at her gold-studded sandals.

'Love your scones,' she said, a moustache of orange yogurt above her top lip. She looked me up and down. 'Those not Leila's clothes, after all?'

I chuckled. 'I know – too conservative, aren't they? Hers are more exotic in colour and cut. I did borrow a lovely skirt and blouse this morning, whilst baking – but then I hurried back to the villa to shower and change.'

I headed back into the kitchen to pile more scones onto plates. Instead of seeing Henrik at the villa, I'd found half of his clothes missing and a hastily scrawled note.

"*Apologies for last night – my behaviour was unconscionable. You know I'm not a frequent nor capable drunk. I have nothing but respect for Grandma. Best that I move out. I shall stay at the Vesteros' hotel with Stavros, until our flight leaves next Saturday.*"

'Need help?' said a familiar male voice, today back to being gruff. My body stiffened as Niko's breath wafted against my neck. Now that my heart had officially severed links with Henrik, I found it increasingly difficult to fight my instincts. Every molecule of my body shouted that Niko and I fitted perfectly like two halves of the tastiest scone, filled with the creamiest, most satisfying... I shook myself and turned around.

'Grandma looks great this morning.' I said.

His shoulders sagged a little. 'Yes... but last night was a reminder of how vulnerable she still is.'

'Hmm, guess she'll need to pace herself a bit over the coming months.' I passed him a plate. 'Last night, Niko... on the beach... you were just about to say something before Stefan appeared.'

His cheeks flushed. 'No matter, now Pippa,' and with that he disappeared.

Weird – but at least we were talking again. I couldn't face going home if I thought he actually hated me. Walking speedily, I followed him to see if I could find out what was up, but the taverna was full, people talking about drunk Henrik and creepy Stavros. I mingled, handing out scones. The plate emptied just as Georgios clapped for silence. I put it on a table and stood next to him, almost tripping over Apollo the cat, who wasn't too old to scout for crumbs.

Georgios rubbed his head and began by asking everyone to share any bookings they'd taken for next week. With the help of several coffees and a sugar rush from the scones, the chat became more animated. Villagers put forward new ideas, whilst expressing worries about future costs. The man Stavros had talked to last night, with the ponytail, stood by the wall.

I jerked my head towards him. 'Do you recognise that man?' I asked Sophia.

She stared for a moment. 'No. Yes. Not sure...' She smiled. 'We may be a small village but it doesn't mean I know absolutely everyone. Sometimes, of course, friends or relatives of the locals come to stay. Why?'

I shrugged. 'No reason. He just seemed quite friendly with Stavros last night.'

'Perhaps he is keen to take the pay-off. Not every single villager is on our side.'

Mr Dellis piped up and I turned my attention back to the meeting.

'I've been thinking all night and have news that might help,' he said, during a brief moment of hush. 'Before I had to give up my job as a... a website designer, my last, um, project was with tax department in Kos Town. Um...'

Even though he was doing a great job in English, Mr Dellis asked if Niko or Georgios could translate for me and carried on in Greek. Impatiently I waited as he continued, the room oohing and aahing, then giving nods and smiles. The thin man at the back listened intently. Finally I poked Georgios in the ribs.

'What's it all about?' I said a bit too loudly and everyone chuckled.

'Mr Dellis – he worked closely with a tax man who loved his job and is very, very strict.' Georgios smiled. 'He thinks if this tax man finds out about the illegal tax breaks that Stavros has offered, then the mayor will be in big trouble and the deal could be off.'

'Really? That is brilliant!' I shook Mr Dellis' hand and glanced around. Hmm, interesting. The thin man at the back was heading out of the front door.

'I'm sure that man with the ponytail was a spy,' I said to Niko over dinner that night, as twilight fell.

'Spies? Here?' He snorted. 'No, this is Taxos with Problems, not Russia with Love.'

We sat on the beach, sharing a picnic – him, me and Leila. She threw some small chunks of bread at the gulls. Niko snapped at her to stop. Over the course of the day, his anger seemed to have switched from me to her. In fact they'd been sniping at each other for hours, from what

I could see. The meeting had dragged on until mid-afternoon and the conclusion had been unanimous. As Grandma said, one day at a time... We would just try to make the next week as successful as possible and collect more signatures on the petition.

After that Niko and Leila had discussed something out on the patio and he'd stormed off to go sponge-diving. I helped Georgios translate some descriptions of birds he needed for his tours. Then I went for a dip in the sea. The Dellis children were there, laughing but clinging tightly to their lilos in the shallows, with their mum. Although even a paddle didn't last long as the wind made the waves several feet high and I only swam for a short while.

'Perhaps that strange man has heard that franchises might be up for sale soon,' said Leila, brightly. 'He could be from another village. Did you see him, Niko?'

He didn't reply. Goodness. They must have had a big argument. It was just as well I'd suggested this picnic, to save everyone cooking. Grandma had wanted to come but Georgios and Sophia insisted she rest after fainting the night before. At least this way, the young couple avoided curious eyes – apart from mine.

'I'm glad everyone believed I wasn't really on ThinkBig's side,' I said and finished my last mouthful of feta cheese and salad sandwich.

'Of course they believe you, Pippa,' said Leila and bit into an apricot. Niko passed her a napkin without shifting his gaze from the tide. 'You are one of us – there is history. Anyway, everyone knows if they speak badly of you, Niko would punch them in the eye.'

She laughed and I marvelled at her total lack of jealousy. Not that I'm bigging myself up and saying she had reason to be envious, but I'm not sure how I'd cope with a boyfriend being so close to a female friend.

I elbowed him. Niko had been quiet all day. 'What's up? The meeting went well – and I like the sound of Mr Dellis' tax man friend.'

Niko looked first at me – then Leila – and sort of groaned before getting up and walking away. He headed left, towards the fig tree and the strip of beach which led to Tyrionitsa.

'Leila?' I raised my eyebrows. She wrapped up the apricot stone in her napkin and gave a sigh.

'Follow him, Pippa. I got to go now – Mama and Papa are expecting me. And everyone needs an early night after the excitement of the barbecue. I'll see you tomorrow, yes?'

'But...' Huh? What was happening? First Niko was hardly talking to me, now he reluctantly does. And I was the object of his glares and bad temper, but now Leila is. '*You* should go after him. I'll pack up, don't worry.'

'Sorry – no, not me. I must leave now, otherwise... I am afraid I might say too much.' She stood up and eyes all shiny, gave me a wry smile. 'I like you, Pippa. Sorry things couldn't be different.'

Huh, again? Was I going mad? It was as if the two of them spoke in code.

'What do you mean?'

'Secrets... they are no good.'

Well, seeing as she brought it up... 'Tell me, Leila...' I stood up, feeling I had nothing to lose in the suddenly very weird parallel universe. 'Is it my imagination, or are you planning to go abroad?'

She stepped back on the sand and swallowed hard.

'I saw you in Kos Town, coming out of an international recruitment agency and Postie said you'd been sent a passport. '

'He should mind his own business,' she murmured.

'Then when we handed out the tourist leaflets, you eyed up new luggage.'

'Pippa... no... I mean...'

'I like you Leila, and find it hard to believe you would deceive Niko and his family, but...'

She shook her head, the thick black hair buffeted by the wind, and hurried away, lugging the picnic basket and muttering something about not lying any more.

For a few minutes I stood gobsmacked, simply staring out at the sea – until a distant figure caught my attention. It was Niko, skimming stones. Sandals filling with grains of sand, I headed over, the outline of him getting closer as darkness continued to fall. Finally I reached him and stood still for a moment, listening to the cicadas and lapping tide.

'What's the point of doing that? You can hardly see the water and the strong wind makes it difficult.' I eventually said.

'Makes me feel better.' Niko didn't turn to face me, so I took his arm, prised a pebble out of his hand and lobbed it into the water.

'What's going on with you and Leila? Neither of you are making sense today. I can tell you've had an argument. Is it about me? She said to talk to you.'

'Mind your own business,' he snapped and walked towards the waves. 'Please, Pippa, just leave me alone – go and see Henrik at your villa. He's your boyfriend, after all.'

I sat on the sand for a while, waiting for him to calm down. Laying back on my elbows, I surveyed the beach and coastline. Taxos truly was beautiful in its simplicity, and reminded me of team-building adventure trips I'd taken with work, to the Peaks, Lakes and Scotland. It took a lot to beat the sky at night, away from the intrusive city glow. Its inky blackness was instead broken up by clear star constellations and an occasional aeroplane. The purity of its darkness made me think of the unpolluted, azure Aegean sea.

'He's not there. Henrik. At the villa,' I said when Niko finally returned and sat next to me.

He fiddled with his leather bracelet. 'Why...? Did he have to suddenly return to England? Or has our fight against his company torn you apart and you've split up?' He looked me straight in the eye.

I pursed my lips together, fighting every urge that told me to shout yes and pull his head towards me, to press my lips against that tender, warm mouth. Damn my inclination to try to do the decent thing.

'No... but, um, with everything going on it's just easier for him to stay with Stavros at the Vesteros' hotel.'

Niko's mocha eyes drooped at the corners. 'Then go see him there. You on holiday – should be spending it with the one you love... Drinking cocktails... taking romantic strolls... discussing intellectual stuff.'

I bit my lip hard, almost drawing blood, millimetres away from screaming into the air that all those horrible things I said about him, I made up. Niko was like a walking encyclopaedia when it came to fishing, sponges and nature. If I died of anything in his company, it wouldn't be boredom but an excess of love. And as our bodies leant against each other, I hardly dared turn my head. If my face met his at this proximity, I couldn't trust my actions.

'Shh – what's that?' Niko suddenly said. He concentrated for a moment. His face went pale, before he leapt up and held out his hand.

Instinct told me to grab his fingers and let him pull me up. My stomach knotted as I saw his eyes widen. Without even knowing why, I ran alongside him, our fingers intertwined.

'What is that person shouting?' I gasped, struggling to keep up.

Niko's pace quickened. 'Fire! Someone shout "Fire!"'

CHAPTER NINETEEN

'Over there!' I said and pointed towards the end of the village, past The Fish House restaurant. Thick smoke salsa-danced with the wind – that meant the woods were on fire; that anyone coming from the villas, along the dusty road, wouldn't be able to cut through the trees, into Taxos.

'Let me check on my parents and Grandma,' said Niko and he dashed into the taverna. Irrational yes, but I understood – far or near, a fire was a fearsome thing. People stood in the street in pyjamas, some shaking their heads, others shouting at neighbours to get up.

Niko soon reappeared. 'It's okay. Everyone is all right. Leila, she went straight home?'

I nodded. Fortunately she lived in a house near the shore, well away from the wooded area at the entrance to the village.

Grandma came into view, hair uncombed, in a rumpled skirt and untucked blouse.

'Go back inside,' said Niko. 'Everything is all right.'

'Don't baby me, boy,' she said. 'I've seen fires like this before you were born. Now do as I say... Wake up everyone in the village and get them onto the beach. Georgios is ringing the fire station, in case no one else has.' Grandma walked into the street and lifted her head, squinting into the distance. 'If that fire takes hold the village will be cut off. If this wind helps it spread...' she sucked in her lips, '...the fire crew will not be able to get through.'

'Henrik... He's staying at the Vesteros' hotel, right by the woods – do you think he'll be all right?' I bit my lip.

Grandma and Niko looked at each other. 'He should be...' she said. 'They will have smelt it first – although its restaurant is made from log and also has a wooded outside dining area... that could feed the flames.'

Grandma sniffed the air. I sniffed too – a pungent smoky cedarwood smell wafted our way. 'It is strange...' said Grandma, '...we haven't had rain for a long time, so yes the woods will be dry, but...' She shrugged. 'Forest fires starting at night is unusual.'

We all looked at each other. Surely no one would do this on purpose?

'Someone must have been careless with a cigarette,' I said.

Grandma nodded. 'We need to control the spread.'

'And I know just how,' said Georgios, coming outside. 'I've rung Mr Dellis – his fireman brother still hasn't picked up the drip torches used to burn down some of his land to build those animal pens. He also left the protective clothes... I think we should try to burn a strip of land, closest to the village, to stop the fire heading down here.'

'But that's dangerous!' said Pandora, who'd just appeared, in her dressing gown, her usually slick short hair sticking out in all directions.

We all fell silent for a moment. No one knew more that Pandora that loved ones could be lost, fighting fire. 'We're no experts and embers can fly through the air.'

'But it's a chance – better than doing nothing... A bit like our fight against ThinkBig,' said an out-of-breath Demetrios who'd just turned up, minus his signature cravat. It was as if Taxos Taverna was now the village hub to deal with any emergency.

'Let's start by getting everyone to the beach,' said Grandma. 'We need the fittest to run and knock on the doors of those closest to the woods.'

'I'll head off to Mr Dellis' house,' said Georgios. 'Find out how specialised this equipment is. He'll know if it's too dangerous for us civilians to use.'

'I need to check on Leila,' said Niko and turned to Demetrios. 'I'll meet you at the Vesteros' place, yes?'

'I'll go with you,' I said to Demetrios. We may not have been dating any more, but I still cared about Henrik and needed to know he was all right. A couple of young men in their twenties, the Angelis brothers, ran with me and the potter. Chests heaving, about ten minutes later, we reached the edge of the woods. The Vesteros' hotel was to the right as you entered the village, just in front of a row of houses which led down the road to the pottery shop and church.

Wow. We reached the building to see a path of thick smoke run from the woods to its front door. I couldn't see flames but heard crackling and the air felt scorching hot, as if someone had just thrown water on the rocks in a sauna. With a cough I took several steps back.

'Henrik!' I shouted and, squinting, saw low flames lick the doorway. A random gust of wind thinned the smoke for a second and I surveyed crumbling remains of the outdoor cedarwood restaurant. 'Henrik! Are you in there?' Eyes wide, I stared at Demetrios. With handkerchiefs over their mouths, like two cowboys, the Angelis brothers ran around the back of the hotel. A noise from behind made me turn. Who was that guy creeping away in a black balaclava? He was very thin, had ash all over his clothes and... I swallowed and strode after him. Sticking out the back of the woollen hat was a ponytail.

'It was you!' I stuttered and pointed a finger. 'You did this for Stavros – but why?'

He started running away and I was just about to follow when one of the Angelis brothers shouted. I span around. He beckoned for us to follow him to the back of the hotel. Holding our breath past the thickest of the smoke, Demetrios and I sprinted, turned the corner of the building and... oh my. Several hotel guests knelt on the ground coughing, as more smoke billowed out of the hotel's back door, like the dirty exhaust of a giant car. I crouched down and rubbed the back of a teenage girl, as she was sick. Mrs Vesteros passed me tissues and a bottle of water. The girl nodded her thanks and wiped her mouth, before heading over to a woman – no doubt her mum – who'd managed to stand up and stop coughing.

'Your boyfriend... he's a hero after all,' said Mrs Vesteros, eyes streaming, nose red, hair flapping violently in the wind. 'He rescued these guests and has just gone in again. We were all asleep – flames spread from outside to the indoor restaurant.' Her face crumpled. 'The smoke alarm downstairs no work. I've been meaning to change it for days, but what with the plans to reinvent the village, my thoughts were elsewhere.'

'Where is Henrik, now?' I said, stomach lurching. 'And your husband?'

'They've gone in to look for Stavros. He must be heavy sleeper and hasn't heard anything. I told them not to...' A sob escaped her lips. 'Ceiling beams have already fallen – it is too dangerous.'

Out of breath, Niko appeared at my side.

'Leila's fine. People are evacuating the village and congregating on the beach. Mr Dellis and Papa are driving the drip torches to the edge of the woodland – they will try to burn ground and contain the fire, so–'

He stopped talking and we listened for a second. Thank God – the siren of a fire engine. They must have made it through the woods. Suddenly a head appeared out of a top window. Stavros?

'Where is Henrik!' I hollered.

'I don't know,' he said. 'Help – my room is full of smoke.'

'This is your fault!' I screamed.

Everyone looked at me and I took a deep breath. Now was not the time to confront Stavros. We had to get the mayor out before anything else.

'No worry, Stavros,' shouted up Niko. 'We'll help you down.' He added on something in Greek, probably more comforting words.

Then Demetrios hollered up at him in Greek – according to Niko the potter told Stavros to block the bottom of his bedroom door with bedding, to stop the smoke getting in.

'But don't jump, whatever you do,' I called. 'The fire engine is on its way. You've got time on your side.'

Stavros' terrified face nodded.

'There is a ladder around the other side of the building,' said Mrs Vesteros, in between coughs.

Niko and Demetrios nodded and within minutes had it leant up against the back of the hotel, to underneath Stavros' window. I rubbed my cheek as a searing heat radiated from the woodland – the smoke was still too thick to see whether the trees right near us were on fire. I couldn't hear loud crackling, just the whoosh of the wind and sirens. All the cicadas and night birds must have fled.

Niko shouted at the mayor, beckoning for him to come down. But Stavros froze, didn't reply and then closed his eyes.

Coughing and spluttering, several figures ran out of the back door of the hotel.

'Thank God,' I murmured and, heart pounding, ran towards Henrik with a bottle of water that Mrs Vesteros had thrust into my hand.

'Take this,' I shouted above the now very loud sirens. Eyes and nose streaming, he gratefully drank it down.

'Pips – you all right?' With a white handkerchief, he tidied up his face.

I nodded and we gave each other a quick smile. I looked up again at Stavros. Then Cosmo appeared on a bike. He stopped, got off and threw the cycle to the floor. Quickly we told him the problem. Without warning he started to climb the ladder, whilst Niko held it steady. He reached the top, just as a big engine revved nearby and the deafening sirens stop. Cosmo and Stavros chatted briefly and the mayor shook his head. Smoke coming out of the building was even thicker now and the woods surrounding us gave out even stronger heat. Firemen helped spluttering guests around to the front and told those of us standing to leave and head for the beach.

However, Demetrios and I stood still, watching Cosmo and Stavros. Finally the mayor lifted one leg over the windowsill and lowered it onto the ladder. He wore a vest top and boxer shorts. Then the other leg came over, all whilst Cosmo chatted and patted him on the back. Slowly the two men came down. As they neared I heard Cosmo mutter comforting words in Greek. Finally he reached the ground and then a fireman helped a shaky Stavros manage the last few steps.

Demetrios passed the mayor a bottle of water. His eyes were bloodshot and voice trembly as we took him around to an ambulance. Now wasn't the time to confront him about the cause of the fire. Instead I slipped an arm around his massive shoulders and squeezed him tight. He looked at me, but no words came out.

The paramedic took over and sat him down in the back of his yellow and orange van. Firemen directed the rest of us away and a pair headed to the edge of the woodland, carrying drip torches and wearing different outfits to the rest of the crew. I looked up at Henrik who'd appeared at my side, just as I walked past a big red and silver fire truck.

'You should get yourself checked over,' I said, and nausea backed up my throat as I noticed the hem of his shirt was singed. 'If anything... I mean, I know we're not together any more but... I'm so glad you're all right.'

'Maybe I'll just get this hand checked out,' he said and showed me a slight burn. 'You go ahead. Go on. See if Grandma is okay.'

I felt Niko watch us as we hugged and Henrik went back to the ambulance.

'You're not staying with him?' said Niko, without looking me in the eye.

'No. The villagers – let's get back. We could probably do with handing out drinks and...'

Niko half-smiled. 'Don't tell me – any leftover scones.'

Quickly we headed down the high street, past the taverna and onto the crowded beach. Families stood in their pyjamas, holding torches, whilst – I should have known – Sophia and Grandma were already dealing with the refreshments. Pandora had also fetched a basket of cakes. Plus a farmer filled numerous takeaway granita cups with his strong homemade wine. Niko went straight to Leila, who was sitting the sand, telling a story to a group of children. He pulled her up and held her tight. She kissed him on the cheek and a stab of pain pierced my chest. Silly really. I'd be gone soon. Niko and exotic Leila belonged together – perhaps he'd go travelling with her.

With a shake, I walked through the crowd, trying to block out the stink of smoke from my clothes, and told those with good English what had happened at the Vesteros' hotel – how the fire had spread; how Henrik had been a hero. After what seemed like hours, the chief fireman turned up at the beach, along with a police officer who spoke for several minutes in Greek.

'What did he say?' I asked as mouths downturned and people started to leave.

'The police have set up temporary beds in the town hall, for those of you who cannot return to their houses tonight,' said Niko, in quiet tones.

'The fire officers have contained the flames – the smoke was worse than the fire, apparently,' said Leila, voice flat. 'The Vesteros' hotel bore the brunt of the damage.'

'But the worst thing, now...' Pandora's voice broke. 'An investigation into the fire and clear up of fallen trees means that tourists will not be allowed near Taxos for several days.'

'Our bookings...?' said Demetrios.

Pandora nodded.

'Our efforts to turn this village around without ThinkBig...? Sophia collecting signatures for the petition from other villages...?' I mumbled. I stared at the others. They stared back.

'With emergency services tape everywhere and certain areas cordoned off, it will be almost impossible to offer a lot of services advertised in our tourist leaflet, whilst the police and emergency services carry out their duties,' said Sophia.

Cosmo sighed. 'Then we have lost. Thanks to Mother Earth, Stavros has won.'

CHAPTER TWENTY

Whilst I might blame Mother Earth, or Mother Nature, for some things – like my propensity to lose weight from my breasts, not my thighs – yesterday's fire wasn't her fault. And once the dust – or rather ash – had settled, new flames, made from raging anger, sprang up inside my chest. Yes, I'd felt sorry for Stavros yesterday and was relieved and happy to see him safe. However, overnight I felt bile shoot up my throat at the thought that corruption had come out on top. I started obsessing about seeing him locked up in jail with his ponytailed friend.

The police hadn't come over to the taverna to take statements, yet, but when they did, I'd decided to give them a full description and say what I suspected about Stavros' involvement.

Not quite sure what to do until then, I sat in Pippa's Pantry. A lump formed in my throat. My teashop dream was now over, although, in a bit of a daze, I'd still put up the "Open" sign and dusted down the tables.

I'd slept over at the taverna again as the way out of Taxos was blocked. Firsthand, I experienced the subdued mood of the Sotiropoulos family, when we got up for breakfast. No one talked of boat trips or birdwatching walks and as if on automatic Georgios mopped the floor whilst Sophia got ready for church.

The door opened and I looked up to see... Blimey, I must have been obsessing over the mayor, because this man looked just like a slimline version of Stavros. He had the same beady eyes and crooked nose. Before I could shoosh him away, he sat down at one of the tables and picked up a menu.

'Sorry... we're not doing business today,' I said. What was the point? The village's hopes had been shattered.

'The sign – it say "Open".' He pointed to the door. 'And I've come all the way from Kos Town to sample these scones.'

Hoping to put him off, I frowned.

'So I try one savoury and one sweet, no? They all sound delicious.'

Still worn out after last night, I shrugged, not in the mood for an argument or chit-chat to find out how he'd heard of my baking. I went into the kitchen, to see what scones we had left. My head cleared for a few minutes, as I filled a roasted pepper one with feta cheese, and a cherry scone with a generous dollop of almond flavoured yogurt.

'Coffee?' I said and put the plates down in front of him.

He nodded and bit first into the roast pepper dough. He closed his eyes. By the time I'd brought through his drink, both scones had gone.

'Super,' he said and wiped his mouth with a napkin. 'Tell me... do scones keep well?'

Was he a fellow baker? Perhaps he wanted to steal my idea for a Greek teashop. Inwardly I thought, so what? Good luck to him, because my plans were going nowhere now.

I indicated to the seat opposite him and he nodded for me to sit down.

'Yes – they'll keep for one or two days in your pantry. A week in the fridge. A couple of month in the freezer. Obviously, don't halve them until the last minute and make sure your fillings are fresh.'

'How you get them to rise so well?' he said and took a sip of coffee.

'Keep the butter cold, during the mixing process.'

'And the dough so light?'

'Don't use too much milk.'

He took another sip and to break the silence I asked his line of business.

'I run a large chain of coffee and ice cream bars.'

'Not Creami-Kos, by any chance?' I said, that being the only one I'd heard of.

'As it so happens, yes.'

'Wow. Congratulations.' They'd been going for years. For a treat, my parents would take Niko and me into the island's capital for one of their tropical fruit sundaes with all the trimmings. 'So, what brings you to Taxos?' I said, curious now. 'Surely not just my baking.'

He drained his cup and held out his hand. 'My name is Orion Lakis.'

Lakis. Where had I heard that name before... I gasped. 'Talk about a family resemblance, I knew it! You are Stavros Lakis' brother.'

He smiled.

My eyes narrowed. 'So what are you doing here? In fact, I'm not interested. Get out. No one related to that monster is welcome in Taxos.'

'Sorry. No can do. Stavros wants to see you. In Kos Town. Right now.'

I snorted. 'He's not royalty and I'm not some subject he can summon to his imagined court. And how did you get into Taxos, all the roads are blocked?'

'Being the mayor's brother opens many avenues.'

'I bet it does!' I stood up. Well if he wouldn't leave, that left me no choice, and before he could say one word more, I tore off my apron and swished out of the shop. A walk on the beach would help, all that salty air in my lungs, the squawk of seabirds in my ears, the breeze blowing against my face... And I was just a few metres from the sand when a flash silver car drove up, cut in front of me and stopped. Someone jumped out and yanked open the passenger door.

'Get in, Pippa,' said Orion.

Huh? I backed away, but he clasped my arm. Yet his grip was gentle and his tone softened.

'Look... I know my brother... It must be hard to have faith in the Lakis family name, but trust me, seeing Stavros today, it is for the advantage of you and Taxos. He is waiting for you and Henrik at the Flamingo Inn.'

'Henrik?'

'Yes.' Orion let go of me. 'We pick him up on the way back. Last night he slept in the town hall. I can drop you both at the villa. You change, then we head into Kos Town together.'

'What sort of advantage?'

Orion simply raised his eyebrows.

I stared inside the car and spotted no rope, machete nor gun. Okay, that was a good start.

'For the benefit of Taxos, you say?'

He nodded and looked me straight in the face without the air of shiftiness his brother seemed to carry around.

I bit my lip. Nodded. Climbed into the passenger seat. Orion shut the door and went around to the other side. He got in.

'You like Barry Manilow?' he asked, and turned on the engine.

Copacabana? The knot in my stomach unfurled. That was hardly the music choice of an axe murderer.

Although I wasn't sure, as having heard that song almost twenty times by the time we got to Kos Town and parked, I was ready to wield an axe myself. As promised, Orion had picked up Henrik. We'd freshened up and both changed clothes in the villa. It was just as well Henrik hadn't taken all his belongings to the Vesteros' hotel. He had no idea what the meeting was about. His burned hand was dressed in bandages, so I helped him button up his shirt.

'So, the villagers' plans to save Taxos are now in ruins?' he asked, as we both sat in the back of Orion's car.

'I wouldn't say that, but, well... Understandably despondency has set in. If tourists can't access the village, their chances of promoting new ventures are stumped.' I shrugged. 'How does it feel to have won?'

'Pippa, please – this is work.'

'And that means everything to you?'

His brow furrowed. 'Yes. I thought you felt the same.'

'Me too.' I glanced out of the window. Who would have thought that a couple of weeks in Taxos would change my perspective – or rather, bring my true perspective to the fore? It had given me a taste of a life I once dreamed of, living within a community where the postman knew everyone's business and feisty grandmas called the shots... Where someone complimenting a scone felt as good as closing a business deal... where a walk along the beach soothed the soul much more than an hour of Candy Crush. Life felt real in Taxos, unlike back in London where most of my time was spent in front of a screen, either professionally at the office or for "fun" at home.

'Stavros started it, you know – the fire,' I said to Henrik, in a low voice, and told him about the man in the balaclava.

His jaw fell open. 'Well, if he did, I can assure you that ThinkBig and I had nothing to do with it.'

'Never thought you did – what I don't understand, though, is why would he go that far?'

Henrik thought for a moment. 'He did mention something in passing – said a villager was friendly with the tax office and might report him for offering those tax breaks. That news unsettled him. I think he wanted villagers to sign on the dotted line as soon as possible.'

Ah yes – the arsonist spying at the meeting and hearing about Mr Dellis' diligent tax man friend.

'But that fire could have killed someone.' Again that anger built within me and was ready to erupt by the time we sat down at Stavros' table, in a discreet corner of the busy Flamingo Inn. Orion fetched four ouzos whilst Stavros stood up to greet us, then sat down again, wearing his signature black suit and white shirt.

'Cheers.' He raised his glass.

'What are we celebrating?' I asked, in a measured voice.

Stavros' cheeks flushed. 'Pippa... last night...'

'You weren't kept in hospital, then?' asked Henrik.

'No. Thanks to you, my friends...'

'I'm not your friend,' I snapped. 'Believe me, organising arson isn't an appealing trait.'

'Shh! Be careful what you say,' said Stavros and looked around. 'You have no evidence.'

'No? That man you were talking to on the beach, with the ponytail... He turned up at one of the villagers' meetings. I saw him last night, wearing a balaclava, before he ran away.'

Stavros sipped his drink. 'I don't know what you talking about. And if such a man existed, he could be anywhere in Greece – anywhere in Europe by now.'

I threw my hands in the air. 'But I don't get it, Stavros, why a fire?'

Ooh. His eyes looked all wet and a kind of sheepish look crossed his face. Stavros cleared his throat. 'If anyone arranged such a fire, I can only think they had heard of the villagers' new business plans and thought perhaps... just perhaps thought there was a chance they could make things difficult if any sort of appeal to the council was put forward. That possibility needed to be removed.'

'Bravo, mission accomplished,' I muttered.

Stavros' voice broke. 'I imagine if someone did plan the fire, they never, for one moment, thought it could be so dangerous – never wanted to hurt anyone.'

'Enough of this speaking in riddles,' said Henrik and looked around the table. 'Why is Pippa here, Stavros? You and I have business to tie up, but–'

'Ah... about that...' Stavros looked at me. 'After everything that has happened last night, I couldn't believe how the villagers pulled together, to save me. There was no question...' his chin trembled, '…no hesitation. It would have been so easy to wait for the firemen and take the risk that professional help might arrive too late. Niko, Cosmo, Demetrios... they put my life above the future of Taxos. And Henrik, of course...' He patted my ex's shoulder. 'Which is why it pains me to say... I have to call off the deal with ThinkBig.'

I gasped.

'Stavros?' Henrik almost dropped his ouzo. 'This is a joke, right?'

'Sorry, my mate.'

'But most of the paperwork is done – ThinkBig could make it very difficult to–'

Stavros held up his hand. 'You knew I rushed through planning permission. ThinkBig could get into a lot of trouble if certain favours I've done came to light.'

Henrik sneered. 'As if you are going to air your own dishonesty.'

Stavros pulled out a handkerchief and blew his nose. 'You are right. I'm no fool – which is why I have covered my tracks. There is no clear evidence anywhere that I fast-tracked the approval. Investigations would find nothing concrete against me personally, just against the planning permission department, and they aren't likely to sack anyone without a solid name to go on.'

'But why on earth would you call off the deal?' I asked.

'I've seen the Taxos tourist leaflet – been impressed with the villagers' efforts. This new Taxos, offering nature and craft experiences provides something the rest of the island doesn't – it could work.'

'Pah – you mean after last night, you've gone soft.' Henrik shook his head. 'You should have gone into hospital, Stavros, and got someone to check out your head. And if you think for one moment that my boss and I are going to back out quietly...'

'Don't threaten my brother,' growled Orion.

'I not ask you to back out completely.' Stavros shrugged. 'I have another proposition.' He stared at me. 'You and the villagers agree that something needs doing, no? Things cannot continue as they have been.'

Heart racing, I nodded. What was he going to suggest?

Stavros turned to Henrik. 'You told me of another project you were considering, that had just come in.'

Henrik's eyebrows knotted together.

'The marine museum, with the aquarium in it – I think Taxos would be the ideal location for that. What with Caretta Cove and the turtle theme, the birdwatching walks, cycle rides... An indoor aquarium would bring in money over the winter as well, with visits from local schools.'

My eyes widened. 'A marine museum? Yes... yes! I could see that working. Henrik?'

He ran a hand through his hair. 'I... I need to think. Yes, I agree, it's a good fit. But ThinkBig would want compensation for all the work we've put in to the former idea. I mean, we've lined up architects and builders...'

Once again Stavros held up his hand. 'I'm sure we can work out a deal. ThinkBig will always have new proposals for Kos, no? I can help... smooth the way. You can therefore guarantee your builders other jobs as well. Plus I can introduce your boss to other *accommodating* mayors that I know on other islands.'

Abruptly, Henrik stood up. 'I'm going over to ThinkBig's offices. This isn't going to go down well.'

'Nonsense!' said Stavros. 'It's the way you sell it – say that you've clinched the marine museum deal and will soon have the contacts in place to garner many other developments in the Aegean.'

'And why should I?'

Stavros glanced at me and Henrik followed suit. Then he sighed and without another word left.

'Stavros... Thank you, I guess,' I said.

He chuckled. 'Did that hurt?'

I shrugged. 'Although the Vesteros family – how will they manage? Whoever...' I gave a sardonic smile, '...whoever started that fire effectively burnt down their hotel.'

'You are a demanding woman – I like that,' he said. 'Although it's a shame they hadn't put new batteries in their smoke alarm, the insurers won't pay up.'

I glared at him.

'All right, all right... I'm sure I can arrange something. They will not be out of pocket.'

'Thank you,' I muttered.

'No... I thank you. Last night taught me a lesson. I see now, how important community life is – how, if possible, it should be preserved. I...' His voice suddenly broke, 'I'm sorry. Money is king to me...' He jerked his head towards Orion. 'We grew up with very little. My dad was ill and on benefits. That's one reason why – believe it or not – I truly thought the redevelopment was great for Taxos. There is nothing worse than no job, because it means no respect from others or yourself.'

Orion nodded. 'That's why I'm always looking to improve my business, talking of which... Stavros told me about your scones. They are something new. Now I know they taste great. So I have a proposition – you supply Creami-Kos with them all year around, no?'

'What? Really? But... how would I manage that?'

'You a businesswoman, yes? Get a loan, bigger kitchens or new premises... run Pippa's Pantry alongside scone-baking for me. To start, just supply my biggest outlet at the airport. If that success, then also the one in Kos Town... and so on.'

'But no... you see, London... my life...'

Stavros gave me a grin and for a moment he looked all together less shifty. 'Pippa Pattinson! Your heart is in the small village life – everyone sees that. As soon as you took sides with the villagers, I knew I had a battle on my hands. Not because you are intelligent with good business acumen, but because it obvious you believe in these people and their way of life.' He shrugged. 'When I mingled at the meeting, Taxos people talked to me about you, the woman who they thought, inside, was still like the little English girl who used to visit with her parents – who fitted in with, and loved, the Greek island way of life.'

'Really?' My cheeks seared with heat. Could I really give up my career? My executive London life? Then that chirpy voice inside me piped up again, reminding me of the stress headaches back home, and sleepless nights.

Stavros nodded. 'And I've seen the change in you, just over the last week – the high shoes and make-up gone. You are comfortable with village life. Is clear you care about the simple things – good food, looking after others, finding pleasure in nature... And is legend now, how you stripped off to save the Dellis boys without a thought for your fancy clothes or your own life. And just now, you make sure the Vesteros family okay...' He shook his head. 'Why did you ever decide to work with numbers and pieces of paper in a clinical bank office?'

'No idea,' I stuttered. 'I mean – I didn't decide, it was always assumed.'

'And our neighbours decided our father was a scrounger and assumed we were the same,' said Orion. 'Expectations don't need to be fulfilled.'

Orion was right. Perhaps now was my time to change and follow my heart – job-wise and in life. Much as I didn't want to hurt Sophia or the family, that would mean I could no longer stay away from Niko. I knew he loved me – there were too many clues... the tender compliments... his glee at seeing me when I first arrived... his concern when I'd been winded... I had no idea what was going on with him and Leila, nor why he fought his true feelings. So, thanks to Stavros (did I really just say that?) I'd just decided two things:

Firstly, I was going to quit my executive London life and instead bake scones and run the tastiest little afternoon teashop in Kos.

Secondly, Nikolaos Sotiropoulos was in for a huge surprise when I got back to Taxos, because the very first thing I'd do would be to press my lips against his!

CHAPTER TWENTY-ONE

'Pippa – I don't know what to say, except... that's amazing!'

Leila grabbed my hands. Laughing, she spun me around and around, until I felt queasy and Grandma ordered her to stop. Sophia showed me to a chair and Georgios passed me an orange granita.

A couple of hours after meeting Stavros, I was in Taxos Taverna and had just announced the mayor's change of heart.

'Tell us again,' said Georgios, and sat down next to me. Everyone else stood up – even Grandma – clapping their hands.

'Okay...' I cleared my throat. 'No quad bike park. No nightclubs. No tacky boat trips. No branded franchises... Instead we expand the new businesses we have started and ThinkBig will build a marine museum with an aquarium in it. The latter will attract business all year around. Stavros believes that with the investment in the area, namely the marine museum, banks will be more open to the idea of loans, so that we can easily pay for the equipment we've needed like new bicycles, improvements to premises or extra insurance.'

Tears trickling down her heart-shaped face, Sophia sat down on Georgios' knee. 'I can't believe it' she said, voice choked. 'After all this worry. Now our future seems more secure.' She wiped her eyes with a napkin. 'Grandma was right.'

'What do you mean, my lamb chop?' said Georgios.

Sophia wiped her face again. 'She read the coffee sediment – said the sea would save Taxos. It has. Sea on land – this aquarium, in the museum.'

We all sat in silence for a moment. 'Ach,' said Grandma, eventually. 'It is Pippa who has saved us, really. My dear little peach who, along with this fight for our village, has helped me find my old spirit. I haven't felt this well in months.'

'Oh um... no... we've all done this together! It's not just down to me,' I said. However one by one, the family members descended on me with a kiss. Even grinning Niko, which resulted in a dart of electricity down that side of my cheek.

'And *Pippitsa* – you have decided to stay here... to run our teashop and supply Creami-Kos with scones.'

I smiled sheepishly at Sophia. 'Yes. It's been my secret dream for years.'

Apollo ambled in and suddenly meowed as if to approve. Everyone laughed, even Niko, who... huh? Caught my eye and winked. Perhaps he'd managed to forgive my insulting comments – maybe even work out I didn't really mean them.

Yet my stomach scrunched as I soon realised the real reason for his happiness. Niko and Leila moved to the doorway and stood hand in hand, as if they were about to make a very important announcement. My eyes felt all wet. So this was it: the announcement of a wedding date. But how... to me Leila and Niko's relationship still didn't make sense.

I guess that was love – irrational; a little crazy. There was no rule book.

Niko clapped his hands. 'Mama, Papa, Grandma... good friend Pippa. We told Leila's parents something very important this morning, and now we tell you.'

Full of tenderness, they looked at each other. Oh God. Niko was positively radiant – eyes shining and smiling straight from the heart. He stood straight and I'd detected a bubble of excitement in his voice.

I felt sick. My heart thumped out a rhythm to a voice in my head screaming *no, no, no*! Niko and I were meant to be! It was fate, all those years of friendship had been building to this point. We "got" each other totally. That magnetised sensation between us was natural chemistry, a rare and uncontrollable thing.

Fortunately, just at that moment, Pandora, Demetrios and Cosmo came in tell us that the firemen reckoned a barbecue had started the fire. They'd found kebab sticks, barbecue fuel and beer bottles. Hmm. Clever planting of evidence. Then cue half an hour of excited chat about the marine museum with hugs all around, ouzo and baklava out of Pandora's basket.

'So, um, what do you think Niko and Leila were going to announce?' I asked Sophia, a tiny part of me still wondering whether to follow through my resolution of giving him a kiss.

'A date for the wedding! There are no worries to hold them back now.'

I had to agree.

'Are you sure?' asked Grandma, as my top lip trembled. 'Recently they argue...'

'Haven't we all? It's been a stressful time.' Sophia got up. 'I fetch the camera to catch the happy moment on film!'

'You okay, my little peach?' said Grandma.

I nodded, not trusting myself to speak.

It was over. I would not interfere if this was about to happen. Niko and lovely Leila looked happy. Sophia looked ecstatic. Bottom line, they were my friends – more than that, my Greek family. If I was wrong and Niko was happy with this destiny then I couldn't be selfish and try to destroy that.

The door squeaked open and Henrik walked in. Silence fell.

'Hello,' I said and stood up. 'Is everything all right?'

He gazed around the room. Georgios poured an ouzo and took it over to him.

'Well done, son – for rescuing those guests from the Vesteros' hotel last night. You are a hero.' As everyone clapped, Georgios clapped him on the back.

Even Niko went over. He held out his hand. After a few seconds' pause, Henrik reciprocated and then knocked back his drink.

'Did you speak with your boss?' I asked. Everyone in the room waited for him to speak. Finally Henrik nodded and sat down at the nearest table, shoulders slumped, hair untidy.

'Yes. He wasn't happy at first. But, well, to quote Stavros, I "sold" it to him and he's agreed we can accept the aquarium project and build it in Taxos.'

'That's fantastic!' I said.

More handshaking. More hugs. Georgios put on music and he and Cosmo started clapping and stamping their feet. I took Henrik to one side.

'Thanks Henrik... I know you are disappointed, the way things have turned out.'

He shrugged. I looked up as Sophia had turned off the music. She pushed Niko and Leila towards the door and lifted up her camera.

'I can wait no longer!' she said. 'Please, make your announcement!'

My eyes filled. Tears streamed down my face. Goodness, what a sap. Since arriving in Greece I'd cried more than in the whole of my England-based life. It must have been the late nights and stress of recent days. A sob escaped my lips.

'Pips, what's the matter?' whispered Henrik.

'Pippa?' How did Niko get to my side so quickly? Just like that night when a drunk Henrik had turned up on the beach.

I got to my feet. 'Nothing. Sorry. Don't feel very well. Need some fresh air. Please... just leave me alone for a while...' I bolted for the door, yanked it open and ran out onto the street. Which way to go?

Vision blurred, I ran as fast as I could, up to the right, towards the woods. I needed to somehow get to the villa, pack my stuff and leave. Who had I been kidding, about starting a life here in Taxos? Thank goodness my parents never got to hear of this ludicrous plan, they'd never have stopped teasing me. And thank goodness it was Sunday and I hadn't been able to email work and hand in my notice.

I sniffed loudly, crying enough tears to extinguish any forest fire. I'd got it wrong. Niko didn't want to share his life with me. I'd never seen him looking any happier than he did today, standing up in front of his loved ones, with his future wife.

'Pippa, stop!' My heart sank. That was no Greeklish but Henrik's voice. Easily his long legs caught up with me. He held my hands, for a moment seeming to forget his burnt, bandaged skin.

'What is wrong? Come back... your friends...' A muscle in his cheek flinched. 'They have something to tell you.'

I shook my head. 'No... um... I feel sick, and, and their future... it's nothing to do with me now.'

'But Sophia just told me you are moving to Taxos.'

I met his gaze and forced a laugh. 'No... that was just a silly dream. She, um, must have misunderstood.'

His face lit up. 'Really?'

'In fact... let's leave for England right now. We can book flights over the phone. Be packed within a couple of hours. Go back to our flat – to our London life.'

'Are you mad?'

'No...' I said brightly. 'Three weeks was way too long a holiday for me, anyway. I need to return to my desk.'

'Well... I could do with getting back to collect the rest of my clothes and meet up with the boss. I've a feeling I'll be spending a lot of time in Kos, over the next few months. But tonight?'

'Let's do it!'

'The police might want to speak to us about the fire.'

I shrugged. 'I doubt it – sounds like they've worked out the cause.'

Henrik's brow furrowed. 'Don't you want to say goodbye to everyone?'

Oh God. Eyes refilling. 'I hate goodbyes!' I squeaked, still in that bright voice. 'And the villagers... they don't need my help any more. Perhaps I'll come over anyway, later this year, and visit you – pop into Taxos at the same time. I'll help fund a renovation of the teashop – look on it as an investment. Georgios and Sophia are already doing a great job of running it. I can email over my scone recipes and always be on call to give advice. I can deal with Orion Lakis from England – I won't let the village down.'

'Really? I mean... okay. Sure. That'd be great. Well yes. Let's get back to London.' He beamed. 'And get back to our executive routine.'

Uh oh. As I packed and booked tickets, an uncomfortable feeling sat in my chest – that Henrik believed I was having second thoughts about him and would get back together. I'd put him straight once we were back in England. But first, I just needed to get on that flight and leave my hurt behind on the island. I hardly said anything in the taxi, wishing, like Chitty Chitty Bang Bang, it could fly.

Finally we arrived at the airport and before checking in, sat down, waiting for the massive queues to subside.

Tears threatened again. All I could think about was missing gooey baklavas, Demetrios' colourful cravats and Sophia's warm hugs.

'Pippa!' said Henrik.

'Sorry, did you say something?'

'I just wondered... next weekend – how about a spa getaway. Just the two of us. The last couple of weeks has been full-on.' He gave a wry smile. 'We need a holiday after this holiday.'

Oh dear. My suspicions had been right.

'No... I mean, no thanks – what a lovely idea, but... but when I said I wanted to return to the London life...'

He swallowed. 'Oh. Now I feel stupid. You didn't mean to us?'

I shook my head. 'Sorry,' I whispered. 'The last thing I wanted to do was hurt you again.'

Those slate eyes glistened for a second. 'I understand. Thank you for your honesty.' He looked at the ground. 'Sorry, if I was ever a disappointment – not being as honest as you hoped.'

'No! Henrik! You've... you've been a... a brill boyfriend. Loyal, supportive, sensitive... And... I kind of get it. Why you kept the ThinkBig deal a secret. Your career – it means more to you than mine does to me.'

'Yes. And this holiday has made me question why. I could have tried to change ThinkBig's mind about the original development in Taxos, so that you and I were on the same side. But I couldn't. It always comes back to my Mum – how she doted on Dad and when he left she had nothing. It's made me feel I have to keep my professional life to myself and not let it be influenced by anyone I'm dating. At least I will always have my career as a reliable constant throughout my life, whatever happens with people I... I love.'

I placed my smaller hand over his and he glanced sideways at me.

'You like him, really like him, don't you... Niko?' he mumbled.

I stared back. 'Yes. Yes, I do, Henrik. It's come out of nowhere.'

'Damn.' he muttered and tried to smile. 'It's okay, Pippa. I should have faced up to this earlier. Look, I'm just going to get a coffee... want one?'

I didn't when he left but by the time he got back, I was absolutely parched.

'What took you so long?'

Henrik stared into his coffee. 'I, um, got lost.'

Lost? Good thing we weren't in a big international airport, then. He looked at his watch as the queue for our check-in desk disappeared.

'Come on,' I said and stood up.

'Just let me finish my drink.'

'Henrik! We'll miss our flight.' My throat ached. The thought of leaving Kos filled me with relief and despair all at once.

Finally Henrik stood up and threw his paper cup in the bin. Slowly he walked towards the check-in desk, every now and again turning around. He checked his luggage in first, moving slower than a turtle out of water and I was just about to ask him if something was wrong when a familiar Greeklish voice called out my name.

I gazed up at Henrik and my eyes went blurry.

'What have you done?' I asked before turning around. Niko was running through the airport, shirt hanging out of his jeans. I turned back to Henrik. He bent down, kissed me on the cheek and pushed my suitcase towards my feet.

'Listen to what he has to say, Pips. And... good luck.'

Huh?

I turned around again. Niko stood half a metre away from me. He picked up my suitcase and headed over to the bench, where Henrik and I had been sitting.

'Now, wait a minute,' I said and followed him. 'I'm going to miss my plane. How did you know I was here?

'Henrik.' he said and took my fingers. We both sat down. 'And what were you doing, leaving without letting me know?'

'I... didn't think you'd mind,' I said and pulled back my hand. 'And congratulations – you and Leila have set a wedding date?' My flight was called to the departure lounge and I stood up. Niko pulled me back down.

'Wedding date? No... we announced that the engagement is off.'

I stopped fiddling with my ticket. 'Off?'

'Yes. Have I said it right? I mean–'

'I know what you mean, but... *why*?' My heart pounded.

'Henrik still hasn't explained to you?'

'He knew?' I turned to the check-in desk. My Dutch Titan had gone.

'Yes. After you left the taverna, we told everyone. Henrik – I think he hoped to get back with you. So that probably why he said nothing before the airport – he wanted to return to London as quickly as possible. But in the end... guess he's a good man. He accepts that you no longer love him and wanted the best for you.'

'I don't understand...' In exasperation I shook my head. 'So, you and Leila... was I right about her travelling?'

'Yes.'

'How long have you known?'

'Months.'

I gasped. 'But... Niko... this makes no sense.'

'Does this?' He leant forward and pressed his soft mouth against mine. Within seconds, my body responded, pressing close against his. Eyes tightly shut, kaleidoscopic magic fairy dust lit up my vision. I pulled away, trying to understand what was happening, before once again finding those tender lips. My skin prickled from head to toe as his fingers cupped my cheek and gently undid my ponytail.

'Oh Pippa... so long I've waited,' he whispered and met my gaze. 'Always it's been you – so hard to pretend... so hard to try and do the best...'

'But... what... when...?' Oh, sod explanations! I leaned forwards and our mouths met. God, his lips felt so sweet and warm. He kissed softly, yet an urgency drove him, a power that said he needed me. I pulled away briefly, for breath, then my need for him kicked in even more forcefully. My body trembled as I clasped his collar and pulled him closer still. A hot glow spread through my limbs and felt unfamiliar yet comfortable... dangerous yet safe...

Finally we parted, me ignoring a mixture of smiling and disapproving faces of passers-by. Niko grinned and my world felt complete.

'Leila and I love each other as friends – and dating, it seemed like the next logical step. Our families are a good match... neither of us met another person... It seemed sensible to get engaged, even though our relationship missed that... that romantic glitter.'

Clasping his hands, I nodded.

'And it cheered Grandma up so much, what with the recession. And then she got really ill. Business got worse. Everyone kept saying our wedding was the only positive thing to look forward to. We didn't dare admit to everyone that we'd made a mistake, in case Grandma got worse... But the last few weeks, especially since you returned, she stronger and stronger...'

My heart beat furiously and, for the first time in days, my chest felt as light and carefree as one of Pandora's sponge cakes.

'That's why you were upset when she collapsed and her health seemed to have taken a step backwards.'

'Yes. Of course, I was upset with worry for her – but also because it made us think if Grandma had deteriorated again, we'd have to go through with the marriage. Then when it was just low blood pressure, Leila thought it was safe to break up, that Grandma was still strong enough. But I was still concerned... probably over-anxious... Leila and I disagreed.'

'That's why you two weren't talking, on the picnic.'

He nodded. 'It's always been you, Pippa. Tomboy. My juicy little fig. My soulmate.'

I ran a hand over his caramel skin. That's why he'd talked of "respecting" Leila and not mentioned the word "love". Everything made sense. He was no playboy. No cheater. All this time he'd been just the opposite, doing the honourable thing, however difficult, for the sake of his family.

'And remember those women I flirt with in the taverna, right at the beginning of your holiday, after you fainted?'

I thought for a moment and then nodded.

'I know them well – they come back here three years now and are gay!'

He laughed but instead – yes you've guessed it – my eyes filled up once more. 'Oh, Niko... how could I have doubted you – so easily tossed away my gorgeous view of you from our childhood?'

'I've always loved you, Pippa, and that last summer, when we were fourteen, seeing you stung by those jellyfish – it made me realise the depth of my feelings. It ignited a spark of romance. But I never thought you'd return. The summers passed without seeing you again.'

My eyes tingled. 'Couldn't you have confided in me about you and Leila's dilemma?'

'No – because you and Grandma have always been so close, I worried you might confide in her. My behaviour must have seemed strange – especially as someone who not a brain person, who would bore you...' He bit his lip and looked straight at me.

'Oh God – please say you didn't really believe I meant that. I know you've been angry and quite rightly, but... but in every way, you are more than a match for me. You see Sophia – your whole family – was counting so much on the wedding. She heard about us on the beach, with the policeman... I think she thought I was leading you astray. I had to knock you back. Do the decent thing. Insulting your intelligence like that was the hardest thing I've ever had to do. I can't think of anyone who would bore me less.'

Gently, Niko ran his thumb across my cheek. 'Mama told me tonight, after our announcement, that she'd heard about the policeman. I guessed that was why you backed off. Like me, you want to do the right thing. And of course...' He grinned and poked me gently in the ribs. 'There are lots of interesting things to learn about fishing.' He leant close. 'Like choosing the right *bait*... like *reeling in* a special catch...'

I leant closer. 'And I have lots of fascinating facts to tell you about the finance business – like how some people like to *massage figures*.' We grinned and kissed again.

'So this announcement?' I said eventually, and smoothed down my hair.

'Leila is going travelling – she has a job as an au pair, something she's always dreamed of.'

'And how did your family take it?'

'Shocked. But, well, Grandma...' He chuckled. 'Remember when you little, she read your cup – said you would marry a foreign man? Grandma says that secretly she always knew you and me would get together.'

'I assumed it was Henrik, what with him being half-Dutch.' Talking of which... I looked at the departure board. The flight had left. Niko squeezed my hand.

'Henrik is a generous man. We must invite him over, when he back in Kos. Let him see how Pippa's Pantry is doing.' Niko cleared his throat. 'There is one more lie I have to admit to,' he whispered as we finally drew apart. 'I really do want to make fuck with you.'

Through tears of joy, I giggled. 'As long as you don't call me Shirley Valentine.'

'No...' he said in a husky voice. 'But one day I hope to call you Pippa Sotiropoulos.'

If you loved *Game of Scones* turn the page for more from Taxos in an exclusive extract from *My Big Fat Christmas Wedding*

PROLOGUE

As if trying to rock us to sleep, the ocean lapped against the fishing boat's sides. However, Niko and I couldn't have been more awake as we lay, lips pressed together, on its wooden bottom. A kaleidoscope of magical fairy dust danced before my closed eyes. Despite the midnight breeze, heat surged through my limbs. Almost two months I'd been in Taxos and the passion of my fisherman friend still left me with wobbly Greek semolina pudding for knees.

Okay. Bear with me. I know this sounded like an extract from one of my favourite romance novels. But a starlit Greek night, during the last humidity of summer, spent with the sexiest man in the Aegean, stirred every soppy cell of my being.

I opened my eyes, pulled away and grinned. Niko leant up on one elbow and an enquiring smile crossed those silken lips. In the moonlight (okay, with the help of our lamp) I drank in that caramel skin, those mocha eyes and the taut outline of a man who did physical work for a living. Then my gaze turned to Kos island's shoreline. Glowing amber lights illuminated the village. The wind dropped and, along with the familiar chirp of cicadas, string music drifted across the waves from the beach, where locals cleared up after a community barbecue. We'd all celebrated building work starting on the much-needed, income-boosting Marine Museum. Thank goodness for the faith of some foreign investors.

'Pippa? You have a joke to share?'

'It's nothing,' I said and chuckled.

He leant forward and with his free hand tickled just above the corner of my hip. His fingers crept up to under my arm and I laughed even harder. Then gently he bent further forwards, so that our noses touched. He batted his lush eyelashes against mine – butterfly kisses, his speciality to make me giggle when we were kids. They still did – but these days made me also tingle in places I never used to know existed.

'Okay, okay,' I said and backed away, longing to once again kiss his firm mouth. 'It's just that in my mind I called you my fisherman friend. A Fisherman's Friend is a decades-old famous cough sweet in England, made from liquorice and menthol – people either love or hate it.'

One eyebrow raised, Niko sat up on the blanket and took both my hands. 'And you, my little juicy fig,' he said, huskily, 'are a *huge* fan of this particular fisherman friend, no?'

'I'm not sure,' I said airily. 'I might need to have another taste.'

Niko smiled and then stared for a moment. He cleared his throat and pulled me up, so that I was sitting too. Cue a more vigorous rocking of the boat. Water splashed onto my arm, like a sudden shot of air-con. This was the perfect night for skinny-dipping, me minus my polka-dot undies, Niko revealing his lower abdominal V muscle, acquired from honest labour, not some clinical gym.

'You see me as *much more* than a friend though, no?' said Niko, cheeks tingeing red. 'And you like living here?'

'Huh? Of course. Nikolaos Sotiropoulos, how can you even ask?'

Since my return to Taxos, the holiday destination of my early years, earnest, gorgeous islander, Niko, had become the centre of my world. This was quite an admission for a mathematician who, only a matter of weeks ago, commuted daily for work in a major London bank. If you'd told me back then that in September I'd be running a teashop in Kos, I'd have sooner believed I was going to relocate to Mars. Okay so it would be nice to visit my favourite restaurant in Soho now and again, plus shop in Oxford Street, but London couldn't compete with the island's freshly caught fish and coastal views.

'I adore you and love living here,' I said. 'Watching the teashop take off has given me such an adrenaline rush – as has me making plans to branch out to make regular scone deliveries to the Creami-Kos café chain. And the summer weeks here have been idyllic. Diving into the refreshing Taxos sea after a hard day's work certainly beats catching a stuffy train home to take a shower. As for the raven-black night skies, untainted by the glow of city lights, and villagers shaking my hand every day… I'd never once spoken to some of my close neighbours in London.'

Niko ran a hand through his curly black hair. Through his tight T-shirt his chest rose and dipped more quickly than usual.

'You speak more poetically since living here,' he whispered. 'Where has that practical banker gone?'

I poked him in the ribs. 'You've ruined her. It's your fault.'

'I can be a poet too,' he said, in a seductive treacle-like tone. 'It's as if you're the antidote to my personal poisons. You extinguish my self-doubt and evaporate my paranoia.' He took a deep breath and glanced away for a second. 'But now, dear Pippa, I have something very important to say.' He looked back at me, all the twinkle gone from his eyes. 'Can't put it off any longer. It's been building up.'

'Is something the matter?' My heart thumped. Perhaps our time together had been too intense, and he wanted to step back. What if Niko had brought me onto the ocean to let me down gently; say it wasn't working out, me living in his family's taverna, baking and selling my scones in the half of the building they'd closed down; poetry aside, that we were too different, with me thinking in numbers, him thinking in shoals; that all those years we'd played together as children, during summer holidays, didn't mean we were destined to spend our lives together as adults?

I swallowed. 'What is it?'

'Yesterday. I spoke to your father.'

'Did he ring?' I sat bolt upright. 'Why didn't you tell me? Is everything okay?' My mind raced. Was something wrong at home? Or was Niko worried I'd have no job if we split up and I decided to return to England? Perhaps he was trying to line me up a position with my dad – not that I'd need anyone's help. I was an independent, modern woman who… aarghh, who melted like chocolate in the sun, when Niko touched me or spoke with his sexy Greek accent that made my skin flush and palms moisten.

'We… I… your father agreed that…'

'Niko! Just spit it out!'

'Huh?' His brow furrowed and he stuck out his tongue. 'See, I am not eating anything.'

'No! In English that means hurry up and tell me. What's this all about?'

'Us. The future.' He pulled a small red box out of his back pocket.

I gasped. 'Gosh. Really? But…' My eyes pricked.

'Your father gives us his blessing,' Niko prised open the lid and looked up at me shyly. 'I hope you don't mind me seeking your father's permission first but…' He shrugged those strong shoulders and I nodded, knowing how important some traditions were to him, especially when it came to family. 'Pippa, you are sweeter than the most honey-filled baklava in Athens. Your first smile of the day is my sunrise. Marry me. Make me the happiest man in the whole of Greece.'

A lump rose in my throat. What an exceptionally pretty silver ring, bearing a sparkling blue sapphire, surrounded by tiny diamonds. It reminded me of the blue and white houses across the island.

'This belonged to my great aunt Alexis. She had no children and considered me her own grandson. When I was a little boy, she gave this to Mama and told me to one day give it to the woman who captured my heart.' A smile crossed his face. 'Of course, at the time I was more interested in capturing carp.' He squeezed my fingers and his face kind of scrunched up. 'I… I know it's not long after Henrik's proposal. And Greece… the economy… So if you need time to think – I would understand if you don't see your future in Kos.'

My heart pounded and I wanted to stand upright and sing! Niko and me married? A tear trickled down my cheek. I couldn't have felt more different to when my practical, down-to-earth ex-boyfriend had proposed in the summer – which was odd. Up until my trip here, I'd agreed with Henrik that slushy declarations of love were for teenagers or the pastel-covered beach reads that I ironically liked to read. But there was something about Niko's seductive words that always softened my logical, pragmatic part. And as for the country's difficulties, I felt nothing but compassion for the Greek people.

'No.'

His shoulders dropped.

'No, no, I don't need time to think!'

His eyes sparked and he pulled me towards him, his warm mouth once again owning mine. I breathed in his natural aroma, a kind of musky, leather masculine scent. My desire for him became more urgent, as our bodies pressed together. Gently, he pushed me away, eyes dancing, cheeks flushed. He took the ring out of the box and hesitated for a moment. Of course – over here wedding rings didn't go on the left-hand finger, but the right.

More tears flowing, I laughed and offered him my right hand.

'We're going to have to compromise,' I said. 'Won't I have to convert to your religion? And then there is the reception venue to choose. Above all else, I don't want an over-the-top wedding.'

Niko's infectious chuckles filled the balmy evening air. 'Good luck with telling Mama and Grandma. We'd better set an early date, if you don't want arrangements to snowball.'

Snowball. Great word. Like so many of the locals, Niko spoke good English, despite sometimes still misunderstanding the basics. Whereas Greek, to me, might as well have been like learning cat or dog, and don't even get me started on its written alphabet.

I clapped my hands. 'Then talking of snow, what about a Christmas wedding? It would cheer up those quiet winter months you talk of.'

In response, Niko – my husband-to-be – gave me a kiss hot enough to turn the sturdiest of snowmen into a puddle.

ACKNOWLEDGEMENTS

Firstly, I'd like to thank my hardworking, lovely editor Lucy Gilmour, along with the rest of the dedicated Carina UK team. Thanks also to Kate Nash for her input. Carina UK authors, I love you guys, thanks for brightening every working day. Hugs to Martin, Immy and Jay for their continued support. Appreciation to my many online friends who always know when to offer virtual chocolate. And a big shout-out to all those wonderful bloggers who generously give up their spare time to help us authors promote our books.

A special thank you goes to Frank de Jong, the very charming KLM flight attendant I met on the way back from Japan who inspired the character of Henrik. Thanks Frank, for putting up with my emails and requests for photos; for not running a mile when KLM tracked you down, having heard me chat about this book's 'hot Dutch hero' on Twitter.

Of course, these acknowledgements wouldn't be complete without mentioning my favourite Game of Thrones characters Tyrion, Daenerys and Jon Snow. George R R Martin, I salute you!

Welcome to the Lonely Hearts Travel Club

Follow Georgia in the *Lonely Hearts Travel Club* series as she travels the world.

The new favourite series for fans of *Bridget Jones's Diary*, the *Shopaholic* series and *Eat, Pray, Love*.

'Katy writes with humour and heart. The Lonely Hearts Travel Club is like **Bridget Jones goes backpacking**.'
- Holly Martin, author of *The White Cliff Bay* series

CARINA™

Visit Us Online

www.carinauk.com

0216_CARINA_P_SM